THE WORLD AS WE KNOW IT

Curtis Krusie

Copyright © 2015 Curtis Krusie
All rights reserved.

ISBN: 1506120016
ISBN 13: 9781506120010
Library of Congress Control Number: 2015900305
CreateSpace Independent Publishing Platform
North Charleston, South Carolina

This story is dedicated to my loving wife, Bryn.

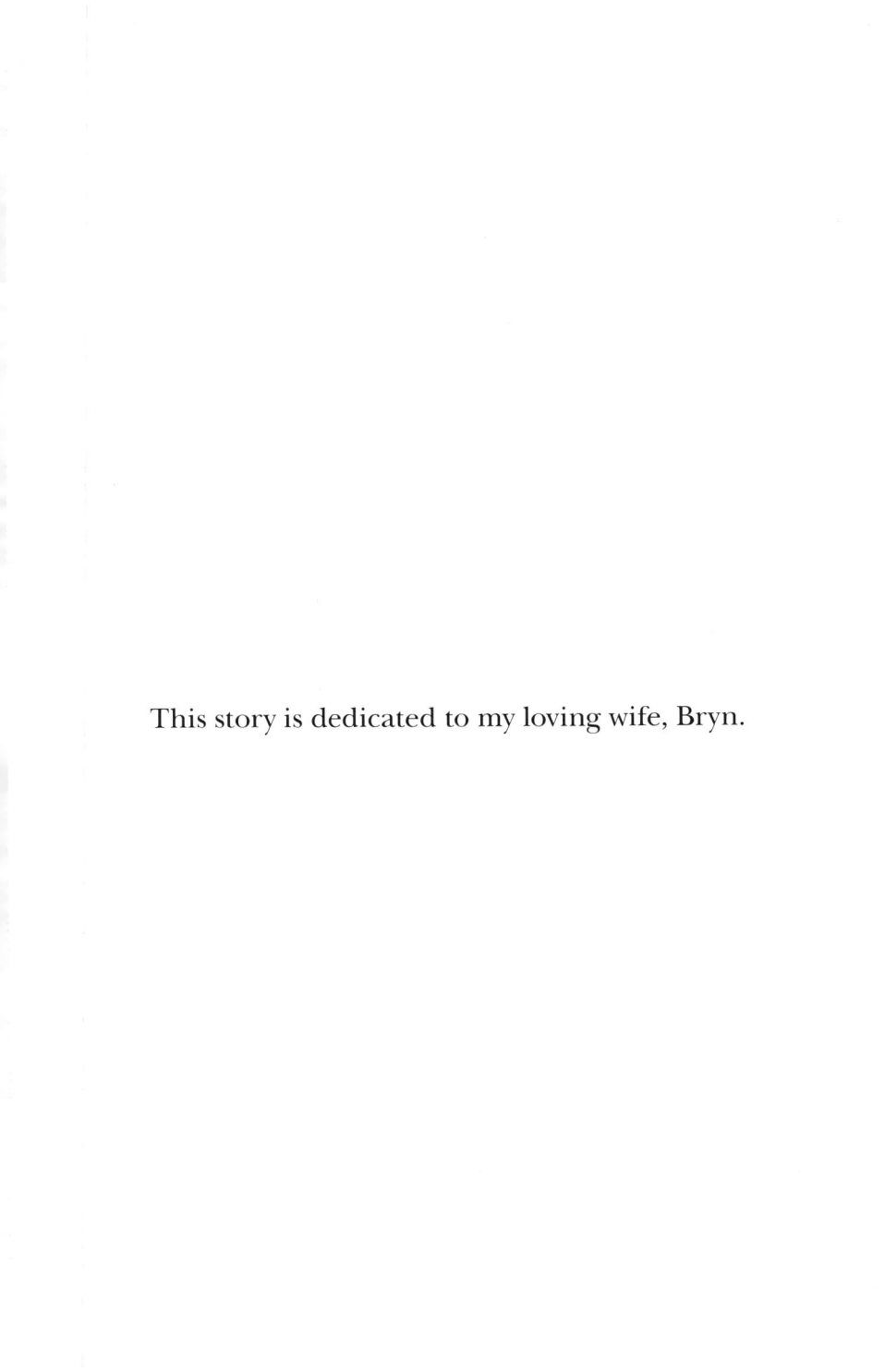

Special thanks to God; to my wife, Bryn; and to all of my friends and family who inspired this story in one way or another.

And now these three remain: faith, hope and love. But the greatest of these is love.

—1 Corinthians 13:13

1

IN THE BEGINNING

I still remember the Y2K scare. *Anno Domini* 2000. That was the first time I remember hearing people talk about a technological and economic meltdown. I was a freshman in high school. My friend Noah's father had a cellar completely stocked with a year's supply of food and water, just in case it took that long for him to find those things once the world went mad, which would occur at precisely midnight between December 31, 1999, and January 1, 2000. Their move from England to the States three years before had been the first step of his eccentric plan for disaster recovery. Of course, by the time the fireworks ended that morning, he had already made the shocking discovery that Windows 98 was still functioning on his IBM, so those first two digits in the "year" column probably hadn't been much of an obstacle for the computers at MasterCard, Starbucks, or Norad, either. His family was really sick of canned produce by the end of the next year. Then came September 11, 2001. Just seeing the date on paper still gives me chills. Three thousand Americans kissed their families good-bye for the last time before leaving for work that morning. Those responsible called it jihad, or "holy war," a concept that might fall into the category of comical irony if it weren't so perverse—that is, if you interpret jihad the way the Western world has been driven to. Rather, if you know it as a spiritual struggle within, then perhaps we're all mujahideen of sorts, all yearning for enlightenment, as misguided as a minority may be. Global markets shut down for days, and when they opened again, they tanked. Just the immediate damage was in the tens of billions of dollars. In response, the US government waged a "War on Terror" in two different countries, which ended up costing trillions more dollars and thousands more lives. People talked about prophetical fulfillments and signs of the Apocalypse.

Before the aftermath was even in our rear view, we saw the world economy upended again. That time, it began with the real estate crisis, caused by a series of irresponsible federal policies and risky bank investments over the course of two decades, but predictably pinned on the most convenient scapegoat: the then president of the United States of America. Why anyone would have wanted that job remains a great mystery to me. It was the worst economic downturn since the Great Depression, perpetuated by the succeeding administration, which continued to rack up federal debt in numbers that even an astrophysicist could scarcely comprehend. In the meantime, the political turmoil on the other side of the world erupted into violent revolutions across North Africa and the Middle East that compounded exponentially. The entertainment media capitalized on the convenient coincidence that all of those events seemed to be building toward the climax of the Mayan long-count calendar, which would come to an end on December 21, 2012. Yes, come to an end, not start over, according to the opportunistic sensationalists. That date, of course, would be the end of the world.

Those "Doomsdayers" had always been out there to warn that Armageddon was upon us. But there was hope—for a nominal monetary donation to Organization X. Some of the more hopeless ones didn't even attempt to profit from it. They were content just to have an audience. It was less lonely that way. At least they'd found a cause.

I never bought into all of that nonsense. I wasn't superstitious or particularly religious. In fact, sometimes I wondered if the latter wasn't simply a specialized breed of the former. I graduated in 2008 from the University of Missouri–Columbia with a BS in Human Environmental Sciences and an emphasis in Personal Financial Planning. "BS" is an equally appropriate acronym for my extracurricular activities during my time at Mizzou as it is for Bachelor of Science. I wasn't much of a student until my fifth year, when I realized that my academic record was the only means I had of convincing prospective employers that I was capable of doing a job, and my grade point average needed a drastic boost in my last two semesters to make me marketable. Suddenly, my grades improved. All along, I had convinced myself that I simply wasn't capable of that kind of success. I wasn't capable until there was no other option. Just as the ink was drying on my diploma, I watched the market crashing to its demise, promising little in the way of employment prospects for a fresh graduate in an industry then loathed by the American public. Some fortunate circumstances, however, subsequently landed me a career as a financial planner, which, though not the simplest of careers to embark upon during a recession, proved to be a decent fit. Maria and I met shortly thereafter, and it wasn't long before I was out shopping for the biggest rock I could afford with which to adorn her finger.

On June 9, 2012, my fiancée became my wife, and our signed marriage license was sealed and filed with the recorder of deeds in the County of what used to be St. Louis, Missouri. Six—nine—twelve. Maria liked it for the pattern. I'll never forget how beautiful she was, gliding down the aisle in that white dress. Glowing like an angel. We had nothing on our minds but the handsome life we were starting together and all of the wonderful years in store for us. We certainly weren't anticipatorily dwelling on an impending catastrophic collapse of the world economic system. In the still aching economy, we were blessed to have jobs, a contract on a picturesque home in the west-central suburbs that we would close on within the month, two new cars trimmed inside with shiny polished wood and leather, and few cares beyond the manageable everyday responsibilities of the average upper-middle class American couple. We were living the American dream.

Our flight to Aruba left the following morning, and we spent the week getting sun kissed in the white sand, roaming the island wilderness, swimming in the blue Caribbean water, and dining on more fish than I had ever before consumed in such a short period of time. If there's one thing they know about down there, it's how to prepare fish. That, and any beverage with a foundation of rum.

Two words: ¡Aruba Arriba!

"One Happy Island" was their slogan. The simplicity of the south Caribbean lifestyle intrigued me. Most of the homes were humbly designed yet distinguishingly colored, and there was seemingly no kind of struggle between social classes. As an indicator of their diversity, every student on the island learned four languages: English, Spanish, Dutch, and Papiamento, which is a sort of medley of the preceding three. The unemployment and crime rates, they said, stood matched at 1 percent. One night we took a late meal about a mile up the island from the hotel where we were staying. We ate at a faded wooden table by the light of tiki torches with our toes in the sand, watching the sun set over the ocean. It was a nice night, so after dinner we asked our waiter if it would be safe for us to walk back to the resort under the stars. As Americans in a foreign country, naturally we had our reservations, but he laughed as if we had made a joke, which I took as a clear "yes." The road was quite dark and vacant and was lined on both sides by foliage and an endless supply of hiding places. It almost seemed unnatural not to fear the possibility of falling victim to the whims of some cracked-out criminal.

"How do you live this way?" I wanted to ask. "How do you make it work? What's your big secret kept from the rest of the world?"

"No secret," I imagine they'd reply with smiling faces. "We're just people. Just like you."

A few months after Maria's and my honeymoon was the marriage of my best man, Paul, to his bride, Sarah. It was the last of four weddings, including my own, that I had participated in over the course of the year. That year—2012—was a year of love, as they all should be. As thanks for our participation in the ceremony, each of the groomsmen—Daniel, Mike, Noah, Gabe, John, and I—was graced with a gift that, at the time, I believe was intended more as a unique mantle piece than as an instrument of life preservation. I opened the modest white box to find an elegant wooden-handled Ka-Bar with my initials engraved into the fuller, or "blood groove," of the matte black blade. The knife would spend the following few years collecting dust at my bedside coupled with the Mossberg 500A that I had purchased, but would never need, for home defense.

When I first bought the Mossberg, it came with a pistol grip and no stock. I got it from a pawnshop in Columbia, Missouri, during a wave of drug-related home invasions in the area. It was designed for room clearing, not for hunting. I took the shotgun to Paul's farm that weekend for its maiden assault on a line of watermelons. Unfortunately, it had been a while since I had fired a shotgun, and I failed to take into account the considerable twelve-gauge recoil. With eight shells in the magazine and one in the chamber, I took aim at my first ripe victim, eyeing its virgin green rind down the barrel, and I squeezed the trigger. Without a stock, my face served my shoulder's purpose in absorbing the recoil, and the sound of the impact rivaled that of the shot itself. I calmly set down the gun and turned toward Paul, blood pouring from my mouth, and said, "Please tell me I still have all my teeth." I still have a fat lip from the resulting scar tissue as a permanent reminder of my embarrassing mistake. Needless to say, I ordered a stock as soon as I returned home. The watermelon did not survive.

"I wish you'd put that thing where people can't see it, Joe," Maria had told me, referring to the shotgun that she, for some reason, found so much more offensive than the combat knife next to it.

"Who's going to see it?"

"We have company."

"Well, if they have a problem with weaponry, they should stay out of our bedroom."

She shook her head at my innuendo and replied with a playful scowl, which I returned. But truly, I didn't want it stored away. A home defense mechanism is useless if it's not easily accessible. Of course, I kept the shells locked away for the sake of safety anyway. The gun was more for show.

Our new home quickly revealed a tendency to accumulate clutter. New Year's. Valentine's Day. St. Patrick's Day. Easter. Memorial Day, conveniently followed by

Independence Day, which necessitated the same décor. Halloween. Thanksgiving. Christmas. New Year's again. We took advantage of any excuse to buy more stuff to hang on the house, stick in the yard, or display on a table or wherever else we could find a vacant square foot of surface area. After a month or so, we'd swap it all out for the next occasion and restock the boxes in the basement between the litter box and the case of antique silverware that would never get used because it was a pain in the ass to clean.

Not to mention the decorating projects that never seemed to end. I insisted that my home office be exempt from the constant evolution of the rest of the house. It was just the way I liked it—olive walls, a solid-oak desk, and an enviable collection of guitars that I still loved, though I could never find the time in my schedule to play them anymore. Among them were a Taylor 614, an Alvarez jumbo twelve-string, a Martin dreadnought once owned by Bob Dylan, an American Stratocaster, and a Gibson Les Paul. Once upon a time, I was an avid guitarist, but my priorities had evolved, and little joys like music had fallen by the wayside. The love for literature that my wife and I shared, though, kept us many nights in the quiet company of one another by a warm fire in the fireplace, framed by a wall of bookshelves housing my prized collection of adventure classics. Maria preferred poetry—that, and the Bible. She sometimes teased that, with my propensity for slipping literary metaphors into casual conversation, I must have secretly aspired to star in some epic tale of my own. In truth, I was more comfortable in my armchair reading stories told by others, but as Dr. Aronnax said, "Man proposes, but fate disposes."

Looking back, I find the media's influence on the American lifestyle hilarious and absurd. Maria had the cat eating gourmet cat food at five dollars a can. That ball of fur never voiced any objection to the crunchy stuff, but the television had convinced my wife that her four-legged baby deserved better. Every time I used the Ultra Plush, lotion-treated toilet paper, I couldn't help but think of myself as "soft ass." She even bought pink rose-scented trash bags. That was where I drew the line. Trash is not supposed to smell like roses. It's unnatural, and it didn't make me like the trash any better. It just made me hate flowers.

Moving in with a member of the opposite sex is like moving in with a creature of another species. You have to learn their habits, make adjustments, adapt to their irritating little idiosyncrasies. Like with a dog.

I was trying to break this down to Gabe, who had not yet been graced with the magic of love, while he was over one Sunday watching a football game. I heard Maria scream from the kitchen, "Are you calling me a bitch?" I guess it was a poor analogy.

"Of course not, my love!" I replied.

"Don't suck up to me!"

"You're my favorite girl."

"I'd better be your only girl," she said. "There can be no contenders."

Despite the inevitable differences that befall any married couple, I loved Maria the way Arcite loved Emily. The way Romeo loved Juliet. The way Gatsby loved Daisy. I would have given anything for her, including my own life. By the time we were married, my business was well established, and it was looking like the next major milestone in our life would be children, though neither of us was in a hurry to get there. I'm quite glad there were no accidents, because I don't know how we would have made it through what happened had we been responsible for the welfare of anyone other than ourselves, let alone a helpless, vulnerable child. I'm also glad to know that when we are ready, they will be brought into the world as it is now, and not as it was then. The transition was an arduous one.

It was some time in midautumn and some years after we got married when it started. The exact dates and sequence of events are of little importance now, but this is what I remember. It was a cool Monday morning. As she did every day, Maria packed my lunch, graced it with a little love note, and handed it to me, kissing me good-bye before I walked out the door. A heavy fog formed a quiet and eerie ambience as I pulled out of the three-car garage and headed to work. Nothing about my drive on that Monday was particularly unusual, other than the sort of sick feeling in my gut that I couldn't explain. The typical banter of my favorite radio morning show was replaced only by the sounds of the road. The air was still. Something felt amiss.

After parking my shiny new wheels of German luxury in front of my office, I remember stepping out and glancing back at the car momentarily, justifying its expense to myself. I have to project an image of success, I thought. This is how success is gauged. I turned and walked in the door, hanging my overcoat on the rack in the chic wood-trimmed lobby and simultaneously greeting my receptionist, whose face I had not yet noticed.

"Good morning, Debbi."

I heard her gasp, startled, as if she hadn't seen me come in.

"Morning, Joe," she replied in an uncharacteristically nervous tone. I turned around and looked at her ghostly white face; she was staring at her desk in a trance. The phone was already ringing in my office down the hall.

"What's going on?" I asked.

"You haven't heard?"

"Heard what?"

"About what happened last night."

"I was at a buddy's farm all weekend. We got back late."

"You don't check your e-mail?"

"I didn't have service. My cell is still off."

"The phone hasn't stopped ringing since I got here half an hour ago."

"OK, why don't you answer it, Debbi?"

"I don't know how to take these calls."

"Why, who is it?"

"Everyone. You know the Chinese manufacturing bubble you've been talking about? I think it burst."

"That bubble's been seeping for a while," I said as my stomach dropped. The bureaucratic powers above me had been pushing a new alternative energy fund that was heavily weighted in China. Too heavily, in my opinion. I had expressed my concerns to Arthur, our regional vice president of business development, but they had been ignored. "Your job is sales and account management, not analysis," he had said, talking over the desk fan that ran constantly because his high lactose diet, combined with an unstable digestive atmosphere, resulted in uncontrollable and foul flatulence. Nonetheless, I was "strongly encouraged" to include the fund in my clients' portfolios whenever possible. It wasn't that I was opposed to alternative energy, of course. I was as green as anyone, but the color was, to me, more representative of the money to be made in that emerging industry. What made me nervous were the questionable manufacturing methods that certain companies had a tendency to employ.

"You haven't talked to anyone this morning? Turned on the TV?"

"No."

"Joe, when the Chinese markets opened last night... it was bad. Really bad. Shanghai, Shenzhen, Hong Kong. And it's only getting worse."

I bolted to my office and turned on the television. I flipped through channels—CSPAN, CNN, CNBC, FOX—it was everywhere.

"CHINESE MARKETS STILL TANKING."

"ASIAN AND EUROPEAN STOCK MARKETS FOLLOWING CHINA."

"GLOBAL ECONOMY HEADED FOR ANOTHER RECESSION?"

More like depression, I thought. I had seen it coming ten miles away. We relied so heavily on the Chinese that I wondered how we would ever recover after a crash like the one I feared had just begun. The mutual dependence of massive economies like the United States and China had become dangerously great. The upside of such a system was that all parties had an equal interest in cooperation and healthy competition. The downside was that when the first domino toppled, the others followed. I looked at the Swiss-made automatic watch on my wrist. US markets had not yet opened, but when they did, they were sure to mirror what was happening on the other side of the world.

Of course, responsibility for the crash rested on all of our shoulders. China was just where it had begun, perhaps simply because their geographic location ensures that they are the first to greet each new day. Like a compression bomb or a bad romantic relationship, when pressure gets too great, it has to be released at some point, and the greater the pressure, the louder the bang. We're left wondering where the damage will end. The distance from rock bottom is always measured based on some point in the past, because there's no way to predict the consequences of crashing through what has been perceived as the lowest point in history.

The phone was still ringing. I picked up the receiver and held it to my ear, speechless.

"Joe?"

"Maria, thank God," I sighed, snapping from my bewildered trance.

"Joe, what's going on? I just turned on the television."

"Just relax, the market's like a roller coaster," I said reassuringly, more for my own benefit. "It's just adjusting."

"But they're saying…"

"Don't pay attention to the headlines. You know how the media is. Good news doesn't sell. The more they scare people, the bigger their ratings. It will be fine."

"Are you sure?"

"Of course I'm sure. It's always fine, right? Trust me. Now, I have to try to take some of these calls before Wall Street opens in half an hour. I'm going to spend all day reassuring a few hundred other people who are trusting me with the security of their retirement, so I really have to go. I'll see you tonight, OK?"

"OK. I love you."

"I love you."

As expected, US markets followed everyone else. The rest of the week went pretty much the same way. I suffered a five-day barrage of frantic screaming from terrified clients as the lines on the charts continued to plummet. By the weekend, it seemed to be leveling out, but that did little to ease the fears of the public. Everyone whose livelihood was dependent on a job or an IRA was nervous, and that was the vast majority of us. Our spirits stayed high around the house, but everywhere we went, the mood was somber.

That Friday night, we went to dinner, as we usually did, to a local pub within walking distance of our house. When we stepped in the door, the place was unusually quiet.

Clientele was light. Even our normally peppy waitress was clearly anxiety stricken. Paul called later and suggested that, after the exhausting week it had been, we needed to get out of town again. I protested, insisting that I had to work through the weekend to see what I could do to mitigate the damage.

"There's nothing you can do, Joe," he said. "Just relax. Let it go."

As hard as that was to hear, he was right.

The next morning, we loaded up Paul's truck, and the four of us headed back out to his farm a few hours southwest of the city, where we had spent the previous weekend. We had visited three or four times over the last few months, and the more time I spent there, the more doubtful I became of the practicality of our "normal" life. He had a few hundred acres of fields and forest, and the colors on the trees were just beginning to change. When we got off the highway, a gravel road wound through the woods and led to a small two-room log cabin with a well in the front yard. The thick wooden walls showed their age. Behind the cabin ran a stream that cut through the woods and the adjacent farm fields, and hidden off to the side was an outhouse as old as the cabin itself.

It was a sunny day and slightly warm for that time of year, but there was a pleasant, cool breeze. With the windows down, I actually slept awhile in the back seat with my head resting on Maria's shoulder. That was probably the longest uninterrupted sleep I'd had since Monday. The ride down had been relatively devoid of conversation, but we all perked up pretty quickly once we arrived around noon. After unpacking, Paul and I headed to the water for some trout fishing, a hobby new to me but one that I was becoming increasingly fond of. Maria and Sarah stuck around the cabin, disinterested in what they deemed to be "guy stuff."

I popped open a beer from the cooler we had brought with us, slipped it into the koozie hanging around my neck, and headed into the stream. As soon as I felt the cold water run across the toes of my waders, I forgot all about the turbulence of the previous week. I cast my fly into the water, basking silently in the beautiful serenity of the wilderness around me.

"I could live out here," Paul said after a short while.

"That thought crosses my mind every time we visit."

The birds chirping in the trees, the water rushing through the rocks, and the gentle breeze in the leaves all seemed to be teasing us. It was as if they were inquiring as to why we didn't join them permanently as we so desired.

"Well, when the world goes to hell, this is where I'll be," he continued. "You're welcome to join me."

I laughed.

"You and Maria both. You know my great grandfather lived in that cabin? He built it himself."

"Is that right?"

"Yeah. If he could do it, what's stopping me?"

"Your wife, for one," I said.

"Right, well, there isn't a mall around here, but she'll get used to it."

"She will? You're already planning?"

"You saw what happened this week. I don't quite share your faith in the modern economy. I don't understand how everything got so complicated. Look around you. Food, water, shelter. Family. Absolute freedom and self-sufficiency. This is what it's all about. Every level of Maslow's hierarchy of needs can be better satisfied out here. What else do we need?"

"A reason," I answered. He looked at me, confused. "You know that'll never happen, don't you?" I continued. "We're too accustomed to our luxuries. Central heat and air conditioning is nice. Indoor plumbing. Electricity. You'll never leave the city without a very compelling reason."

"We'll see," he said.

We both took a sip of our beers and let the conversation float away down the stream.

It was nearing dusk when we returned to the cabin with our catch. We built a fire in the old iron wood-burning stove, fileted the fish, and cooked up dinner while Maria and Sarah set out candles to keep us in light as the sun fell behind the Ozark hills. While Paul and I were fishing, they had been in the garden gathering herbs and vegetables that we sliced up and sautéed to complete the meal. A pitcher of clear well-drawn water graced the table, coupled with a fresh-born amber ale that Paul had been brewing for the previous weeks, all ingredients grown on site. No pesticides, no genetic modification, and no preservatives anywhere. Such high-quality naturally grown produce could scarcely be found in stores.

After dinner, we reclined awhile, bantering into the night by candlelight. The events of the previous week never made their way back into our conversation. Honestly, I don't think they even crossed our minds.

We all slept well that night. I awoke first on Sunday morning to the dawn breaking through the windows, and Maria and I were still tangled warmly together. Even in her sleep, she had a beautiful, carefree smile on her face. She was so sweet—so pure. That moment was the first time I remember truly understanding what an extraordinary gift she was to me; a gift for which I would never bear the capacity to give the thanks deserved. When she opened her eyes to meet my gaze, her smile only grew. She felt safe in my arms.

"Good morning," she sighed with a sleepy, labored blink.

"You were smiling in your sleep."

"Was I? Maybe I was having a nice dream."

"About me?"

"Probably."

The two of us headed out to the stream to bathe, where we were met by Paul and Sarah once they had risen. The cold water was exhilarating. Then we got the stove going again for a hearty bacon-and-eggs breakfast. At that time, Paul and Sarah's "farm" was more of a loose interpretation of the word. Because nobody made their permanent residence there, livestock was out of the question, so meal selection was relatively limited. If we wanted variety, some items had to be brought with us. As much as I enjoyed the detachment from modernity, I was glad to have brought the bacon. Had it been a choice between murdering a pig and going hungry, I would have chosen the latter. The prospect of slaughtering anything didn't appeal to me. Perhaps years of that lotion-treated toilet paper had made their mark. At the same time, though, my dependence on that connection left me with a veiled sense of isolation and helplessness.

Parting with the farm that afternoon was somewhat painful. As we headed back to the city, I tried to remain optimistic about the week ahead, but my tendencies toward realism dominated my expectations. The evening was slow and quiet as it faded inevitably into night, which seemed to last forever.

2

THE COLLAPSE

When I stepped into work the next morning, Debbi told me that Arthur was already waiting for me in my office. He was sitting in the farther of the two burgundy leather chairs across from my desk, half-asleep and struggling to keep his head upright. He didn't acknowledge my presence in the room until I sat down right in front of him.

"How's it going, Art."

"Oh, you know, just livin' the dream."

I love when a courteous greeting is met with a morbidly sarcastic response like "just livin' the dream." Perhaps I should have felt guilty finding comedy in such complacent hopelessness. I smiled slightly.

"What can I do for you? Got another fund you want to pitch?"

"Funny, Joe. You know, we're all treading water here."

"I know, I know. It doesn't matter anyway. Everything is headed south now."

"Even so, I came here to apologize. Sometimes I'm too willing to give into pressure from above and not willing enough to listen to my people on the front lines."

War analogies. Who was the enemy?

"Well, it's a new week. Let's see if things turn around."

They didn't. That Monday was as bad as the previous, if not worse. Markets around the world continued the trend that had begun the week before, and there was no indication that it would let up any time soon. A decline of that magnitude was unprecedented. It was more rapid and more widespread than any in modern history had been. Economic peaks and troughs are expected, and in hindsight, they're usually explainable, but this was baffling. It was as if the entire school of economics had ignored some unseen and all-important variable that had finally decided to show its hideous face. Nobody understood it. The world's top economists gathered to try to reverse the trend, but even they didn't know where to start. It was far more than a natural adjustment to overinflated stock prices. The lines on the charts crashed right through their futile attempts to slow the momentum.

It lasted for about a month before the protests began. Mobs formed outside of corporate offices around the world to point fingers and demand revolution. They began picketing mostly in relative peace, but unrest grew quickly, and within a week, riot police and tear gas were necessary to maintain order. I remember watching the news one night as it broadcasted footage of law enforcement unloading rubber bullets into a crowd in Boston, and then it switched over to a journalist in Houston who seemed to be covering the same event under slightly different lighting. That reporter was the first person I heard put a name to what was happening. She called it "The Great Collapse," a headline that would be permanently etched into history books.

The fact that it all progressed so quickly reflected the lack of faith that the citizens of the world held in the system. When I say "system," I mean the entire machine and each of its components that made up the modern world, which determined how society operated in every country large or small, first world to third. The economic system, monetary exchange, corporate conglomerates, government in every form and at every level, social hierarchies—all of it. Wherever you lived, you were a part of it in one way or another. In the eyes of the working and middle classes, they had followed the rules, gone to work, provided for their families, and invested in their futures, but that hadn't been enough. They were losing everything they had worked for their entire lives, day after day, watching it happen on the television, despite having taken every possible step to ensure the security of their lifestyles. They were finally coming to the realization that even after thousands of years of what had always been deemed "progress," nothing man-made could be taken for granted. They were sick of the roller coaster, distrusting of the system, and the collapse was the final straw.

Although she pretended to be satisfied with my reassurances, Maria was no fool. She knew as well as anyone that things were changing, and she knew that my line of work put us in a particularly vulnerable position during that time. She would smile and nod and hold my hand, but her eyes always gave away her true feelings. They seemed constantly glazed with tears of fear that would break the barrier of her eyelashes and come rolling down her soft cheeks if she didn't blink frequently enough to absorb them. That was the worst part for me—seeing her in such a state of distress, knowing that there was nothing I could do to stop it, and watching her try to hide her fear to make things easier on me.

After about two months, a lot of people just quit showing up for work. Those of us who still denied the inevitable, blindly carrying on like a depleting herd of confused sheep, should have been more careful about our use of the resources at our disposal. Stores and gas stations were shutting down, some for lack of business, some for lack of staff. I, at least, began walking to work to conserve gas. My office was less than two miles from our house, but the thought of getting there on my own feet had never before crossed my mind. When it snowed, I had to stuff my shiny leather shoes in a gym sack slung over the opposite shoulder from my messenger bag and walk to work in snow boots, which were not flattering to my suits. The winter days were growing shorter. I would leave before sunrise and return home after sunset. Fortunately, Maria worked out of our house, so I didn't have to worry about her walking the streets alone in the dark. Just a few months prior, she wouldn't have thought twice about a midnight jog through our suburban neighborhood. Even the place where we lived no longer felt safe and predictable.

Rather than put their minds to conservation, as the wise would have, most people began to consume energy and food in excess, afraid that those things would soon be scarce. Electricity. Batteries. Gas. Had I known where things were headed, I would have stocked up on ammunition for my gun like some of the others. We spent the little money that was left even more frivolously than we had when it was abundant. I could see the value of every currency in the world dropping day after day, and I decided it would be irresponsible not to put it to use before it was worthless. That was my justification for self-indulgence. After all, I had earned it. One night, I went to an underground wine auction to which I had been invited by one of my clients, and unbeknownst to my wife, I placed the ten thousand–dollar winning bid on a Bordeaux claret. I brought it home and slipped it into an inconspicuous slot on our wine rack under the bar, intending to save it for some special occasion in the future. Perhaps our anniversary. A big promotion, maybe, if the world economy's free fall miraculously ended in a soft landing. If nothing else, at least we could celebrate the end with class.

The next morning as I walked past the bar, I noticed what looked like a pool of blood creeping around from behind it. My first thought was one of death. It was not my wife, I knew. I had just left her in the bedroom. Perhaps it was the cat, though I couldn't imagine so much blood coming from such a small creature. What could she have done to create such a mess? Had she exploded? I poked my head around the corner of the bar, where I found my bottle of Bordeaux still resting in the same spot on the rack but open and empty. The cork lay ten feet away. I pulled out the bottle and turned it up, pouring the remaining few drops into my mouth while standing barefoot in the ten thousand–dollar mess on the floor. I was later told that the wine had undergone an unintentional refermentation process that had caused a buildup of carbon dioxide, and pressure had compounded inside the bottle until, at one clandestinely climactic moment in the night, it had ejected the cork.

My business declined like everyone else's. Soon, the total value of the portfolios in my care was next to nothing. The angry phone calls from distraught clients ceased, and my office became a quiet, lonely place. I hadn't heard a word from Arthur since his apologetic visit, and I had to let Debbi go. She was paid out of the profits from my office alone, and there wasn't enough money coming in for me to keep her on. When she left, I told her I would call her when things came back, but realistically, we both knew that wasn't going to happen. I wasn't even generating enough revenue to pay my own salary. I had to start pulling from savings every week just to buy groceries and pay bills, though I don't even know why I bothered at that point. Money had become virtually worthless. Our neighborhood grocery had shut down, but they had left the doors unlocked so that looters wouldn't have to smash the glass to get in. The police force was too concerned with its own desperation to interfere.

Despite my insistence that we continue to honor our financial responsibilities, services began to go out. First it was the satellite television, which was only playing news and reruns at that point because there was no money anywhere for new production. As much as we enjoyed those old sitcoms, they lost their appeal. We really only watched about five out of the two hundred or so channels we got anyway.

Cellular phones went next. I was talking with Maria one day when her voice abruptly went silent, and the signal strength icon on my smartphone was at zero. It seemed archaic to have to resort to the old wired phone plugged into the wall. As awkward as it felt, though, I also felt a certain sense of liberation, a freedom from that omnipresent need to be available. Less than two days later, the Internet was out and landlines were dead. The radio said that it was happening everywhere. A lot of places had already lost power. That was when I left work for the last time. It was time to refocus my attention on what we would need for survival once the electricity went out and gas lines went down. December in the Midwest can be brutally cold.

I began walking home to check on Maria, but my reluctant saunter soon became a run as I noticed angry crowds beginning to form in the streets. I knew then that that was it. There was no coming back. Maria was startled when I burst through the door and broke down crying when she saw me.

"What's happening, Joe? I'm so scared," she sobbed onto my shoulder as I held her tightly.

"Everything is going to be OK. I promise."

So many thoughts were rushing through my head. We needed food. We needed water. Soon we were going to need heat. We needed to secure the house. Where were our friends and family? Were they OK? What was going to happen next?

First things first.

"Maria, I need to go get food before there's nothing left."

"Where?"

"The grocery store."

"It's closed."

"I don't think that matters now."

I continued talking as I headed into the bedroom for the Mossberg.

"Joe! What are you doing with that?"

"You're taking it."

Maria was shaking as I loaded up the shotgun and forced it into her hands, giving her the briefest firearm tutorial in history just in case anyone tried to get in. *Safety off. Point-shoot-rack-repeat. Eight shells in the magazine, one in the chamber.* She stayed at the house with the doors bolted, the blinds drawn, and the lights out. Any place that had food was potentially dangerous, and I couldn't put her at risk. Human laws are ignored in such times of desperation. All that matters is staying alive. I grabbed the Ka-Bar from our bedside, rushed out the door, jumped in my car, and headed quickly to the grocery store with a duffel bag.

In my haste, I had left my coat, but there was no time to go back. There would be others scrambling for food too, and I didn't want a fight. The frigid air bit the bare skin on my arms. My breath froze before it even left my mouth, and my dry fingers could hardly grip the slick leather-wrapped steering wheel. It had been raining for days, and the ground was coated in a thick layer of black ice. The engine roared as I slid through the grid of streets, and the antilock brakes grabbed repeatedly but did little to slow me down. The car bounced off curbs and street signs as I sped toward downtown, completely destroying its once flawless metallic beauty.

I drifted around the last corner, smashing directly into the side of an armored personnel carrier. The National Guard had arrived, and not a moment too soon. It was anarchy. I got out of the car and stood watching in horror with so much adrenaline rushing through me that I couldn't even feel the cold anymore. The historic center of our little suburban town was engulfed in flames. Brick facades were collapsing onto the sidewalks and streets, and a furious mob was engaged in brutal hand-to-hand combat with the armed forces, who were doing everything in their power to control the chaos without resorting to gunpowder and lead.

"What are you doing out here?" I heard a voice yell. I spun to find myself looking down the barrel of a military-issue assault rifle in the shaking hands of a terrified kid who looked like he was fresh out of high school. A patch on the breast of his uniform read "Peterson" next to the American flag on his right shoulder. Surely pointing his weapon at fellow Americans was not what Peterson had anticipated when he had signed those enlistment papers.

"You can put the gun down, Peterson. I'm just getting food for my family."

We both glanced over at the half-destroyed grocery store and then back at each other.

"The liquor aisle is empty," he said, still pointing the M16 in my face. I wanted to ask if that was where he had just come from while his friends were all down the street brawling with a crazed mob, but I decided that that would not be in my best interest. How ironic that the most powerful government in the world would arm the kid with deadly weapons but wouldn't trust him with a beer.

"Food, not liquor," I said. "For my family."

He kept on his glare for a moment until a voice yelled from down the street, "Peterson, get your ass over here!" With that, he left me alone and headed toward the riot. I grabbed the duffel bag and bolted into what was left of the grocery store.

Peterson had been right about the liquor aisle; it was completely empty. I would guess it was cleared out within twenty-four hours of the store closing. Someone had come through and torn apart that whole section, probably enraged that they had arrived too late and missed the party. The rest of the shelves were pretty stark too, but I filled the bag with as much nutrition as I could, focusing on items that would preserve well.

Bottled water.

Canned fruits and vegetables.

Summer sausage.

Peanut butter.

Crackers.

Nothing frozen or refrigerated. It was cold enough outside to keep those things for the time being, but I had no idea how long the madness would last.

I wasn't the only scavenger there, nor was I the only one wearing a white collar, but none of us were interested in interacting. We didn't make eye contact. The shame was palpable. I was one among a random assortment of people just like me—people I would have met at conventions and seminars. People who had prided themselves on their work ethic, earning everything they owned, we were then reduced to the same primal acts of desperation that we had found utterly despicable not long before. It's all too easy to judge the poor from a plush couch in an air-conditioned living room. We suddenly filled the shoes of those we used to pity as we had dropped pocket change into their dirty hats outside of Cardinals games.

I had never thought of myself as a looter. Some years earlier, a hurricane had devastated New Orleans, and I remembered two particular photographs in newspaper articles, both of which depicted men in the exact same position that I was in. One man was white and the other was black, and though they were engaged in the same act, the captions described them quite differently. One was a looter. The other was gathering supplies for his family. I'm certain the disparity was unintentional, but societal roles had become so ingrained in us that one was automatically viewed as a criminal. I never felt like a criminal, as I'm sure neither of the men in the photographs nor the people around me in the grocery store did. We were doing what was necessary to survive.

Once I had filled the bag, I found myself stopping at the checkout counter and taking my wallet out of my pocket. Social habits aren't all easy to break. For a moment I waited, looking around at the wrecked shelves and the overturned payment register, the white collars around me scrambling for sustenance. I laid my wallet on the counter and walked out the front door, leaving behind my driver's license, six credit cards, insurance certificates, and a few hundred dollars in cash. None of those had any value anymore.

I stepped out onto the street just in time to see a freight train with its horn blaring barreling past the station in the center of town. It blasted through a car that had been abandoned on the tracks, leaving a trail of flames as it separated the brawling mob into two halves. I jumped back in the car and sped home, coming to a screeching stop in front of the house just as Paul and Sarah's truck arrived from the other direction.

"What are you guys doing here?" I asked, getting out of the car with the bag of food.

"We wanted to make sure you were OK," Sarah said. "Where's Maria?"

"Inside."

Paul and I just looked at each other without a word as we headed toward the house. I think the same thing occupied both of our minds: our conversation at the farm.

"I'm home, baby," I called to Maria through the door before I opened it. "Sarah and Paul are here. We're coming inside, so don't shoot us."

The shotgun was lying on the floor just inside the door with a fresh shell lying next to it. My stomach dropped. We passed through the kitchen and into the family room. Dining room. Living room. Home office.

"Maria!" I called to her. "Maria! Talk to me! Where are you?"

She didn't respond, but the cat did. I heard the meow from the bedroom, where I ran and threw the closet door open to find them both huddled in a dark corner. Maria was shivering in terror and clutching the cat tightly in her arms. I lifted her up and pulled her to me. She seemed to snap from a trance and picked up her crying where she had left it when I had gone to get food.

"What happened?" I asked. "Are you all right?"

"Please don't leave me again," she begged.

"Are you OK? Talk to me!"

"Someone...I thought someone was trying to get in. Please don't leave me again. Please don't leave me again."

"I won't. I promise."

I held her tightly, her body quivering in my arms.

Once Maria had settled, we all tried to relax. We pulled some chicken breasts out of the freezer to thaw for dinner and prepared a nice marinade from various bottled items in the refrigerator. Everything in there would have to be eaten within a day or so anyway. We wouldn't have electricity much longer, so we might as well enjoy it while we could.

We had to get our family, I thought, to make sure they were OK. Throughout dinner, I couldn't get them off my mind. They all lived in safe, or what had been safe, parts of town, and I figured they had enough sense to stay in their homes. For the moment, everyone was probably OK. That could change at any time. Conditions outside were deteriorating at an exponential rate. What we had experienced over the last few weeks was only the beginning of what was to come. When refrigerators and pantries were emptied and there was no food left in the abandoned grocery stores, then where would people turn? It would be a free-for-all. Every man for himself. I thought of the farm again.

In the light of the next day, Paul and I left the girls with an arsenal at the house and headed off to round up our family around town: my parents and sister, Maria's parents, her brother and his wife, their two children, and Paul's and Sarah's families. We spent three or four hours breaking traffic laws and gathering relatives from all corners of the metropolitan area. The freezing rain seemed like it would never let up. I remember suggesting that we build an ark. Paul laughed and said something about the *Titanic* having been sunk by less ice than what we were facing; a boat would do us no good. Traffic, needless to say, was light. The fortunate thing about the current situation was that it kept every sane person at home, so we had no trouble finding the ones we were looking for. The collapse had happened gradually enough that none of us had been isolated anywhere. That was also fortunate. I remembered hearing some years before that you should always have a plan and a meeting place for a natural disaster, but I never knew anyone who actually did. Except for Noah's father, of course, as ill timed as his preparations were. These things always happen when you least expect them and never when you're planning for them. What we were dealing with was a rather unnatural disaster, but a disaster nonetheless. That's what it felt like at the time. I lacked the faith and foresight necessary to see it all as birth pains.

As we drove, I glanced down at my hands on the steering wheel and noticed how bitten down my fingernails were. Some were bleeding. I looked up and realized that I hadn't seen a plane in quite some time. Perhaps it was the overcast sky that kept them out of sight, but I was pretty certain that nobody was flying anymore. The train I had seen crashing through town was probably the last one I would see for a while. I pitied anyone who hadn't managed to make it home before the long-range transportation systems had gone down. Wherever they were, they were probably stuck there. If home was across an ocean, it was time to find a boat and some patience. Across the country, they would need a car, or, more likely, a few of them, as fuel was no longer commercially available. We were reliant on whatever was in our tanks. But then what? I looked at the fuel gauge. Less than a quarter of a tank. I decided not to mention it yet. Gathering our family was the first priority. Once they were all with us, then we could start thinking about fuel.

But I overestimated my gas mileage. We ran dry on our way to Sarah's parents' house and had to walk awhile to get there. Fortunately, they still had a car with enough left in the tank to make it back to our house, and on the way, we passed my abandoned and unlocked chunk of metal on the highway. There were an increasing number of those accumulating on the roads and an unusual amount of people walking on the shoulder. Most were headed away from town.

Our house was then full of relatives and food, a scenario reminiscent of every holiday gathering since my childhood, but without the joyful ambience. We had taken as much food and water with us as possible from each house we had visited. Every container we could find, we filled from the tap, and we boiled what we intended to drink later because we didn't know if the water treatment facilities were still operational. Our booty would sustain us for the next few days, and nobody left the house during that time. Conversation was not abundant. Neither was laughter. We all just sat around, waiting, wondering what would happen next.

The electricity went out in the middle of the day. That meant the ignition on the furnace, the thermostat, and the blower were no longer functional. We lit the gas oven with a barbecue lighter and left its door open to produce as much warmth as possible, but the natural gas line quit producing later that night. I had a fire going in the fireplace. Unfortunately, all of the extra firewood was stored on pallets outside and was then completely soaked after days of ceaseless rain. Paul and I carried some into the house, but we would be frozen by the time it was dry enough to burn. We all huddled close together that night, shivering as we tried to sleep.

The following day was Christmas Eve. The temperature inside the house gradually continued to drop throughout the day. We tore the wrapping paper and opened boxes from the gifts under the tree to restart the fire, but there was no dry wood left to sustain it. We had no choice but to start burning our belongings. We threw in books, picture frames, and various household items. Eventually, we started breaking up furniture to burn. It was devastating. Piece by piece, we watched old memories and family history literally go up in flames, producing heat that seemed to dissipate immediately as it rose to the high ceilings.

Maria and I held each other and shivered, staring into the fireplace as if entranced. It wasn't the fire that captivated us. It was an overwhelming sense of grief and helplessness that crept up on us both as we realized that the life that we had been working for was gone forever. Things would never go back to the way they had been. The house no longer felt like our home. It felt more like an oversized cardboard box with nothing left to offer us except for rooms that were too big to heat.

None of us had ever known true desperation. The feeling of having nothing was an unfamiliar one, and we didn't know how to cope. As the sun went down that Christmas Eve, I almost envied the homeless or the people in third world countries who had never had a car or a computer or a cell phone. Their lives probably hadn't changed much over the last few months. I lamented the inexorable loss of all my worldly desires—a big house, fancy cars, a corner office, and a six-figure salary—that would never again be fulfilled.

We could hear explosions and screaming not far away. They were still rioting outside, and it was getting worse. People were cold and hungry. I think Paul knew all along what needed to be done. He was just waiting for me to say the word. I looked past all of our family toward him and Sarah, who were cuddled together in the same position on the floor that Maria and I were in. When he glanced back at me, I silently mouthed the word "farm." He replied with a nod and then turned back to the fire. We would leave the next day.

3

THE ESSENTIALS

When the sun came up on Christmas day, there was not a cloud in the sky. We began packing right away with the sounds of rioting still in the background. Our burden was kept as light as possible, but there were certain things we knew we would need. First, of course, were food and water. Then came warmth. All the clothes we needed we were already wearing, having donned layer upon layer to keep from freezing in the night. Every sheet, blanket, and sleeping bag in the house came with us. The cabin at the farm was smaller than our house and, though a bit crowded, would be much more efficient to heat. It had a large fireplace in addition to the wood-burning stove. There was an abundance of wood there, so having a fuel source for heat and cooking wouldn't be an issue as long as we were prepared and kept it protected from the weather. There was an axe and an open shed for that purpose. We also brought a tent, just in case. Then toiletries—soap, shampoo, toothbrush, toothpaste, and dental floss—all of the hygienic necessities to keep us civilized and whatever medicine we had in the cabinet. My Mossberg came with us too, along with Paul's assortment of hunting rifles. The Ka-Bar he had given me was still on my belt.

We set off to the highway in a convoy of five cars, knowing that we were running on the last bit of fuel we would have for a long time. Our Christmas gift to ourselves that year was a new home at the farm. Two of the cars ran out of gas on the way, so we had to consolidate gear and people in the ones still running and leave the others behind. It was a tight trip.

There were around twenty of us to begin with. Over the last few weeks, we had all been so consumed by adapting and coping with the collapse that none of us had had much communication with our extended family or other friends. We never had the opportunity to tell them where we were going. Some of them had been to Paul and Sarah's farm before, and I hoped that they would make their way to us. It was no secret that the farm was Paul's safe haven. I got the impression that he wasn't very troubled by the state of the world. To him, it seemed that it had all been inevitable. It was as if he possessed an understanding of human nature and, in particular, of our inherent need for a connection to the natural earth that few of us enjoyed. His aura of peace throughout that time brought the rest of us at least some comfort. A few times

I noticed him looking to the sky with his eyes closed and a slight smile.

As we wound through the woods on the gravel road that led from the highway, a light snow began to fall. It was a perfect powder snow. The trees glistened beautifully, and as the snow accumulated, the sunlight sprayed a bright, angelic glow through the forest. The air was quiet and still. When we pulled up to the cabin, the roof was covered in a fine white layer, completing the image of the quintessential gingerbread house set on a picturesque rolling landscape. I could hear the stream still babbling, though it was then half-frozen.

"Make yourselves at home," Paul said as we started to unload the cars and Maria's niece and nephew ran off to play in the snow. A few of the men collected wood from the shed and got a fire going inside, and the cabin warmed up quickly. We already felt more at home than we had in a while, with a sense of safety that had vanished from our own homes. The farm was the same as it had always been, untainted by the deterioration of the modern world. It was nice to feel some consistency somewhere.

Our food supply was getting short, but Paul said there was a neighbor down the road who would help us out—an old man named Abraham. Abraham was a farmer who had lived out there for Paul's entire life. I would guess he had been there even before Paul's grandfather had built the cabin. Paul's description of the old man painted a picture of an eccentric hick—the kind of person I would have scoffed at in days past. Then, it seemed, that was precisely the kind of person we needed to help us find our footing out there. He had skills and resources that most of us lacked entirely.

Paul and I took his truck and headed toward Abraham's farm while everyone else got settled. The few homes out there were separated by many acres of undeveloped land, and the drive took some time, but it was peaceful. I wasn't used to driving without the sounds of music or a radio show. Instead, the muffled sounds of rubber on snow-covered rock and the hum of the engine took me back to the last quiet moments of ignorance on the morning that it had all begun. The old man's driveway branched from the same gravel road as our new home, but it was invisible under the snow. The only landmark was an old wooden mailbox with no street number that I imagine was seldom used. It was a long driveway, and Paul kept the pace slow since we could not quite tell if we were on it or not. I think we probably created more of a path than we followed.

We crested a hill, and I caught a glimpse of Abraham's house just as I heard the grinding sound of the truck's antilock brakes. We slid off the road where a tree caught the front passenger side fender and spun us around, and the momentum carried the truck over onto its side, creating a puff as it tumbled softly into the snow. The engine died on impact, the wheels stopped spinning, and for a moment, the two of us were frozen in silent confusion as we tried to regain our bearings.

"You all right?" Paul asked after catching his breath. I looked over and saw only snow and dirt outside his window.

"Yeah, you?"

"Yeah. The bridge is out ahead. I was trying to stop."

We smashed out the windshield and climbed out of the truck. Down the hill in front of us were a creek and an old wooden bridge that had collapsed into it. From the looks of it, the bridge had been out for a while. Beyond that was a vast open field where Abraham's small house stood all alone, surrounded by wooded hills that spread upward from all sides of the quiet valley.

"Well, I was almost out of gas anyway," said Paul as we brushed snow and glass off of our clothes.

We began the half-mile walk across the white field toward the house, leaving footprints in the snow behind us. There was light in the windows and smoke rising from the chimney in a thin white ribbon that dissipated gradually as it reached the sky. The old man emerged from the door and stood on the front porch puffing on a corncob pipe as we approached. He was bundled up warmly, and under the beacon of his red nose was a huge white beard through which I perceived a sly grin. A short distance away was a stable, and I could hear horses uneasily rustling at the sounds of unfamiliar voices. Two dogs ran from the side of the house and greeted us, barking and jumping excitedly.

"Whatchyu boys want?" the old man called to us. "Y'all junkin' up my prop'ty? Damn city kids."

"What's the deal with the bridge, Abe?" Paul asked as we stepped onto the porch.

"Don't use that driveway much no mo'. Got riddama truck."

"Why?"

He raised his eyebrows and looked past us at the carcass of Paul's truck lying on its side. "Unreli'ble," he said. "An' Tennessee Walk'n Horse don't need no gas."

Paul scoffed and shook his head. "Listen, Abe, we moved our families out to the farm."

"'Bout time. Don't see folks too much no mo'."

"Well I expect you'll be seeing quite a bit more of us. We're running low on food, though. This is my friend Joe. We were hoping you could help us out."

Abraham smiled and shook his head.

"Oh, you city kids gots lotsa learn'n ta do. But da good Lode blessed me wit' mo' den I need here. I think I can help y'all out. Come on inside."

Abe never asked why we had all moved out to the farm. I still don't know if he had any idea what was happening in the rest of the world. He probably figured that regardless of our reasoning, we were better off, so the *why* didn't matter. He took us to a series of underground storage containers with straw bedding where he had stocked away more than enough produce to last through the winter. The yields of his harvest were divided and stored by type. He had potatoes, cabbage, spinach, carrots, broccoli, celery, onions, beets, winter squash, and varieties of nuts and grains. They were kept separate not only for the sake of organization, but also to maximize the life span and quality of the produce, as different varieties have different shelf lives. It was an underground smorgasbord of commodities from the garden, orchard, and vineyard. Some were fresh, some canned, and some juiced or dried for preservation. There was no way we were going to go hungry.

Abraham helped us fill sacks with his produce to take back with us. He told us that his surplus at the end of the winter was normally the first stock on the tables at the local farmers' market when they opened in the spring, but that was only so it wouldn't go to waste. He didn't need the money, but he kept on harvesting his crop season after season and year after year, simply because the farm was his life. It always had been. It gave him purpose. He would deliver his produce on a wooden cart pulled by a pair of his horses, which he then graciously loaned to us so that we could deliver the same load to our own families for no compensation.

Once the cart was filled and the horses hitched, Abraham pointed us in the direction of a new path back to our farm through the woods. The horses knew the way, he said, and he would be over later with some chickens, milk, butter, and various other items that we would need. We thanked him and set off.

In the months that followed, I realized that my skills scarcely exceeded those of a plecostomus, but those months were made easier by the old man's presence. He never stayed overnight, but he visited every day to make sure we had everything we needed, and he provided instruction on every aspect of our new lifestyle. Although he had lived alone out there for years, I think he was grateful for the company. He continued to bring us produce regularly until our own underground storage bins were complete. In the spring, he said, we would learn farming techniques so that we could start producing on our own. Then he would bring us livestock. In the meantime, we absorbed the basics of a truly self-sustaining farm. We churned butter from milk. We pressed oils from seeds and nuts. We grew yeast to raise bread or collected the yeast from nearby woods, and we ground flour from wheat grain. We heated well water for bathing, and Abraham taught us how to make soap the old-fashioned way. Cleanliness was vital to preserve our health. Without doctors to diagnose illness and to treat us when we got sick, it was up to us to ensure that didn't happen.

Lye was vital to the manufacturing of soap, and since we couldn't just run out and pick some up at the hardware store, we had to make it using fresh rainwater and hardwood ashes from the fire. Our lye solution was combined with animal fats and fragrant natural oils to create a versatile bar soap that was even suitable for hair cleansing and conditioning. Oral hygiene was just as vital. To clean our teeth, we used various mixtures of ground fruits and vegetables with a more grainy texture, such as carrots and celery, mixed with strawberries to whiten or with mint for those who were still partial to the classic toothpaste flavor. To their parents' amazement, Maria's niece and nephew actually enjoyed brushing their teeth. Thorough rinsing was important so the acids from the fruits didn't sit too long and corrode enamel. Those of us who could tolerate the flavor and the temporary blackened mouth even made paste from wood ashes. Toothbrushes and picks could be made from twigs.

Abraham taught us a variety of personal care recipes composed of natural ingredients from our own land. More and more, we found that those products kept our bodies healthier than the ones we'd had before, and the recipes could easily be manipulated depending on the preferences of the user. If you had dry skin, you could add more oils to your soap or use less potent lye. If you had delicate teeth, you used fewer acidic fruits in your solution.

Everything slowed down. Our sleep cycles gradually synchronized with the setting and rising of the sun. The work required to maintain a minimum level of comfort was exhausting, and by the time night fell, we were usually more than ready for it. I spent so much time chopping wood to keep the fires burning that I could already see significant improvement in my physical ability. My muscles toned. My belly vanished. As we began to adapt, the laborious evolution into this farming lifestyle got easier by the week. It became our new normal. Every few days, more people fleeing the chaos of the cities would arrive looking for a place to stay, and we always took them in. They came from all over—from St. Louis, Springfield, Memphis, and Little Rock—from every urban center within a couple hundred-mile radius. Even the unfamiliar faces became family. Some of us made occasional trips back to the darkened town that had once been our home; we went by horse to gather tools, whatever supplies we could find, and people we knew to bring them to the farm, and every time I saw the city, it looked more and more desolate. The violence was dying down as it became necessary to focus on survival rather than on destruction. Groups of migrants passed by on the old highways, looking for new places to settle away from the hideous urban skeleton. We moved the cars back to the highway, stripped them of any components that could be useful, and left them there so that we wouldn't have to look at them on the property anymore. The sight of complex machinery, plastic, and rubber was a constant reminder of the collapse that we just didn't need.

Our tiny community continued to grow, quickly surpassing a hundred people. Most of them slept under brush piles around open fires to keep warm. At the first sign of spring, we began to build more cabins to accommodate everyone. The smell of fresh-cut cedar and oak lingered constantly in the air. We chopped trees down to size, fit them together like the old Lincoln log toys I remembered from my childhood, and used the remnants for firewood. With our growing workforce, each cabin went up surprisingly quickly. The foundations were built of stone, which came about eighteen inches above grade, so the wooden walls and floors were less accessible to termites and carpenter ants. We packed the gaps between timbers with mud and clay. The means to manufacture glass and metal products were not yet readily available, so for the time being, windows and doors were simply rectangular openings in the walls with wooden planks that fit within them to keep the cold out. Every cabin was equipped with a door on each end for circulation and with a large fireplace to be used for heating and cooking. The roofs were also framed with notched logs at three-to-one slopes to minimize wasted space underneath while still ensuring proper runoff and the strength necessary to support the weight of snow in the winter. The roof surfaces were coated in mud to seal them and would eventually grow grass, the roots of which would absorb moisture and act as a binding and insulating blanket that would protect the house from the elements. Our cabins varied in size depending on the number of people who would be living in them. Nobody wanted to heat more space than necessary.

We also needed beds, blankets, and pillows. Few of our new arrivals had brought any more than the clothes on their backs. Bed frames were built of wood. All of the soft components were made from animal skins stuffed with feathers or wool since it had grown warm enough to shear the sheep that Abraham had given us. They were held together with wool thread or with twine made by cutting the inner layer of bark from a tree branch, tearing it into strips after removing the brittle outer layer, boiling the strips, laying them out to dry, and finally cording them together. Sometimes we used vines or shrubs that could be broken down and stripped into fibers. Rope was made the same way, but thicker.

After some months, there weren't many things we had that we couldn't make on the farm. Among those still leftover were our clothes, though they were becoming worn, and we were starting to make new ones from wool and cotton and sometimes even by felting the fur of our household pets. My Ka-Bar was constantly on my waist. I still had my kinetic wound watch that would keep time as long as I wore it daily, and my shotgun was stored in the one-room cabin that had been built for Maria and me. And then there were our wedding rings.

There were some things that we missed more than others. Indoor plumbing was at the top of that list. It was something that we had always taken for granted. I had never invested much thought in the massive network of pipes that routed water under pressure directly into our house for our disposal at any time and for any reason and then took it all away to a treatment plant somewhere once it had served our purposes. At the farm, we were collecting water from the well or the stream and heating it over a fire, which was another burden we had to adapt to. We couldn't turn a knob or flip a switch to turn on the oven or the stove. Cooking meant building a fire. Paul and Sarah were the only ones in the community with a wood-burning iron stove, which then seemed like quite a luxury in comparison to the fireplaces the rest of us cooked in. They were also the only ones with glass windows and a door on hinges. I remembered when that cabin had seemed so primitive.

Much of our food was still coming from Abraham's farm, but our increasing population was depleting his livestock. Paul had been hunting for a while to keep us all fed and to lighten the burden on the old man. Mike and Gabe, a couple of our friends who had recently arrived, usually joined him. I had never been interested in hunting. Fishing, I could get into, because I felt no connection with a cold, scaled water-dwelling creature. Killing a mammal was different. I had always enjoyed the flavor of meat, but I had never wanted anything to do with the process that put it on the table. I was realizing that hunting meant more than just food. A deer, for example, had served many of the needs of Native Americans. The hide was used for clothing, moccasins, tents, and satchels or pouches, among other things. Hides and hoofs could be boiled to produce a strong adhesive. Antlers and bones could be made into tools. Sinews, or tendons and ligaments, were used for thread and bow strings, particularly the back strap sinew. We also used them for dental floss. Almost every part of the animal served some purpose, and because we had no store-bought synthetic substitutes, I felt an increasing intimacy with and respect for the original inhabitants of the land.

It was inevitable that I would learn to hunt. Paul preferred a bow to a rifle, and he insisted that it was important for me to learn that way. Although we could make gunpowder using guano, coal, and sulfur, those commodities were limited, and we only acquired them infrequently. Abraham, who was never short of useful wisdom, came with us on my first trip out. He met us—Mike, Gabe, Paul, and me—early in the morning, and we headed into the forest when it was still dark outside. They had given me some lessons on the bow and arrow, and I thought my shot was decent, but the shot itself was just a small part of the hunt. We wore camouflaged attire made from the very woods from which we gathered so much of our sustenance. My steps were hasty, and more than once I was reproached for the noise I made when I walked. "Boy, you mak'n a racket," Abraham said. "Scar'n deer next county over."

When we were deep in the woods, we separated until we were far enough apart that we couldn't see each other, and I found a sturdy tree and climbed about ten feet up. After half the day I hadn't seen anything close enough to take a shot, and suspecting that the height of my perch might have been inadequate, I decided to climb higher. Heights were not my favorite of things. I reached about twenty feet or so and settled into the pit of a large branch where it met the trunk and secured myself with a leather strap around the tree. Then I waited.

The sun was going down when I spotted her—a young doe. She strolled casually right under me and stopped nearby to gnaw on a dogwood branch. For a few moments, I just watched her, admiring her beautiful presence in the quiet setting. Birds were chirping. The yellow light on the leaves changed as the breeze blew and their shadows flickered, and the stream babbled faintly behind me. Her bronze fur glistened as she ate. She was like the finishing brush stroke on a long labored-over painting, the graceful completion of which finally granted rest to the artist.

I was there to ruin that serene masterpiece. I might as well have been tearing up the canvas. Although I tried, I could not feel any other way about it. I had never killed before, and though I knew it was then my responsibility to provide for my family in the most primal of ways, I was still not at peace with the idea. Was the life of that doe less valuable than my own simply because she lacked the capacity for deeper reasoning? It would certainly have been improper to suggest the same of a human being who suffered the same deficiency, and I would have had no trouble naming more than a few of those. There was no time for justification. Though perhaps not at that very moment, there would come a time when such a decision would mean the difference between life and death, and at that time, my deeper reasoning would be meaningless to predator and prey alike. The conscience will only interfere when there is a choice.

My stomach felt uneasy as I took up my bow and aimed the arrow just behind her shoulder. I had the perfect shot. She was completely vulnerable and unaware, but I didn't release right away. I kept on watching her, the bone tip of my arrow never leaving the invisible line that would take her life, her fate resting on no more than three of my fingertips. In my mind, I couldn't help but personify her. I thought of the old cartoon, *Bambi,* and how tragic it had seemed to me as a child. I had become the hunter. I was the villain.

My hesitation cost me the shot. I felt a bead of sweat drip down my face, and as soon as I realized that I was perspiring, she smelled the stink of my humanity. Her head jerked sharply, and just as I released the arrow, she bounded off, leaving it stuck in the ground having not even grazed her. I called the day then and headed back home, where I was welcomed by Maria's beautiful and ever-forgiving smile when I came in the doorway.

"Get anything?"

"No."

"Hm," she replied softly. I sensed a tone of relief.

The other four arrived after dark, and a bunch of us already had a fire going outside while we waited for them. Paul, Mike, Gabe, and Abraham each dragged a deer behind them, already field dressed and ready to be skinned and hung.

"Already back, Joe?" Gabe asked. "You must have had better luck than we did. Didn't see a thing all day, but a whole group came through just a little while ago."

"I didn't get anything," I said, looking away, more ashamed then of my tarnished masculinity.

"Well, don't worry about that," he replied. "I didn't kill anything my first time out either."

Abraham laughed and said, "Yep, sometime the deer git away. Sometime he win, an' sometime you lose. Ya hafta lose sometime. People always win git cocky, an' that'n a worse loss than a deer, but they too cocky to know it." Then he gently laid out the eight-point buck he had brought back, knelt over the carcass, and bowed his head for a moment.

There was a time when I had always won. I didn't explain why I had come back empty-handed.

It was weeks later when I shot my first deer, and that was a bittersweet moment. It was my hardest kill, both physically and sentimentally. Between Abraham's farm, the woods, and the stream, hunger was seldom a problem, which was more than I could say for anyone who was still in the city. We used Abraham's plow and Clydesdales to cultivate more land for crops, and he generously provided all the necessary seed as promised.

We rose early every morning to our respective trades. I had not adopted one in particular yet, so I was sort of learning them all until I found one that fit. I wasn't much good at anything. Every occupation, though, gave us time for thought, whether we were hunters, fishermen, farmers, or craftsmen.

There was a lot of contemplation happening on the farm—more than there ever had been during our former jobs. Not that we didn't think before, but it was about different things. I used to think about market capitalization, price/earnings ratios, derivatives, dividends, and interest rates. After the collapse, I thought mostly about the consequences of failing to provide for the one person who depended on me and how to ensure that those consequences were never realized. That used to be accomplished with a steady paycheck. Some things had become simpler, and some things were more complex.

I thought a lot about the rest of the world. I wondered how people in other cultures were adapting to the new condition. Many were certainly better equipped to adapt than we were, which was a strange thought. We had considered ourselves so advanced. The terms "first world" and "third world" no longer had any meaning, and the places that had once been so labeled were no longer separated by invisible lines.

I also thought about war. Most modern wars were rooted in differences that seemed more and more inconsequential. Anyone who still had the time to look for someone to blame for their problems had fewer of them than the rest of us. There wasn't much point in placing blame, just like there wasn't much point in attempting to recover the lifestyle we had left, even if that was sometimes all we wanted.

The people of the new world did have one advantage, though. We had seen the way the world was before and everything that had been wrong with it. Most of our luxuries had been lost in the collapse, but with them had gone most of the corruption that we had all despised. Based on what we had heard from other refugees and seen with our own eyes, it was reasonable to assume that there was no more government and that there were no more corporations. Never before had we possessed the influence to fix such powerful entities. In the aftermath, we did. From experience, we knew what worked, and we knew what didn't. It's far more difficult to change a culture set in its ways than it is to create a new one. We no longer had ways to be set in. Our only way then was the way forward.

4

THE JOURNEY

I immediately regretted volunteering for the journey. It had seemed sensible at first, as I had not yet found my niche on the farm, for me to be the one to leave it in order to find out what was happening outside of our community. I was not particularly good at anything useful. It was a glaring fact I had to face and the reason it was always I who volunteered for scavenging missions and searches for nearby settlements. We had found two other villages with which we shared food and supplies, and the barter system between us brought a literal meaning to the term "horse-trading." I never knew where they were getting all of the livestock that we procured from them, but we were in no position to judge anyone for stealing. After all, they never stole from us. It seemed that the commodities we produced were too valuable to jeopardize the relationship.

People there would ask me if I had heard anything of the outside world. My reply was always the same: "I know of you. How far outside is the outside world?" Among those of us who did leave the farm, we all agreed on one thing: it was quiet out there. Some of those who went back to the city in the later months didn't want to talk about what they had seen, but I felt there was more happening than we knew.

Over a year had passed since the Great Collapse, and the springtime sowing had begun again. The forest and fields were greening for the second time since we had moved to the farm, and still, I was a broken man without direction. Perhaps accepting a new and unclaimed responsibility was my way of compensating for my shortcomings, giving myself some degree of importance. Maria loved me no matter what, she said, but there was this primal need to prove my worth.

"You're so brave, honey," she used to say patronizingly when I would kill a spider in the kitchen or toss a garter snake from the yard with a rake. Then she'd follow her words with a kiss on my cheek. Bravery had been defined differently then.

Our curiosities had been discussed over campfires for a while. *I wonder how my cousins in Colorado are holding up— yeah, I have friends in Florida. I hope they're doing OK—this winter must have been rough on Chicago.* I don't remember whose idea it was originally, but eventually, it was suggested that we send someone to find out.

"I'll do it," I said. It had been a particularly emasculating day of hunting, and I'd had a few drinks. Everyone just looked at me. I took another sip.

"Joe, come on," Maria stopped me.

"What, no faith?"

"Of course I have faith in you, but have you forgotten I'm your wife, Joe? You need to stay with me," she mumbled. "You promised you'd never leave me again."

"Maria, sometimes a guy has to take responsibility."

"Fine, then I'm going with you."

"No way." I laughed. "That's too dangerous. We don't have any idea what's going on out there."

Everyone was quietly watching us.

"Exactly," Paul interjected, "you don't know, Joe. It wouldn't be a good idea to send one guy out alone." He looked around at the group. "Anyone else willing? Daniel? John? Noah?" Nobody spoke up. "Gabe?"

Silence.

"Then I'll go," he said.

"No way, Paul," Sarah jumped in.

"You're way too important here," Noah followed quickly. "Nobody knows this land like you do."

"You've got Abraham," replied Paul.

"We can't just rely on him. He's an old man, Paul. What if, God forbid, something happens to him while you're away?"

Paul smiled. "Somehow I don't see that happening."

"It doesn't matter," said Sarah. "We need you."

"They're right, Paul," I slurred. "I, on the other hand, am expendable, and it's about damn time I did something productive. What's the problem? You'll trust me with your IRA, but now that that's all gone—"

"Joe, relax, that's not what I'm saying."

"Well, let me tell you something. All of you. I didn't put us here, but I can put things back the way they were."

"Well, look at you, big man," Mike laughed, pushing me over.

"I'm not so sure everyone wants things back the way they were," Gabe said, "but it would be nice not to feel so isolated. We've got to find out what's happening out there."

"Let it go, Joe," Maria whispered to me. "You and I can talk about this later."

I shut my mouth and took another drink, and the conversation awkwardly evolved to a lighter one.

The next morning, I realized what I had done. I'm never drinking again, I thought, a sentiment I had awoken to so many mornings in college. After the previous night, the journey was on everybody's mind, and I had committed myself. We all knew that we needed some connection to the outside world, and thanks to my big mouth, everyone was looking to me. Nobody talked about it, but I knew they were waiting for me to bring it up again—to reaffirm my commitment.

My true emotions, those that I was always straining to disguise, had been publically exposed that night at the fire as I had wallowed in my own sense of failure and drank myself into buffoonery. I had been important in the world before the collapse. I had worn a suit to work. People used to come to me for advice on all sorts of things, not just on where to put their money. I had been a success, somebody that people looked up to. My marriage had been happy. My life had been good. As soon as the system came crashing down, nobody was interested in anything I had to say anymore. It was as if I couldn't be trusted, but perhaps that feeling was simply my own conscience interpreting the guilt I felt over having been part of that system. I had enjoyed the rural lifestyle, but only as an occasional weekend escape from the fast-paced routine that we had fallen into. Although I may have dreamed of a simpler life, I had never actually planned to live that way. But I was completely immersed in it. I was angry, and though on a clear day, I knew that things could and should never go back to the way they were, I often wished that it were all just a dream I would wake up from.

Under the stress of the last year, my marriage had been struggling. Maria and I had been fighting more than we ever had. Every little thing set me off. I didn't hold her when she slept anymore. Given the current state of things, I didn't understand why she had asked to come along. The more I thought about the journey, the more I realized that it was something I needed to do and that I couldn't bring my wife with me, even if I wanted to. Based on what I had seen and heard, I suspected that there was no law anymore in our country or in any other. The only thing keeping a man honest was his own set of morals, and in the world we had known before, that simply hadn't been enough for most. The human factor was just one of many dangers. The environment was another. If I were to embark on such a journey, it would be a slow one, and there would be no Hiltons along the way. My fear grew by the day, as did the knowledge that I would inevitably have to face the challenge for the sake of everyone there. James Neil Hollingworth, under the pseudonym Ambrose Redmoon, wrote that, "Courage is not the absence of fear, but rather the judgment that something else is more important than one's fear." That definition could not be more accurate.

While working in the fields one day, I confronted Paul with my thoughts.

"What do you think?" I asked him.

"I think somebody's got to do it. There are billions of people out there right now going through the same things were are. We can learn from them, and perhaps they can learn from us. We can't stay isolated the way we have been."

"And I volunteered."

"And you volunteered."

"I was thinking. If I'm going out there, we could use a long-distance system of communication. I could help set it up."

"The Pony Express." He laughed.

"Well, yeah, something like that."

"Postmaster Joe. You'll be like Kevin Costner in that movie."

"*The Postman?*"

"Yeah, *The Postman*."

"I hope the world hasn't come to that."

Then I took the conversation to Maria, which is probably where it should have started. I had grown less concerned with considering her in my decisions. She sat stroking the cat to calm her nerves, not speaking, just listening as I explained why I had resolved to leave. The job could only be entrusted to a person of great ambition and persistence and integrity, and I was the one person willing and able to take it on. I didn't say it, but it gave me that sense of success and purpose that I'd had before the collapse.

When I was finished speaking, I turned to leave, and that was when she stopped me to ask the question that I would find myself agonizing over for some time to come.

"What happened to you, Joe? Where is the man I married?"

"Right here, Maria!" I yelled at her. "Success or failure? Your choice."

"You never gave me a choice, and I think you and I have different ideas about what those things mean. Look, we're OK here. God's given us everything we need."

"Your superstitions are useless, Maria. Where was God when the market tanked and people lost their jobs and destroyed everything?"

"He was right there. But they were looking the other way."

She began to cry.

"Nonsense," I said. "We lost everything. Don't you understand that?"

"We don't need all that stuff, Joe."

"Oh, really? So all those hours I worked to give you everything you could ever want meant nothing to you?"

"Of course they did," she answered, "but you're more important to me than any of that."

"So you'd rather I stay here in this aimless existence, living off of the generosity of successful people?"

"You're obsessed with success, Joe! Stop thinking that way. You have me here."

"Do I?"

"Joe, what do you mean?"

"I mean I don't know what's going to happen with us. I need a change."

"Joe, please don't abandon me."

"It's done, so deal with it."

She sat down on the bed, and I left her there alone in our cabin, still crying.

We spoke less and less after that, and when we did, she couldn't look at me. It was as if she were speaking to the floor. There was no backing out after that argument, and my resentment festered. It was easier not to ask myself why. Perhaps it was that I envied her faith, or that she remained so content after losing all of the things that I had worked so hard to provide.

I asked around, trying to recruit a companion with some kind of useful skill. I knew that Paul was too important to the livelihood of everyone at the farm. He knew the land better than anyone, and he had learned so much from Abraham through the years that our community would have been doomed without his expertise. All of our knowledge about how to survive, everything we manufactured, and everything we grew came from the two of them. I had no doubt that without them, most of us would have died long before, and the rest would still have been struggling to survive. Mike and Gabe were the best hunters behind Paul, and the growing population needed all three of them and many more to keep everyone fed. We had expanded to the size of a small village by then, and our population was well into the hundreds, much larger than when we had started with just Paul's and Abraham's farms. Daniel and John had the fields and livestock, and none of the newer arrivals possessed the same combination of physical endurance and farming knowledge that the two of them had gained from the old man. The number of their apprentices grew as our population did. Noah tended all of our horses, and he had become an invaluable groom and trainer to our growing herd of mustangs. Beyond them, I could think of no other person who wouldn't be more of a burden than an asset. I would be traveling alone.

Word of my impending journey began to spread throughout the community. Talking to Abraham, I started to realize just how trying that journey would be. We no longer had cars, so I would be traveling by horse, and I couldn't expect to cover much more than thirty miles each day. The route we had planned, however, was close to nine thousand miles. Taking into account time spent at other settlements, assuming I could find them, it would be nearly a year before I would see home again. It was a shocking realization. A knot began to grow in my stomach.

We drew the journey out on an old map that we had taken from one of the cars the year before, figuring that the major population centers of the past would be the best places to look for new settlements nearby.

New Orleans.
Miami.
Washington, DC.
New York.
Chicago.
Seattle.
San Francisco.
Los Angeles.
Phoenix.
Denver.

My course traced a line around three-quarters of the perimeter of what used to be the United States of America and then straight through the Midwest and back to our Ozark home. I would experience a range of climates from hot and dry to cold and wet, and I would see landscapes from flat to mountainous and fertile to arid. I would visit more places in the next year than I had over my entire life combined, and I would certainly see them all in a way in which they had never been seen before, either by me or anyone else. Most importantly, hopefully, I would meet many people who shared our burden and our need for a new beginning. And a new beginning it would be. It was a new world, just as literally as it had been when Amerigo Vespucci had coined the term over five hundred years before, and I was in a position to pioneer a whole new culture and way of life to go with it.

I would like to say that leaving Maria was the most difficult part. When I was a single man, there would have been no hesitation before embarking on such an adventure. Before I entered what people had called the "real world" of adult responsibility, I used to take thousand-mile road trips on a day's notice. But things were different. There was a person relying on me, trusting me to keep her safe and to provide for her, but I was too ambitious and selfish to be concerned with that. Instead, I looked upon her as a burden—a hindrance to my potential. What if I didn't make it back? She might never know what had happened—or how or where. For her, there would never be closure. She would spend every day of the rest of her life waiting for me, still hoping I would come riding in with some extraordinary and heroic explanation of where I had been. I knew that because there was a time when, had our roles been reversed, I would have done the same.

Some nights when we were curled up in bed, warm under the covers but cold to one another, I could feel her body tense as she choked back sobs. She thought I was sleeping, but I wasn't. I imagine those dark nights brought back memories of times when we were happy in our old home. Nights when we used to lay wrapped up together—when we could sleep until morning without being awakened by nightmares. Perhaps those memories of a time when the two of us had been so blissful in the company of only each other made her feel the most vulnerable. Happy memories brought her pain and a tormenting fear that she was losing me. Sleeping in the dark cabin without me would be different. Maria was afraid of both the dark and of being alone, which was a dreadful pair she would have to face every night while I was gone. She would always wonder when I would be coming home. Would I ever? I suspect we both had our doubts. Eventually, her breathing would slow, her muscles would relax, and I would know she had fallen asleep. Then I could.

As her agony became more evident, I became more frustrated and anxious to leave. I grew unsympathetic and bitter toward the one person for whom, not long before, I would have given my life. We had debated breaking up the journey into shorter, more manageable trips to places close by, but I always rejected those suggestions with tenacity. I needed a change—a momentous one. Though I couldn't explain why, I had reached a point where just looking at Maria made me angry, and I hated that feeling.

One day, she told me how proud she was of me. "You're a great man, Joe," she said. "I'm so blessed to have found you, and I'm so proud of you." It was an undeserved approval I had not heard from her in so long, and rather than taking it as I knew she had meant it, I called her a liar.

Preparation took weeks as we gathered the supplies I would need for the journey: the map, a tent, minimal clothing for warm and cold weather, toiletries, my Mossberg and Ka-Bar, bow and arrows, a fishing pole, a compass, a water skin, flint and stone, rope, a mug and pot, and a journal would all go with me. Carrying any more than I needed would mean an even slower trip.

I rode every day to build up my endurance on horseback. I studied edible plants and how to prepare them. The common weeds that had been such a nuisance in my green suburban lawn would serve as nourishment. Dandelions. Certain species of honeysuckle. Some could be eaten raw, some boiled. Although most of the journey would follow the old highways, there were deviations here and there to minimize excess mileage. I missed my car. Traveling any kind of distance was a proposition far more involved than it would have been in the past. It wasn't a matter of making sure the tank was full and hitting the gas. I didn't have heat or air conditioning to keep me comfortable or a roof to keep me dry. It would be slow and rough.

My responsibility on the journey was threefold. First, I was to accumulate knowledge—especially that which would be applicable to our own lifestyle back home—in every place that I traveled to. Second, I was to share what I had learned on the farm with people along the way. Third, I was to establish a postal center, if one had not already been established, at every major settlement I came across. It was likely that I was not the first to embark on such a mission. There could have been hundreds out there doing the same. I hoped there were.

Construction began on a cabin that would serve as our post office. We called our settlement "Eden Valley." That was how it would be known under the new postal service. We were far from having the capacity to deliver to each home individually, so instead, the cabin would be a central location where residents of the settlement could send or receive mail. That method helped to simplify the inevitable logistical complications of a mail service that would be used by hundreds of millions of people over millions of square miles—and that was just in our part of the world that used to be called the United States. Ultimately, a global mail service would be necessary.

I made a commitment to send letters from each place once I had deemed the company safe and to update Eden Valley on my wellbeing and progress.

"At least do that for me," Maria asked as we lay quietly by the fire after dinner one night, "so I know you're OK." Her eyes glistened and she pressed her lips together. In less than a week, I would depart, and every time we spoke of it, that was the face I saw. She never ran dry of tears.

"I'll be fine," I said. "Think of it as a long vacation. And when I get home, it'll be like I never left."

"I hope that's not true," she whispered. I didn't reply. "Take that book of Abraham's," she said. "The one with all the plants that tells you what to eat and what you can't."

"Of course."

"You're not used to cooking for yourself. The last thing you need is to make yourself sick out there. I won't be around to take care of you. And wear your hat so you don't get sunburned."

"I will."

"Are you all packed?"

"Not yet."

"You can't procrastinate, Joe. You'll forget something. Are you sure I can't go with you?"

"You'll be safer here, and I'll be faster alone."

"Will you dream of me?" she asked sweetly, hopefully, looking into my eyes. Her beauty made me weak, and for a moment I bared enough humanity for a glimpse of the man she had loved.

"Of course I will," I said. "Night and day. I'll never stop dreaming of you."

She smiled, put her arms around me, and rested her head on my bare chest.

"I love you," she said. She didn't complain when I replied with silence.

5

HEADING SOUTH

On the day in early April when I was to leave, I awoke anxious. Maria made a wholesome breakfast for me, covering the table in plates of eggs, fruit, and bread. She had begun preparing the meal before I had risen that morning to occupy the time that should have been spent sleeping if she could have. I was awake the whole time, but I didn't let her know it. It was better to avoid the awkward silence that was sure to overcast the morning. I could hear her crying as she cooked. When I finally did rise, I savored my breakfast slowly and pensively like the civilized person I had once been. It was, as far as I knew, the last time I would enjoy such a meal for quite a while. Maria didn't eat much that morning.

After breakfast, we met Paul under the communal canopy to go over the final details of my trip. We gathered my gear and reviewed the route, reiterating the need to avoid going directly into the old cities, at least until I had determined that they were safe. God only knew the manner of people left lurking in them. It would be wise to stick to the outskirts, where I would be more likely to come across civilized people—places with land and trees, open spaces and forests. I didn't expect much difficulty in finding what I was looking for. Population centers had adjusted and spread out, surely, but the population itself, I hoped, hadn't changed in number.

Noah joined us with my horse, who was already saddled, and tied him up so that we could load my gear. He was a beautiful red stallion strikingly marked by a jet-black mane and tail, chosen for his power and stamina that was unsurpassed by any of the others. I was told he had been a daunting challenge to tame. I liked that about him. In the weeks we had been riding, I believe he had begun to develop a reverence for me that matched my own for him. It was as if he recognized the journey as his calling and me more as his companion than his master. I preferred it that way. His spirit was free with a persistent desire to see the world, a characteristic that gave him his name—Nomad.

Good-byes were tearful, but Maria was strong—stronger than I had expected her to be. When I held her for that last time, it felt like it lasted forever, but at the same time, only for a moment. She seemed finally at peace, if it only sustained the morning. Though I didn't know it then, the last look on her face would linger in my mind until I returned, and that was a better way to remember her. Not tormented, but proud. So many days I had cringed at her inability to look at me, but not that day. I could feel her love for me despite the cold, callous machine I had become.

My family and friends came for the somber send-off. All were encouraging and wished me well, but it was one of the most difficult days of my life—up until then, that is. There would be many worse to come, and had I known then the trials that awaited me on the road, I might never have left. I'd never had to say good-bye quite like that before. It was possible, I knew, that I might never see any of them again. I would be facing danger I could not yet comprehend or predict. The memory of that day is one that leaves knots in my stomach, even now. Such a range of emotions had been previously unfathomable, but they had to be endured. The eyes of those I loved glistened with the rising sun so brightly that their colors shone, even through the tears that blurred my own vision.

"I hope somewhere in all those miles you find yourself, Joe," Maria said, holding my hand tightly. The soft skin of her cheek rested on my tanned and hardened shoulder. In the light breeze, I felt her warm tears turn cold on my neck. "I miss you already," she said. "I've been missing you for months."

When we finally let go, she stepped back and looked into my eyes. I looked back into hers, straight-faced, without a word.

"You had better come back to me," she said.

"I will."

As I began to step away, she grabbed my left hand with hers. "Wait," she said, gazing at me for a moment as if entranced. "I love you."

"I love you," I replied. I had not uttered the words in so long that I could not remember the last time. I wondered if I even meant them.

A tear rolled down her cheek, and the faintest of whimpers escaped her lips. I turned away before I could change my mind, and as our trembling fingers slipped apart, I heard the click of our rings as they tapped together.

By noon, I had set off alone on my horse and without the mathematical confidence of Phileas Fogg, headed south toward what used to be New Orleans. I looked behind occasionally as we trotted into the woods, watching the silhouettes of all of the people I loved shrinking behind me, still standing together, watching forward as I did the same. When they had vanished, we broke into a gallop that would persist until the fall of dusk.

Once we had emerged from the woods, Nomad and I followed the highway, riding down the grassy median. The roads were like a scene from the dark parts of Cormac McCarthy's imagination. Cars were abandoned everywhere with their doors open and their paint turning to rust. Many were stripped of parts that had been salvaged for tools, but there were few people in sight. Occasionally, we would pass small groups walking down the middle of the road or pitching a tent or gathering around a fire. Some of them gave a courteous nod. Some avoided looking at all. I was wary of every passing drifter, and I could see that they were wary of me. At the sight of another person, my heart would beat faster, and I would instinctively take my gun in hand. They didn't seem so desperate, though, as they had those months ago. "Roughing it," as we used to say, had become a way of life for all of us.

It was clear that I was better equipped than most of the others out there on the highway, anyway. We—my family and I—had been blessed with resources that not everyone else had. Very few, I imagined, had had a farm to run to when the cities had become inhospitable. Most had left without direction, without the slightest idea of how to survive in the wild, and nothing but hopes and prayers to keep them going. But they learned. We all had to learn.

When the sun had gone down, leaving only an orange glow over the western horizon, it was time to turn in for the night. The first day had been light and uneventful but exhausting nonetheless, more emotionally than physically. But neither Nomad nor I were used to covering that kind of distance in a day, I on horseback and he burdened with the weight of a man and his gear. We stopped near a lake and a field of tall grass off of the side of the road where he could drink and graze. I built a fire, dug for earthworms, and went fishing, and then I enjoyed my filet with a healthy side of clovers, dandelions, and redbud flowers. Gathering food, however, proved significantly more difficult in the dark than it would have been in the light. Had I been thinking, I would have stopped to eat at one of the many farm fields that had lined both sides of the highway for most of the day. It hadn't occurred to me yet that someone must still have been cultivating them all and I was never quite as alone as I might have felt. Waiting to stop until the sun had gone down was my first mistake. Fortunately, it was one easily recovered from the next day.

The stars were like an exaggerated stage backdrop across the entire pitch-black sky. They were the brightest stars accompanied by the darkest night that I had seen, even since the electricity had gone out so long ago. The loneliness of that night was unlike anything I had ever experienced, but it was nothing compared to what would come over the following months. I lay on the pavement in the middle of the highway for a while, looking up at the stars, watching them slowly creep in formation through the night. Not a soul made a sound beyond Nomad's occasional heavy breathing as he slept tied to a tree nearby. Even the springtime crickets were silent. My fire crackled as it died down, and memories rushed in of vacations we used to take in the old world. How different that road was from the four-star hotels in which we used to sleep.

I remembered a trip that Paul, Noah, and I had taken to New Orleans during college, where we had booked a room in a high-rise overlooking the French Quarter. After checking in, I had been inspecting the bathroom for cleanliness, as was customary when staying in any foreign place, when I heard Noah out in the room yelling, "What the hell? What the hell is that?" I had bolted through the door to see what was the matter, and I had found him holding the room phone with a dry washcloth half a foot from his ear, a look of repulsion smeared across his face.

"What's your deal?" I had demanded. He had pointed at the mirror hanging above the dresser as he started in on the front desk operator.

"We need maid service in room fourteen twenty-one immediately. No, no, we need another room! Someone ejaculated all over the mirror! Yes! The bloody mirror! You know he was looking at himself when he did it!"

Paul had started rolling on one of the beds in hysterics.

"That's what we get for taking a room on the thirteenth floor." He had laughed.

"It's the fourteenth," I had said.

"Did you see a button for thirteen on the elevator? It's a trick to make the superstitious more comfortable. Think it worked?"

He had looked at Noah's animated expression of repugnance and erupted with laughter.

I found myself laughing too, lying there in the middle of that highway with nothing but the moon and stars lighting the silent wilderness around me.

I tried to count the stars, and the next thing I knew, the sun was rising, waking me to a beautiful bright blue morning sky. I must have been more exhausted than I had realized, because I had passed out on the hard pavement before I'd even had an opportunity to pitch my tent. My skin was sticky with dew. I got up, sore all over from my asphalt bed, and joined my horse in the shade where I broke in the first page of my journal. Then I got the fire going again for breakfast. Though I may not have mastered the art of archery back at the farm, I had no choice out there on the road. There was nobody else to rely on, but I was only hunting to feed myself, and small game was far more abundant than large. Missing the first few shots, however frustrating, was not devastating.

We started off again after breakfast. As if adapting after the collapse hadn't been difficult enough, the journey certainly found a way of topping it, which I guess was to be expected. I had no experts in nature or survival traveling with me to make up for my shortcomings anymore. You're never as prepared as you think you are for such things.

Over the next couple of weeks, I spent some days almost entirely alone, save for my horse, and a few with great numbers of people. We crossed rivers and creeks on old highway bridges. We passed through settlements outside of what used to be Memphis, Tennessee, and Jackson, Mississippi, spread out in vast camps of people. Both seemed to be at about the stage we were at back home, which was comforting in a way, disappointing in another. At least we were not alone in our struggle, but I wished to see more of the world as I had once known it. I spent a day or so in each place, paying for food and boarding in labor and explaining my mission. I began a list of the settlements I came across and asked a member of each to designate its exact location on my map for record.

They committed themselves to building local postal centers, and they would spread the word of the new system throughout their own communities. As future carriers passed through, they could begin to send and receive letters. I wrote my own letters home, and a man from each place vowed to head north and deliver them. In addition to his deliveries, during the period of genesis, each carrier was also responsible for informing each place down the road of new locations to keep the network growing. Other carriers were recruited to establish regional routes to places I would not pass. Recruiting new carriers was easy. There were plenty of people like me who were looking for direction and purpose, and such a great responsibility provided exactly that. So began the New World Mail Network, as it would come to be called.

The weather grew warmer as I moved south. I got used to traveling in the rain, and some days I even welcomed the cool cleansing it brought with it. It was liberating and exhilarating to travel in the open air, unconstrained by a need for luxury and comfort. Sometimes, that is. Other times, I could hardly bear it. The landscape grew increasingly lush and wet. Palm trees began to appear. I thought back to a vacation Maria and I had taken to Florida one February. We had left home with snow on the ground and blowing from the tops of tractor-trailers in front of us, and then we had passed under palm trees within the same day. People wondered then why we had decided to drive when a flight would have taken only a couple of hours. I just liked to drive. I liked to watch the scenery change as we passed from place to place. There was humor to be found in the irony. After the collapse, the same trip would take me weeks, and I longed for the convenience of a plane.

Eventually, I came across a settlement outside of what had been New Orleans, and at a fascinating moment. The sounds gave away its location. The first of its inhabitants I met were the six armed sentries posted on the highway outside who blocked the road as I approached and surrounded me.

Who are you?
What is your purpose?
Are you alone?
How long will you stay?

When they were satisfied that I wasn't a threat, they allowed me to pass. I hadn't seen the water yet, but the community spread immensely and abutted Lake Pontchartrain and the bayous. It was massive—there were thousands of people in dense crowds reminiscent of refugee camps in Africa or the Middle East or wherever that I had seen on CNN. Everyone seemed to be passionately involved in some kind of job.

I dismounted and led Nomad on a stroll through the place, looking for someone in charge. It looked as though it *should* have had someone in charge, and that was the person I needed to meet. How, I wondered, would that person have been chosen? Would he be the smartest? The loudest? The most cunning and clever? Would "he" be a "she," and would he or she be white? Black? Would he wear a suit? No, certainly not, I thought. Nobody in a suit and tie would be taken seriously. If you didn't have a layer of dirt on your shoes, you weren't to be trusted with much.

I say it was a fascinating moment because after a short walk, I came across a group of laborers who were singing like they'd just struck gold. But it wasn't gold they'd struck; it was water. I approached next to a man standing with his arms crossed and a grin on his face, watching the revelry.

"The fun part will be digging the well," he said, shaking his head. "You can't miss the water table down here."

"I'm Joe," I said with a chuckle, extending my hand.

He turned to me and shook my hand with his, which was coated in dried mud. "Glad to meet ya, Joe," he replied. "I'm Dr. Lazarus Heron, formerly of the USGS. Sorry about the dirt."

"No problem, Dr. Heron."

"Call me Laz," he said. Then he looked me up and down. "Where ya from, Joe?"

"St. Louis, originally."

"Rode that horse all the way down here?"

"Well, we've been building a community in southern Missouri for a while. That's where I came from."

"That's quite a ride. How are things going up there?"

"They're coming along. We're adapting, you know?"

"Yeah, I know what you mean. We're all adapting. I can't believe it's taken this long to get a well going around here. You see all these people? Thousands of us. Millions, maybe. We've been drinking out of lakes and rivers and creeks. Depending on where you're coming from, it can be quite a walk, and they get crowded. And you just have to hope there isn't someone taking a leak upstream. I feel like a barbarian. I'm hoping we'll have readily accessible running water within the year—*hope* being the operative word. We'll have to pillage some supplies from the city. Lord knows I'm not looking forward to going back there. The things I saw…The first step, though, is a well. Will you be sticking around a little while?"

"That's the idea."

"Good. Got a place to stay?"

"Not yet."

"All right. Let's see your arms, Joe. Yeah, you'll do just fine."

"Just fine?"

"We start digging tomorrow."

"I'm exhausted."

"You'd better get some rest then. Gotta earn your keep around here. Come on, I'll give you a place to lay your head."

Laz and his wife, Beth, had a cabin of their own where they put me up for the night. It was nestled in the bayou and shaded by cypress trees and Spanish moss. A rowboat was beached at the water's edge. Next to the house was an old tree stump coated in the remnants of fish, which reminded me of how hungry I was.

Beth had a personality as beautiful as her appearance. She was quiet but friendly, and she was a wonderfully accommodating hostess. A great chef, too. Most of our luxuries had been abandoned, but the ethnic creole and Cajun fare was too important to go by the wayside, as I came to learn. People there valued their heritage like nothing I had ever seen. During my first night with them, we shared a meal of blackened catfish and shrimp gumbo with a few welcome neighbors. We sat at a long table in the grass outside and watched the sunset through the trees, which were reflected in the water as we ate. After the time I had spent feeding on weeds and the monotonous soy fields while I traveled, I would have been prepared to ravage that fish raw had I seen it before the fire, but fortunately for all of us, my manners were not so compromised.

It was a banquet unlike any I'd had since before the collapse. By that I don't mean better, just different. Half the ingredients we couldn't even get in the Midwest, which brought a whole new meaning to this mission. Of course, I had been focused on the essentials, and a line of communication was vital. I hadn't considered that I was establishing shipping routes as well. I wanted to eat like that back home.

It was nice to have a soft, warm place to sleep, but once I blew out the candles, I couldn't get my mind off of Maria. Lying in a safe and comfortable bed with a full stomach, my mind slipped away from my task and away from survival and gravitated beyond the things keeping me alive toward the things that made life worth living. I felt there were so few. When I thought of her, I became angry, though I could not justify why. I scoured my memories for some betrayal, some transgression to rationalize those feelings, but in all our time together, I could find none.

It was around ten o'clock. My beautiful wife was, I imagined, alone in our bed, save for the Siberian cat keeping her feet warm. I wondered if she had grown accustomed to the sounds of the night by then. We had never been apart for so long since the day we had met, and certainly not since we had been married. I could count on one hand the number of times I had been away from home on business for more than two days. But it had been weeks. I wondered if she had secretly reciprocated my resentment all that time and perhaps she had been better at disguising it than I. Despite all that had happened between us, I was beginning to miss her. Homesickness was something I hadn't experienced since my childhood days at summer camp, and back then, it had been my parents who I had missed. My caregivers. Roles had changed as I had grown older and taken the first step toward a family of my own, and as a man I felt more like the caregiver. It was my responsibility to provide for Maria, yet another at which I had failed, and I wondered if she didn't share in the feeling that was already beginning to haunt me: that I had abandoned her. After all, she had used the word when I had told her I was leaving. I wondered if she was still crying herself to sleep as I was.

Beth was gentle about waking me the next morning, almost reluctant, as if she had some moral objection to disrupting such a peaceful state. Little did she know that behind that calm façade was a dormant volcano of a man.

"Good morning," she said with a smile. "I'm making breakfast. Come on out when you're ready. The boys are getting ready to start work."

By the time I emerged, there was a crowd of men outside, some sitting, some standing, drinking beer as they filled up on ham and eggs. I declined the former at that time of morning, but a good breakfast was just what I needed to start the day. It was cool for that time of year on the northern Gulf of Mexico, but the sun was bright in the clear blue sky.

"How'd you sleep?" Laz asked, slapping me on the back.

"Better than I have since I left home."

"Good. We've got a long day ahead of us."

"You drink beer with breakfast?" I inquired.

"Ah, beer is a staple of human civilization, my friend. A culture can be judged by the quality of its beer." He laughed. "Even the ancient Egyptians knew that, and look at what they did with their bare hands. You ever been to the pyramids, Joe?"

"I haven't."

"Someday you should."

I met a few of the others who welcomed my assistance and company. Many of them harbored an unusual curiosity about my journey, and they saddled me with a barrage of questions for half the morning. They asked about what the collapse had been like during the winter in St. Louis, about our move south, and about all of the places I had been between here and there. My impression was that moving to that place after the collapse was the farthest they had ever traveled from their previous dwellings in and around New Orleans.

Laz didn't ask questions, though. He was unguarded and friendly, but he never boasted about himself, though I suspected he had much to boast about. There was an air of humble intelligence about him that had been apparent from the moment we had met. I must not have been the only one who noticed, because he was the guy everyone came to for directions and answers, the same role Abraham played back home. Lazarus, though, was much younger. I would guess he was somewhere in his midthirties, perhaps only a few years older than I was.

"You sure picked the wrong day to show up, Joe," Lazarus laughed as we walked toward the future site of well number one. "Drilling is a whole lot easier than digging, but since we don't have a drill rig and couldn't power one even if we did, we're going to be getting a workout."

"Well since I missed the easy part, tell me, how do you find groundwater?" I asked him.

"It's under there almost everywhere you go, actually. There's more fresh water underground than there is in all the lakes, rivers, and streams in the world combined. Out at my place in the bayou, of course, we've got all the fresh water we need at the surface, but it's far less convenient for the folks inland. There it's just a matter of depth. You've got to look at what's around. Do you see water anywhere? Is there a stream? A river? A lake? There will probably be water under the ground nearby. Look in low areas and for trees that thrive in wet conditions. Then start digging until you've broken past the water table and can't dig anymore through the water rushing in. You'll need a guy up above with a bucket on a rope and pulley helping to bail you out. When you think you're going to drown, it's time to start lining your well with stones to filter it and keep the soil from filling it in. With a drill, you could pass a thousand feet if you had to, putting your source deep in the aquifer. Unfortunately, you can't get nearly that deep by hand, but I think the man-made pollutants near the surface will be less of an issue than they used to be. Maybe the fish will even return to the gulf now that they aren't being decimated by toxic urban run-off and chemical fertilizers."

"You filter it after it's drawn?" I asked.

"You afraid of a little sediment, Joe? You must have made out better than most of us when things came down. Sure, you can filter it. Pour it through a strainer or a cloth if you want, which is more than most of us have been doing with the lake and river water. Eventually, we'll have a spigot, but for now, a bucket on a rope will have to do. We're going to need quite a few wells to accommodate this many people, especially since we can't reach the aquifer. They'll save us some walks to fresh water on the surface, and this will be cleaner."

"You keep saying 'us.' You live on the water, Laz. What do you need a well for?"

"We're all in this together, Joe."

About that, he was right. Those who lived in the bayou had a surplus of fresh water and seafood, but their produce came from farms outside and further inland.

There were so many men in our crew that we knocked out three wells that day, set in various places around the community. We finished digging the first one they had begun the day before, walled it with stones, and built a crank structure above to raise and lower a bucket into it using salvaged materials from the old city. Then we moved on to the second, about a quarter mile away. Then the third. They got easier as we went, and we cycled our shifts frequently enough that nobody dropped from exhaustion. By the end of the week, we had around ten wells finished, and my arms were so fatigued that I couldn't hold a cup of our fresh water without my hands quivering.

Having never worked in what we called a blue-collar field, I couldn't help but adopt with intrigue the cheer that seemed to cloak every man laboring by my side. We worked together like family. Some had done the same work many times before, and others, like me, had come from behind a desk. Yet there was no power struggle out there—no envy of the next man or a perception of his overcompensation. We would all profit equally in the freedom our work would provide.

In the meantime, a man had been sent to deliver my latest letter home. They would be relieved and amazed, I thought, to learn that that sort of fellowship extended so far beyond the boundaries of our little Midwestern village in the hills. It flourished as if things had always been that way. People seldom spoke of the way things used to be, even down there. In the beginning, we had avoided the topic because it conjured painful memories of loss, but that avoidance was gradually evolving into a disinterest in the old world.

A large group of us gathered for meals in the evenings, sometimes nattering until the sun came up. When I spoke of things I had learned back home about farming, hygiene, and survival, they usually already possessed the knowledge I had brought with me. I began to realize that there were people like Abraham everywhere I went—people we used to discount and ridicule as hicks or nerds, depending on what sect of society they had come from. But we would have been lost without them.

The great team of men with whom I worked during the days followed Laz's directions dutifully. They seemed to recognize and respect his expertise and asked few questions, other than to clarify his instruction. Never did I hear an argument, though that wasn't because they feared him or needed the job. When I pointed that out to him, it seemed to be the first time he had taken notice.

"Yeah, most of these guys are used to taking orders from a white man," he said, "but they don't seem to mind the color of my skin. Maybe it's my PhD." He laughed. "When we move on to the next project, I'm sure someone else will take over. Electricity is not my forte."

Electricity, I pondered. I had abandoned futile hopes that we would ever enjoy such a thing again in my lifetime.

"Neither is hunting," he continued, lifting his shirt and rolling his sleeves to reveal a collection of scars that would rival those of a veteran Roman gladiator. "Urban hunting, scavenging, whatever you want to call what we did after it all came down. We tried to stick it out in the city for a while, but people were desperate. Food was scarce, so we had to fight for it. First it was one-on-one with fists. Sometimes knives. I fought a guy with a sword once, briefly. He left me with this souvenir. You didn't argue with a guy who had a gun. It usually wasn't loaded, but it wasn't worth the risk.

"People started forming gangs. They would fight over a carcass in the street like vultures. Sometimes even a human carcass. Little by little, the population in the city became less dense as people chose between leaving and dying, and we decided we had a better chance facing the gators in the bayou. At least they'd bring us food. I figure the people still left behind will eventually realize they're better off working together rather than killing one another. Each of us has at least one strength—one talent applicable to any way of life. Just have to find out what that is.

"Be careful of those guys though, Joe. They're still out there. I haven't been back into the city for a while, but I hear stories of what it has become. You may want to avoid it. I'd keep that shotgun handy if I were you."

As more wells became functional, life quickly grew easier in the gulf community. The time its inhabitants used to spend walking to and from fresh water could then be spent on other things. Some of the crew continued working on more wells, while I joined others in the construction of their own postal center.

Shortly after we began, however, a log left me with a rather unpleasant splinter half the length of my forearm lodged deep under my skin. I took that as a sign that it was time to move on, and I headed back to Laz and Beth's home to rest before setting off again. Perhaps I was getting too comfortable there anyway.

"Sometimes they splinter," said Beth as she was treating the wound, "but the tree doesn't mean harm, and it doesn't mean we need the wood any less."

On the day before I left, I was out in the rowboat fishing on the lake sometime in the early afternoon when a woman on the shore started yelling something about boats on the horizon, stirring the placid sounds of nature. Looking out in the direction of the gulf, I caught a view of the oncoming bows of three sailboats. Intrigued, I rowed back in and beached to watch the approach with a gathering cheering crowd.

"What's going on?" I asked.

"The Good Samaritans!" replied a child next to me. His mother took his hand.

"Over twenty have come through in the past few months," she said. "Nobody knows how many more there are."

"Who are they?" I asked, observing that they flew both Mexican and American flags.

"They bring people home, wherever home may be. They've been moving between the Florida Keys, the Yucatan peninsula, and everywhere along the Gulf Coast."

They anchored off the shore, and some forty men and women rowed in on beaten and salvaged dinghies. Restless feet splashed into the water before the boats had even moored, and some collapsed in tearful ecstasy when they finally set foot on land, rolling in the sand alongside their children and crying and laughing with joy. The people of the civilization were there to adopt them with open arms and rushed toward the water with baskets of food, welcoming the weary into their homes. Basic human decency and compassion have a way of burying any language or cultural barriers when a person sees another in desperate need.

I followed the crowd helping the strangers from their boats. The last to disembark were the sailors.

"Is there a place to sleep around here?" one of them asked me. Before I could answer, I felt a hand on my shoulder and heard Laz's voice exclaiming, "Of course! Stay with us. You guys are always welcome."

"How much room have you got?"

"As much as you need."

Laz and Beth welcomed four of the sailors of the Good Samaritan Fleet into their home that night. They, as I, would depart again the next day, and though their vessels housed more than adequate sleeping quarters, a person can spend only so much time at sea. Over dinner, they invited me to travel with them to the places that had been

Tampa or Fort Meyers, where I could cross over to Miami, my next defined destination.

"It would be faster," one said. "Or, if you're willing to trade the time, you could stay with us all the way. We'll be stopping in the Keys on our way around the Florida Peninsula. It's a bit out of your way, but it would be much easier on you and your horse."

"You have space for him?"

"We unloaded just about everyone, and we shouldn't gain many more until we reach Miami. Space shouldn't be a problem, as long as your friend isn't afraid of the water."

"That's very generous," I said. "I'll think about it."

It might have been faster and certainly easier, I knew, but I had to pass on the offer. I could not in good conscience make a decision to neglect the millions of people living along the Florida Panhandle and my route south, particularly in the presence of the selfless mariners whose sacrifices reunited so many families.

"People are amazing creatures," Lazarus said. "Look at what we've accomplished. Months ago, we were all homeless. Now we have roofs over our heads. A week ago, thousands drank from a river. Now they drink from wells built with their bare hands. And you're here, Joe, reconnecting the disconnected world, like these fine sailors with whom we're sharing this meal. Just think, if we can do all this, what else are we capable of? What will we have tomorrow?"

Early the next morning, Nomad and I were on the road again, headed east along the Gulf shore.

6

SHE'LL HAVE A HOME

Mobile.
Pensacola.
Tallahassee.

The billboard advertisements lining both sides of the road were fading. Some were torn, some covered in graffiti. Those old icons of Western culture reminded me of just how alone I was. Businesses that no longer existed were still marketing to the one person left wandering the road. The highways we traveled were already showing signs of deterioration, and the tropical foliage on the sides of the road was converging upon it like a slow and steady adversary.

Some days, Nomad seemed restless, as if he was anxious to reach our next destination. When the weather was on our side and we were both up to it, we could cover sixty miles in a day. That, I thought, was an accomplishment. I had decided to challenge myself to a race against the sailors to the place that had been Miami. I would be following a similar route to theirs along the Gulf Coast, and it gave me something to strive for. I needed all of the motivation I could get.

The morning aroma of the fresh gulf air was the same as it had always been, sometimes sweetened by the perfume of peaches and citrus. The flavor of freedom.

Tampa.

Fort Meyers.

Naples.

I found that it was sometimes easier to find settlements at night. The nights were so black that I could see the glow of a fire miles away. Once we reached the Everglades, however, there were no lights at night save for the stars and the moon. There were no sounds but those of nature. It took two long days to cross from the Gulf side to the Atlantic side of the peninsula, and sleeping in the wetlands between rattled my nerves.

I had heard about the influx of Burmese and African rock pythons there for years, showing up in suburban swimming pools and destroying native wildlife populations. Having never lived nearby, however, I had thought little of it until I was there. Then it was all I could think about. These creatures could reach over twenty feet in length and three feet around, which was plenty big enough to crush my bones and swallow me whole. They truly were monsters in the way we only imagined them in Africa or South America or Southeast Asia. The government of the state of

Florida had labeled them invasive species and had offered rewards for a capture or kill. Fortunately, I was armed. If the moment did arise, speed and accuracy would be absolutely vital.

I didn't sleep well that night in the Everglades. Between the pain from the splinter in my arm, which I suspected had become infected, and my fear of what lurked in the wilderness around me, there was no rest to be had. Every time my horse shuffled his hooves, I stirred. Every time the wind blew through the mangroves and cypress trees, I held my breath, my sweaty fingers tightly clasping my loaded shotgun. Masses of mosquitos buzzed constantly just outside the walls of my tent. The few times that I was able to doze off, it was only moments before I was awakened again by the sounds of some creature in the night.

The morning finally came with no sign of any reptilian foe, and as I emerged into the daylight, I had to laugh at my own paranoia. This expedition and the humid tropical heat were getting to me. My clothes were drenched in sweat and smelled awful, and I thought it an opportune time to cleanse them and myself, not just of filth, but also of my fear. Contrary to the night's cape of darkness, in the daylight, the Everglades were peaceful with an intriguing aura of mystery about them. I grabbed my bar of soap and headed toward the murky swamp unarmed, leaving Nomad by the road.

To reach the water, I had to peel away a section of the chain-link fence that bordered both sides of the long, straight highway through the nature preserve. After a brief walk, I stripped off my clothes and stepped in, feeling the mud squish between my toes. The road was barely visible through the trees behind me, and I glanced back occasionally to ensure that my horse had not left. I cleaned my clothes with the bar of soap and hung them, piece by piece, from a nearby branch to dry. The tropical birds chirped and chattered in the trees around me.

My mind wandered back to our old home in the suburbs, cleaning laundry in a machine, drying it in another, and folding it neatly to be put away in a drawer. Maria had never liked the way I folded laundry.

"Why do you fold yours first?" she had asked me.

"Because if I get the big stuff out of the way, it's easier to get to the smaller stuff, which happens to be yours." There was method to my madness. The conversation paused as I placed my folded clothes in my dresser and went into the bathroom for a shower. After a few minutes, she called to me over the sound of the running water.

"How come you didn't put the towels away?"

"Because they made a nice foundation for your stack of clothes. Actually, I need one of those. Will you bring one in here for me?"

I turned off the shower and slid the glass door open, and I was hit in the face with the towel she had thrown. Fresh out of the wash, it still smelled like a wet dog. There must have been something wrong with the machine, but I'd never had the motivation to hunt for the source.

In the swamp, I bathed among the mangroves with no clothes to fold, because the only ones I owned were the ones I wore every day. I was scrubbing the wound in my forearm that was beginning to swell when the soap slipped from my hand and splashed into the water. I felt it bounce off my foot, and I leaned down to search for it, my fingers combing the mud and mangrove roots. Something brushed against my arm beneath the water. Figuring it was only a fish, I paid it little mind. I found my bar of soap and submerged myself to wash my hair, scrubbing the dirt and salt from my scalp. I could feel the grains under my fingertips. Haircuts had not been a priority, particularly through the winters. My hair had been long before and had only grown longer since I had left home, tangling from humidity and sweat. In the constant heat, I considered shaving it all off with my knife, but it was necessary to protect my scalp from the sun. The clothes I had been wearing were lightweight but long sleeved to serve the same purpose. Sunburn could turn an already trying journey to misery.

With my head under the water, I felt an ever so subtle wave pass over, and though it might have been caused by a breeze, I suddenly felt I was not alone. I emerged again to find myself staring back into a pair of green eyes just at the surface of the water ahead of me. For a moment I was frozen. It was no snake. It was another reptile, perhaps more fearsome, that had somehow managed to slip my mind as I carelessly cleansed myself in its indigenous habitat. I suddenly remembered a passing warning from Lazarus of the formidable prehistoric beast that resides in the swamp: the alligator.

He glared at me as if debating the attack. Whether he was hungry or territorial or both, I was not sure, but he could see my vulnerability, and I could see the intent in his eyes. Even for an animal with the stigma of a ruthless predator, the 'gator would normally have been less interested in a challenge than I, but those eyes were unmistakable. I knew he was not backing down.

The mud oozed around my toes and heels, my feet stuck with suction. I was slow in the water and certainly no match for him, but the ground was just behind me and I was surrounded by trees. A decision had to be made before he made his. Hesitation could be fatal.

I threw my bar of soap, hitting him between the eyes. That distracted him just long enough for me to scramble out of the water and into the tangled trunk of the nearest mangrove tree as his jaws emerged and took a snap, missing my foot by mere inches. I climbed up the branches just out of his reach. He sat below, watching me, pacing, waiting as I moved higher. He groaned with disappointment at the initial strike, but he knew he had me. It was only a matter of time before I had to come down. Then I was doomed.

Naked and treed like a hunted raccoon with the dogs barking below, I searched around for a way out. Tree trunks wound together, and I began to climb between them, my grip slipping in the mud that coated my hands and feet. The 'gator followed, still looking up at me. I must have wandered too near his nest to be pardoned for my trespass. I watched him through the leaves. He was at least ten feet long and black with a tan belly and stripes on his tail that blended with the swamp. One blunder and he'd have his meal. If only I had been blessed with the long arms of a primate, I thought, I could simply swing from my vulnerable position between the mazes of branches above. Humans are not built for trees.

"Nomad!" I called in desperation. He could be of no help as anything other than a distraction, but I saw no other options. Perhaps the sound of another creature might lure the beast far enough for me to make my escape. I could faintly see his figure stirring through the trees, searching for me by the sound of my voice. He could never fit through the hole I had cut in the fence. The gator looked in his direction momentarily and then back up at me as if to boast that my attempted baiting had failed to entice him.

Looking up to the clouds, I pleaded in desperation, "Send me a way."

Suddenly, the branch on which I crouched began to creak, and before I had a chance to react, it snapped under my weight. The green world turned to blue as I plummeted toward my inevitable demise. A moment later, the same green scene returned upside down as I found myself dangling by my legs, wrapped around what remained of the broken branch. My body had answered quicker than my mind, and in that same moment, the trees and the sky had vanished, replaced by a mouth full of teeth and the pink geography down the inside of nature's throat lunging at mine. I swung up just before the bite took me, reaching my hands to my feet and hanging by all fours with my back to the grounded 'gator.

Then I found my opportunity. Through the matrix of trunks and leaves, I saw a clearing that I had not seen from above. Nearby there was a patch of ground blocked entirely by roots that he would have to climb through to reach. They would slow him down, but they would not stop him. He was too determined, pacing back and forth just below me. From the spot where I intended to land was a clear path back to the hole I had cut in the fence. The only problem was the horizontal distance I would have to span to reach it. It would have been a good jump for an athlete, which I was not.

This was it. I shimmied back to the trunk and climbed through the tree toward the nearest point to the clearing, my heart racing and my skin dripping. I gripped the branches on either side of me, positioned my feet for the best spring, and then leaped. I passed over the alligator's head and tumbled to the ground, rolling into a dead run without even looking behind me. I could hear his claws vigorously scaling the ground and his leathery belly dragging. He was after me, jaws snapping at my bare heels. I felt his hot breath on my ankles and heard each swift step crunch in the ground cover as I stumbled as quickly as I could through the trees toward the hole in the fence. I had to reach my shotgun. That would be my only chance against the beast.

When I reached the fence, I dove through it, rolling in the grass toward Nomad, who was standing exactly where I had left him. The alligator got caught up on the fence, but he managed to unhinge himself, persisting just as quickly. Those few lost seconds might have saved my life. Nomad reared at the sight of the beast and turned toward me, putting the weapon just within reach. I slipped my hand into the leather sleeve where my shotgun rested and in one motion pulled it free and racked a shell, spinning toward my pursuer. Just as he approached me and opened his mouth for one final strike, I squeezed the trigger, unleashing a load of buckshot into his throat. The sound echoed for miles. Flocks of birds squawked and retreated from the trees nearby. Then there was silence.

I sat for a moment of reflection next to the smoking carcass of my assailant. He would make quite a meal. The level of adrenaline rushing through my bloodstream had numbed me to the sensation of pain, and I didn't realize until I saw it that I was wounded. My leg was painted red. I wiped away the blood with my hand, but more gushed through the torn skin. The 'gator had not eaten the entire load of buckshot, and some had ricocheted from a nearby rock and caught me in the calf. After the battle was won, the only injury I had sustained was self-inflicted.

I took some time to gather myself together before reluctantly and carefully limping back through the fence for my clothes and the soap I had thrown. That time, the gun came with me. Prying the pellets out of my leg with the Ka-Bar was excruciating. I cleaned the wound and tore a section from my shirt to tie around my leg and stop the bleeding.

I learned two things from that terrifying experience. One: don't ever wander a hostile wilderness alone and unarmed. Two: alligator tastes like chicken, but kind of fishy. I smoked the meat before leaving that day, and there was more left than I could bring with me even after I'd had breakfast. It would keep me satisfied until I reached the Atlantic.

The Miami and Fort Lauderdale metropolitan area came into view immediately east of the Everglades, and I wasn't about to cut through miles of swampland to avoid it, particularly then, with the knowledge of its natural dangers. The city, I hoped, would be safe enough to travel through so long as I didn't linger and call attention. As time passed and I met new people, I was becoming less concerned about the prospect of a hostile human element. Certainly the rioting had died down.

I headed north along the western edge of the city outskirts. As expected, tenancy was scarce, except for a lonely few who were either too stubborn to leave or too terrified of what it would mean. I found a young child starving in the street and stopped to share my smoked alligator with her.

"Where have the people gone?" I asked her.

"No people around here," she replied, ravaging the first bit of food she'd had in days.

"Why do you stay?"

"Nowhere else to go."

"No family?"

"I had family."

"Where are they?"

"I don't know."

"Come with me then. Maybe we can find them together."

"I'm not supposed to talk to strangers," she said.

"Did your mom teach you that?"

"Yes. Mommy and Daddy."

"Smart people. I can't argue with them. You know, I don't think there are bad people anymore, though."

"Really?"

"Really."

"What happened to your leg?"

"I had a fight with an alligator," I said.

"In alligator alley?"

"Is that what you call it?"

"Yeah. What's your horsey's name?"

"Nomad."

"What kind of name is that?" she asked.

"He's a drifter. A perpetual wanderer. Like me."

"Can I pet him?"

"Of course you can."

The little girl began to follow me, as did other lost souls we happened upon. Perhaps all they needed was a final sign of hope—a simple man on a horse emerging through the palms. I put the child up on Nomad's back while I took to my feet. My companions and I traveled for a couple of days before we came across the new population center of southeast Florida, which spread, as I learned, throughout the vast farmland surrounding Lake Okeechobee and stretched all the way to the Atlantic Ocean. It was centered on the lake for both its fresh water and fishing.

Even in the eastern parts that had once been saturated with development, it appeared that many of the existing structures had been demolished and the whole area—or at least the part that I saw—had been flattened to start over. It just made more sense than trying to build upon the mistakes of the past, I guess. The old methods had worked in the old world, perhaps, but they would only hinder the creation of a new civilization. If we're going to rebuild, I thought, we might as well do it right from the ground up. It was beautifully executed. A great number of wells had already been completed, and significant progress had been made toward development of new housing stock.

From our perspective inland, most of the homes appeared to be constructed as domes built of earthbags, which are just what the name implies. Organic woven sacks are filled with soil or whatever ground material is available on site, and then stacked in a brick-like formation to create vertical or curving walls. There, the dome shape was preferred for its stability and simplicity. Once the walls were complete, they were coated inside and out with adobe. Some of the curved roofs flowed directly into small hills surrounding the homes, making them appear as if they had grown from the ground. Most consisted of a single room with a single arched doorway and perhaps a fireplace or a hole in the roof to draw smoke from a central fire pit.

Near the shore, construction was different. Rows of wooden homes were built on stilts to mitigate hurricane damage, and they had hip roofs to reduce drag in strong winds. Networks of trenches spread throughout to direct floodwaters away from neighborhoods. Solid, thoughtful construction is particularly important in geographic areas prone to regular bombardment from the environment. They had to be prepared for the coming hurricane season and many more that would follow annually like clockwork.

We passed through a number of farms, small and large, nestled within the community. An old woman named Esther operated one of them.

"What happened to your leg, boy?" was the first thing she said to me. Before I could answer, she was preparing stitching and insisting that I let her fix me up. She gave me a shirt of her husband's to replace the shabby rag on my back. Then she went to work on my swollen arm, which was then clearly infected. She scrubbed vigorously with soap and a coarse sponge from the ocean, and I had to bite down on a stick to keep from breaking my teeth as I screamed through them. I took the sponge from her to work at it on my own, but the pain was no less agonizing.

"You'll need antibiotics," she said.

"You have any?" I asked, lying on the floor with my arm outstretched when I could no longer take the pain.

"Not here," she replied, "but there is a place where you can get medicine."

"Where?"

"It's a clan that keeps it. I don't want to send you there, but I don't think you have a choice."

"Is it dangerous?"

"They're pirates," she said.

"Pirates?"

"You've had a long trip. Rest here a few days. Then we'll talk more."

Esther took me in for the duration of my stay on the peninsula. The refugees who had come with me were all given room and board at neighboring residences, but the child didn't want to leave my side. She had to stay with Esther and me. She needed someone to look up to until her parents could be found and, for whatever reason, liked me for the job. Esther reminded me of my grandmother. She was generous and friendly to me and to the child, but outside our company, she was quiet and seldom smiled. When the collapse began, her husband had been on a trip to Asia somewhere, though I was never clear on exactly where or why. He was one of those unfortunate souls who had not managed to make it home in time. So Esther was just waiting. She spoke little of him. I figured his absence caused her deep pain, so I didn't ask for any more information than she volunteered. I empathized with her. Her heartache was something I felt more deeply than most.

Esther got up at an ungodly hour every morning, earlier even than the predawn hour at which I had become accustomed to rising. I couldn't feel right about sleeping in while the old woman worked, so naturally, my own schedule had to suffer. She said the animals needed her, but I think she just couldn't sleep. She would make breakfast, and the three of us would eat together by candlelight. I would help her on the farm for a few hours each day until the rest of civilization began its morning. The child stayed with us always, feeding the goats or chasing the chickens in the field.

Then I was off, meeting the citizens of the place and teaching as much as learning. I helped to build homes for the people in the community, filling earthbags, stacking them, mixing adobe from sand, clay, straw, and water, and coating the earthbag walls with adobe. I understood how so much progress had already been made. Their construction was quick, simple, and beautiful. Surely demolition of the old structures had been the hard part. Rebuilding came naturally.

Several postal centers had already been erected across the expansive commune, from which one was selected to serve as the primary stop for long-range mail and the couriers who were sure to follow me. A more complex communication system was already taking shape. Large provincial centers would be spread hundreds of miles apart, where mail would be received by and dispersed to less widespread regional centers. Daily transfers would be made between the regional centers and the local ones within their districts, which would serve as the drop-off and pickup points for individuals within a particular radius. I figured the burgeoning population of mail centers would simply adopt those roles as new civilizations grew. A piece of mail would be addressed this way:

> *Provincial Center Designation*
> *Regional Center Designation*
> *Local Center Designation*
> *Name of Recipient*

The new provincial center there was where I posted and dispatched notice about the child in search of her parents. I was always thinking of her, which helped to take my mind off Maria. I couldn't imagine an innocent child surviving so long alone without food or access to clean water. What had happened to her parents? Were they alive? Could they have left town and abandoned her? And if they had, did they even deserve her? In a city that massive, the best hope for finding them and answers to those questions would be to spread the word via post. Surely someone there missed the child.

I met many new friends with whom I shared recipes for both food and hygienic products. Flora was far different there than back home. The flavor of toothpaste and the aroma of soap changed. Residents cleaned their hair with a blend of cucumber and lemon; the lemon cleansed, and the cucumber conditioned. They used coconut oil for lotion and in soap as well as cooking. Toothpaste was made from dried bay leaves and citrus peels. I was running low on hygienic products, and I had to make more as I traveled. We ate oranges, grapefruits, and bananas among other produce that could not easily be grown outdoors in the Midwest.

I could also add salt to my meals, a treat that I suddenly realized how much I had missed since we had moved to the farm. They say salt doesn't actually have a flavor of its own; rather, it simply enhances the flavor of whatever is seasoned with it. Even more importantly, it was used to cure meat stores. Salt was something we had taken for granted before, and I understood why it had served as currency for hundreds of years in many places across the earth. Unless you lived near the sea or a salt lake, it was not easy to come by. Even extracting from a salt mine was difficult and dangerous without industrial equipment, which, of course, we no longer had use of. Thanks in part to my sacrifice, I thought, the day would soon come when we could ship such commodities around the continent.

I mentioned that in conversation with some of my new friends while peeling a fresh grapefruit at lunchtime; only I used the word "country."

"The lines separating this country from the next don't exist anymore," suggested Andrés, one of those who had joined me as I had passed through what had once been Miami.

"Well, I guess you're right about that," I replied.

"Geographically, 'continent' has always meant far more anyway, and not just in terms of size," he said in his thin Latin accent. "Nature never recognized the invisible lines that humans drew between states and nations among the same land. I forget them too, now that even my own native country has grown as foreign to me as this one. Really, what is the difference between you and me and the Canadian down the road? For that matter, between me and a Peruvian or a Nigerian or a Pakistani or a Korean? If every person on the planet chose a husband or wife from another country and made children, within a few generations, there would be no distinguishing between cultures based on appearance.

"'Give me your tired, your poor, your huddled masses yearning to breathe free.' Those words are from a plaque at the Statue of Liberty. It's a sonnet written by Emma Lazarus. Do you know it?"

"I've seen it in pictures," I replied.

"That sonnet is why I came over here," Andrés continued. "It filled me with hope. It was a statement that Americans could proudly adopt and stand behind in recognition that this truly was a nation of immigrants, as we always heard the politicians say. But instead, we were referred to as 'illegal aliens,' as if our search for a better life was in some way criminal. What were we supposed to do? It seemed like everywhere we looked, the cartels were killing people, leaving body parts in the streets. We didn't have the time or money to do things the way the government wanted us to—the legal way. We just had to get out. The value of a person shouldn't be determined by the location of his or her birthplace in relation to some imaginary line. None of us makes that decision."

What Andrés said made me wonder how Esther's husband was faring in Asia, and I imagine the same thought had been troubling her all the time he had been gone. In many parts of the world, white Americans were not always welcomed with open arms. Perhaps wherever he was, the transition had passed more smoothly.

Although scrubbing my arm regularly seemed to slow the infection, after a few days I knew it would not be healed unless I had the antibiotics to treat it. If it got much worse, I might lose my arm. I would have to go see the nefarious pirates. Their stores were kept on a boat at anchor in the Atlantic, where approaching customers or adversaries were visible a long way off. Their position ensured they always had the upper hand, and only desperate souls with no other choice dared to meet them in their waters. Even fishermen avoided the area for fear of a confrontation. The clan had pillaged all remaining medicine from the coastal hospitals shortly after the collapse and kept it all under close guard ever since.

I was told not to bring anything of value that I didn't intend to trade for medication. The pirates were likely to take everything I had. Bringing a weapon would almost certainly get me killed. I hadn't taken anything with me on the journey that I didn't need for my own survival, but Esther was endlessly generous. She gave me a hen and a rooster to barter with.

It was about a six-hour walk to the coast, where I borrowed a rowboat from a local resident. He was reluctant to loan it at first, but when he saw my arm and heard where I was headed, he took pity on me.

"Good luck," he said. "I'll be praying for you." Then he pointed me in the direction of the clan's floating fortress. I placed the two crates in the boat and set off.

The ocean waves smacked the hull of the little rowboat like a heavyweight boxer with a punching bag, and it was all I could do to keep a straight heading as I was tossed about. The flightless birds squawked in confusion within their crates. My stomach grew ill and my arm ached as the pirates' ship came into view—a massive white yacht that never moved because it had run out of fuel, which was even scarcer than medicine. As I drew near, I could see silhouettes of men moving around on the deck. Five of them boarded an orange lifeboat and began rowing toward me.

"What do you want?" one called from a distance.

"My name's Joe!" I yelled back.

"I don't care who you are!" he replied, still rowing closer. "I asked what you want!"

I could then see guns in their lifeboat.

"Antibiotics!"

They said nothing else but continued to approach. I stopped rowing, the waves still rocking me from side to side. When they reached me, they drew alongside, peering into my rowboat. Then they hooked a rope to the bow and began towing me toward the yacht. My stomach grew sicker. What had I gotten myself into?

We reached the stern of the yacht, where more of the crew on board pulled me in and tied up my rowboat. All of them carried automatic weapons. They directed me to come aboard their vessel, and I collected the crates and climbed from one boat to the other. We rose up the steps that led from the water level at the stern to the main deck, and I was led alongside the cabin out to the bow. They're going to rob me and throw me in, I thought. I was too far from the shore to swim. Would they just shoot me?

I was told to stop at the bow and to turn facing toward the stern, still holding a crate under each arm. Three pirates stood guard on either side of me. Across the deck their spoils were strewn—stacks of coins and cash, cardboard boxes full of jewels, and clear plastic packages of marijuana that could have been stolen from a medical supplier or traded by a desperate customer. Among their treasure laid empty cans of food and trash they hadn't bothered to throw away. There was a grimy filth covering most of the exposed surfaces of the boat.

A few moments later, a young man, perhaps not even twenty years old, emerged from the cabin wearing a red robe and a tricorne hat. A black patch covered his left eye. His boots clapped on the wooden deck with every slow and menacing step he took. The only thing stifling the humor of the spectacle was the terror I felt in the presence of those men who wanted so desperately to emulate pirates as portrayed by Hollywood that they would kill me for any mockery.

"What do you want?" asked the boy in the tricorne hat.

"Antibiotics," I replied.

"You'll address him as 'Captain'!" demanded one of the men beside me.

"Antibiotics, Captain," I said again.

"What do you have for us?" he asked.

I held up the crates in my arms.

"Chickens?" he asked incredulously. "What do you expect us to do with two chickens?"

"Breed them, Captain," I said. "One is a hen, and one is a rooster. You can breed them, and you'll have more chickens."

He stared at me for a moment and then asked, "What else have you got?"

"Nothing," I replied.

"Search him," he commanded of the men standing guard. They did as they were told, and he watched sternly and expectantly. I stared back at that black patch and the one good eye with its heartless expression as they jerked me about and patted me down. His disappointment was plain when they produced nothing of further value.

"Are you a poor man?" he asked me.

"Not sure I would put it that way."

"You don't carry gold."

"I don't carry much of anything. Where I'm from, we don't trade in money or precious metals. We trade in commodities and labor."

"Where is that, exactly?"

"A woodland in southern Missouri."

The boy in the tricorne hat took a seat on a plush bench built into the deck of the yacht.

"What did you say your name was?" he asked.

"Joe."

"Would you like to know how I lost this eye, Joe?"

"Yes, Captain," I humored him.

"It was a duel with a man over a single gold coin. I killed him. It belonged to him, and then it belonged to me. Do you know what I bought with that gold coin? Lunch. He lost his life so that I could have lunch."

"And you lost an eye," I replied, immediately regretting the slip. His face turned angry for a moment, and then his frown grew to a grin.

"Yes, well, I would do it again," he replied.

I stood still, looking at him, doubting whether his eye patch actually served any purpose other than as an ominous prop for some nonsensical anecdote. He sat silently as if he was waiting for me to respond. When I didn't, he said, "Perhaps you'd like to swim back to shore."

With that, a man on either side of me grabbed my shirt and dragged me to the edge of the boat. They leaned me backward over the water, still holding onto my chickens, who were squawking with madness.

"Wait!" I exclaimed. "These birds are far more valuable than some coins!"

"Do you see any place around here for us to breed chickens?"

"I don't, Captain, but what is the big plan here?" I asked at the risk of offending him. "What happens when you run out of medicine to trade? These chickens are an opportunity, Captain. What if you went down to, say, the Caribbean, and commandeered an island the way you did this ship?"

His eyebrows rose.

"Let him up," he said. They reluctantly lifted me back to my feet.

"You could build an empire," I continued, "but you'd need food. You'd need farms. Perhaps these two chickens are just the beginning, Captain."

He continued to stare at me for a moment, his gaze slowly drifting out to sea. After a while, he turned and nodded to another pirate, who grabbed my arm for a look at the infection and then disappeared into the yacht's cabin. The minion returned a few minutes later with a jar and handed it to me.

"Leave the chickens," said the boy in the tricorne hat. The pirates led me back to the rowboat.

I returned to Esther's farm, relieved to still have my life, and began treating the infection with the antibiotics I had bartered for. I owed her so much for her generosity. I hadn't mentioned to the boy the abundance of chickens that roamed free on populated Caribbean islands, but we would be worlds apart by the time he realized he had been duped.

Esther, being the grandmotherly figure that she was, had been reprimanding me about the disheveled mop on my head since she had taken me into her home. "A man should take pride in his appearance," she had said as she was stitching up the wounds in my leg. Of course, she came from an era when men donned suits and ties to walk picket lines. I came from an era when they wore jeans and T-shirts to church. In her eyes, God deserved more respect. In ours, He would accept us despite our attire. Perhaps we were both right. After all, we're born naked.

I finally gave into her persistence and allowed her to cut all of my hair off. She said that would be adequate payment for the chickens, and that was the only time I saw her laugh during my entire stay with her.

"I should make a sweater with the leftovers," she said.

"I knew there was an ulterior motive."

"Now, when I'm done here, you'll shave that beard."

"Yes, ma'am."

"See? There's hope for you yet."

"Can I ask you something?"

"Sure, honey," she said.

"Do you think you'll ever see your husband again?"

She looked at me and thought for a moment, and then she asked, "Do you think you'll ever see your wife again?"

"If I make it home."

"You aren't sure that you will?"

"I've got a long road ahead of me," I said, "and it will only get rougher. My journey has barely begun."

"We all have a journey that's just beginning. I imagine my husband is in about the same place you are. And your wife probably looks upon life much the way I do. She's just waiting for her love to return. It doesn't usually help to make plans. The world has a way of changing them without our permission. All we can do is have faith that things will work out in the end."

"I'm not so sure about that," I mumbled, looking over at the child sleeping peacefully nearby. "I lied to that little girl."

"What do you mean?" Esther asked.

"I told her there weren't bad people anymore."

"You're talking about the pirates?"

"Yes."

"Maybe they're not all bad. They just need someone to show them the way. There's a bit of evil in all of us."

"At least a bit of good in all of us too, though."

"I think, yes."

"You think she'll find her parents?" I asked.

"Well, she'll have a home here as long as she needs it."

That night while the old woman and the child slept, I came across a framed photograph of Esther and a man who I assumed to be her husband. It was a candid shot of the two of them, carefree and happy on the steps outside of an ancient temple with snowcapped mountains poking through the clouds in the background. Hundreds of colorful flags were strung about them. The pair stood out from the crowd in their western garb, but aside from his attire, the man blended in with the locals.

I dreamed of Maria. I dreamed of fights we'd had at the farm and of fights that had never occurred. I woke up with tears in my eyes, anxious to move on, eager for another change in scenery in the hopes that it might ease my pain.

Soon, I was headed north again, taking with me a sack of tropical fruits that I was sure to miss again when they were gone in a few days. Esther and the child stood in the doorway waving as I departed on the back of my horse. Nomad and I passed through the settlement toward the ocean, and I could see three boats in the distance, sailing toward the shore.

7

MONUMENTS TO PRECEDENTS

In some weeks, I reached what had been Washington, DC, after brief stays outside the remains of Jacksonville, Savannah, Charleston, Raleigh, and Richmond. It was midsummer, and the heat was brutal. I had been trying not to watch dates too closely. Independence Day came and went without fireworks, and I didn't know it until days later. Dwelling on the time served no good purpose and would only amplify my anxiety, but I happened to glance at my watch one afternoon, and I realized it was my birthday. It was a milestone I hadn't thought once about since we had left the city. For the first time in my life, I spent my birthday alone. Well, not entirely alone, but Nomad, as loyal a companion as he was, could not substitute for my family. I remembered the cake that Maria had made for me on my last birthday in our house in the suburbs and the watch she had given me that had come to be torturous.

"It's powered by movement," she had said. "As long as you keep moving, it will always work. Now you don't have an excuse for coming home late." Then she kissed me.

That night, I couldn't bring myself to stop, and it was then that I saw the lights of fires in the darkness outside of Washington, DC. I thought of a time when Maria's cousin was flying into St. Louis from DC and Maria had asked me how I planned to pick her up from the airport. Of course, she was asking how we would coordinate the retrieval in the middle of a weekday, but my response was, "Well, I was thinking we could get some ski masks, rent a black van with tinted windows, come to a screeching halt in front of the airport, jump out, throw a shroud over her head, and toss her in the van before speeding off again. Would you like me to call Enterprise and see if that vehicle is available?" My sarcasm was not always well received, but in the months I had been gone, I wondered if she was beginning to miss it.

Nomad decided he was done for the night, and we finally stopped to sleep in the shadowy outskirts of the new settlement. Abandoned cars covered the road around us. The next morning, I awoke to the voices of men outside of my tent. I listened for a moment, but they spoke so quietly that I could not make out the conversation. I was unsure of their intentions, and out there, there would be no witnesses to a crime. The lesson I had learned from the pirates had not yet been lost. Certainly humans can be dangerous creatures—more dangerous and territorial even than an alligator. As a precaution, I racked a shell as quietly as I could before emerging from the tent.

"That's cheating," was the first thing said when they saw me. There were three of them standing around me with bows but no arrows drawn. They looked relaxed.

"You can't be too careful," I said, fearing again that I had lied to the child.

"Easy to say until your finger slips."

For a moment, nothing was said. I eyed the three of them with suspicion as they glared back. Finally, one spoke.

"Are you going to put the gun away?"

"I haven't decided," I said.

"We thought you might be hungry. If you prefer, we'll move on."

I paused to look them over. Their attire suggested they were out to hunt, not to rob drifters on the side of the road. I reluctantly slid the gun into its sleeve attached to my saddle.

"There you go. We're all friends here."

"You guys from DC?"

"The vicinity. But we don't call it that anymore." One of them laughed.

"What do you call it?"

They looked at each other for a moment and then looked back at me and shrugged.

"Well, I'm Aaron," said one of the men. "And this is Dave and Jake."

"Joe."

"You hunt, Joe?"

"When I have to."

I was suspicious still. Caught off guard and outnumbered was not a position into which I relished being placed, particularly in an unfamiliar and lawless land. Even if their intentions seemed innocent, I hoped they wouldn't invite me to join their hunt. Not only would it be an excuse to draw weapons, placing me in an even more vulnerable spot, but it would also certainly expose my weakness in that particular trade. I was still not the best shot with an arrow, and worse at keeping quiet and still. Both the fear of the strangers and my own insecurities left me apprehensive.

"Why don't you come along with us?"

Damn it.

"I don't know. I am pretty hungry."

"Good, so are we," said Aaron. "You've found the right company. When you hunt with Dave and Jake, you never stay hungry."

The pair smiled humbly at the praise.

"All right," I said, "I'm in."

"That's the spirit. You can leave the gun."

Aaron was right about the skills of his companions. The four of us ate well that morning before we headed toward their home, and the camaraderie brought back sensations of my first days hunting at the farm. That eased my tension, and gradually I began to look at them as friends. There was nothing hostile about them. How primal it is to immediately prepare defense in the presence of a larger, more dominant, or greater number of the same species. In time, I think, that reflex will fade away in humanity. Our capacity for comprehensive reasoning sets us apart from every other creature, and cooperation, as opposed to competition, was clearly in everyone's best interest.

The lawless place where we then lived sometimes seemed safer than it ever had with rules. As we strolled into the new city that had grown from what had once been the capital of the United States of America, southwest of the old ghost town with a Blue Ridge Mountain backdrop, I wondered if we would ever again see government and law as we had known them before. And should we? As Thomas Jefferson said, "The natural progress of things is for liberty to yield and government to gain ground."

Without government, without modern technology, without many resources beyond the natural earth and the knowledge we had brought with us, we were all forced to start from scratch. For the first time since Europeans had set foot on this continent, it truly was a land of equal opportunity.

"You're welcome to stay at my house if you like, Joe," said Aaron, an offer I, of course, accepted. His home was similar to the one-room cabin that Maria and I called home. It sat among a neighborhood of similar houses where Dave and Jake also lived. Between our kill from that morning and the dishes supplied by the neighbors, nobody went hungry. That was the way things went.

We reminisced about our former trades, and I found that the professional skills and experience of my new friends had rendered them about as useless as I was after the collapse. Jake wouldn't exactly say what he did, but he told tales of the military coming into town during the rioting and imposing martial law and a citywide curfew, which only escalated the bedlam.

"That's when we knew it was time to get the hell out," he said. "They blocked the streets with tanks so that nobody could get in or out, at least with a vehicle. Then they turned on us. We had to sneak in at night to collect family members one by one. The ones that were left, anyway. You always assume the government is there to protect you, but when people lose sight of what they're fighting for, then they're just fighting."

Dave, who had once been an engineer on the DC Metro, had become a facilitator for the clandestine exodus from the old capital. He had acted as a guide for refugees and had helped to establish their new settlement there. That was how he and Jake had met. I suspected his skills in hunting had been particularly useful for sneaking in and out of the city unseen. Or perhaps that was how he had learned those skills—out of necessity.

Aaron, ironically, had been a lobbyist for rail transportation, a luxury I yearned for. He told a story of the trip that had gotten him hooked as a child—a train ride from New England to Southern California. Day after day, he had watched the scene in the window change as the train passed mountains, deserts, forests, plains, and cities, with a view of those things from a whole different perspective. "You're closer to the earth in a train," he said, "like you're really a part of it all." From then on, he had wanted to see the world, and by rail was the finest way to do it. That was his passion. Not the politics. But lobbying was more lucrative than engineering and afforded him the stately brick manor in Arlington that he had called home.

I'm sure all of my questions must have seemed like an interrogation as I probed to learn the dark secrets that had powered the political machine, but he took it all with humor. It wasn't as though I could blow any whistle. "Ultimately," he said, "it was all about money. Big government was always in collusion with big business. It's just the way it was. Not always in the best interests of the American people, but it was profitable." He told us about secret meetings with congressmen behind closed doors, anonymous campaign contributions, media manipulation, and envelopes passed under the table. "One on one," he said, "it didn't feel like what we called 'corruption.' We thought of it as 'collaboration.'"

Things usually look different from a macro perspective.

His stories were like a blend of *The Godfather* and *House of Cards*. The definitions of honor and patriotism were bent to align with business interests. Aaron had operated that way simply because everyone else had. There had been no other way to compete or to be heard. He had believed in his cause, but every industry from tobacco to renewable energy had implemented the same tactics regardless of their ethics. Even the best ideas would have been doomed in the marketplace if their representatives hadn't been willing to make the necessary sacrifices, which sometimes included their integrity.

Gerald Ford said, "A government big enough to give you everything you want is a government big enough to take from you everything you have." We had lost the corruption inherent in such a massive organization. What had come about in the new city, and I can't imagine a more appropriate place for such a thing to have had its genesis, was a new form of peacekeeping that didn't allow an opportunity for rampant immorality. It was explained to me as simply "the ethical way." There wasn't a word for it. The community had democratically selected a council based on virtues, not on politics or campaigning, to simplify the important decisions. When there was misconduct significant enough to warrant attention, which was rare, the council would determine the appropriate resolution and always leave an opportunity for the community as a whole to reject the decision and propose an alternate. That rarely came in the form of punishment. As we had learned, punishment seldom solved a problem. That should have been evident by the percentage of repeat offenders in our archaic "correctional system."

"The idea now is to focus on why the offense was committed rather than to avenge the victim," Aaron said. "Then we make an effort to correct the problem and help the offender to understand why his or her action was unacceptable without being patronizing. I don't know what it's like where you came from, but violent crime is almost unheard of here. For one, most of the social failures that bred that kind of behavior are long gone, and now we pay more attention to people as individuals. Usually, we can catch flaws early before a person reaches such a state of desperation that they feel hurting another is the only way out."

It was my first evening with them. We had been talking awhile around a fire, and as Aaron spoke, I suddenly realized that Nomad was no longer in sight. He had been tied up near Aaron's home, no more than fifty feet from where we were all seated.

"Where's my horse?" I interrupted him. I had been listening with such fascination that I had ignored my periphery. I stood to look around. Nobody else had noticed either, and their puzzled gazes met me with silence.

"My horse," I repeated.

I began to pace, looking into the dark distance.

"You all right, Joe?" Dave asked.

"My horse was tied up over there. He's not there anymore."

"You sure?"

"Yes, I'm sure. He doesn't wander off, and it was a tight knot."

"He must be around then."

"I have to find him," I said, growing frantic. I had a terrible feeling. I grabbed a flaming branch from the fire.

The three rose to follow and we spread in a search. It was so dark that I could hardly see what was ahead or remember where I had already been as I wound through paths between cabins and trees and tramped through tall grass.

"Nomad!" I yelled at the top of my lungs. "Come here, boy!"

Nothing.

"Come on! Where are you?"

I felt my eyes watering.

"Try to keep it down, Joe," Aaron called as he began to move farther away. "People are sleeping."

"I don't care! I have to find him!"

I began to panic. It was late in the evening, and most everyone was already in bed. Fires had died down. Everything was black and profiled by the moonlight. I saw the glow of the other torches in the distance.

"Anyone see anything?" I yelled.

"Nothing," Jake called back.

"Keep looking."

Tears of dread ran down my cheeks. Nomad was my only companion on the road and my only connection to home that I had to cling to. I would be lost without him. The horse had become the closest thing to family I had known in months. He would never leave me, I knew, which terrified me even more. He had not caught a wind of inspiration and run off on his own accord. Someone had taken him. I was sure of it.

We were reaching the outskirts of the village, and I could see the tree line in the distance when I heard Nomad's neigh. I knew it instinctively. "Here!" I yelled, breaking into a sprint in the direction of the sound. I saw his silhouette in the moonlight, and then I saw a man tugging the reins against Nomad's will. He became more forceful when he saw me approaching.

"Drop it!" I screamed at him. "I'll kill you!"

I charged at him with every intention of fulfilling the promise, the ground cover crunching beneath my feet. My skin grew hot with rage, and my vision blurred. The man released the reins and tried to run as I rushed upon him, but there was no escaping for him. I ran past my horse, drawing my knife to take the life of the thief, and I tackled him to the ground. He slid through the dirt and leaves face down as I grabbed one arm, twisting it behind his back, and slipped the knife around to his throat.

"You know what they used to do to horse thieves?" I screamed into his ear, my voice cracking.

"I'm sorry!" he pleaded, spitting out dirt, his face pressed into the ground.

"They used to shoot them on the spot, and nobody protested. You should have taken my gun off my horse. That might have saved you from me."

"I'm sorry! I'm just so hungry."

"You were going to eat him?"

The teeth on the blade snagged the skin of his throat, tearing grooves in his flesh. My grip only tightened.

"I'm so sorry. Please don't hurt me."

I heard footsteps behind me and Aaron's voice yelling at me. "Don't do it, Joe," he said. The lights of torches glowed around us and grew brighter as neighbors approached to see what it was that had woken them.

"Don't touch me. I'll kill him."

"Joe, take a breath."

"He was going to eat my horse!"

"But he didn't," Aaron said. "Think, Joe. How will you feel when he's dead?"

"I don't care!"

"You do care. Take a lesson from Buck Grangerford and don't start down that road. The world has seen enough violence."

I said nothing. I felt warmth on my cheek and then a rub from Nomad's moist muzzle. I turned to look at him and he looked right back, and I saw the compassion in his dark eyes. He was calm and still.

"Please," said the thief, the dirt under his head turning to mud from the tears.

Slowly I released his arm, took the knife from his throat, and stood. He lay on the ground crying.

The next day was different. I had lost it, and I was ashamed of what I'd done. I had nearly killed a hungry man. His name was Thomas. As it turned out, Thom had just come out of hiding from the city, and the ways of the new world had not yet been introduced to him. He had no skill for wilderness survival, and he had taken the first opportunity he had seen for food without conflict. When he felt my knife at his throat, he had fully expected death to come next, but when he lay there crying afterward, they weren't tears of fear, he said. They were tears of joy. The mercy and compassion that had been shown to him in that single moment had renewed his faith in humanity.

Thom was not a violent man, I learned. Nor was he a career thief. He was a desperate man who, from his limited perspective, saw only one way to survive. Afterward, he was offered food and work, and I even assisted in building a cabin for him when I was around. Thom and I had about the strangest introduction that I can imagine a pair of friends can claim. One stole from the other, who in turn nearly killed him for it.

After that incident, though, I began to grow more attached to my horse. I kept him with me as much as possible, and when he wasn't, I made sure he remained in the company of someone I trusted. I couldn't go through that again. Everybody needs someone to care for, be that a spouse, a child, or even a horse. We aren't complete without somebody relying on us.

Over the next several days, I had time to explore the new settlement, and it became evident that everything from Washington to New England had spread out so much that it was like one immense single-level megalopolis. There was no longer a government center or a commercial center. Just farmland, primitive architecture, and people sparsely scattered between the cities and suburbs that were still standing.

I took a few days and headed to the Chesapeake for some fishing. I was always expecting that a change in geography would change me as a person, and perhaps the vast sea could help to ease my mind. Since that nearly fateful night, I had been on edge constantly, tense, and anxiety stricken. Whatever barrier had existed in my conscience to keep me under control had snapped, and I was losing my grip on who I was and what exactly I was doing there. That had to change before we set back out on the highway, and fishing helped to calm me while I made a contribution to the neighborhood I had become a part of. It reminded me of my home. I met some fishermen in the harbor who welcomed me aboard their old wooden schooner in exchange for a small percentage of whatever I caught.

The beautiful thing about the sea is that it never changes. Once we were far enough out of the harbor, the land behind us looked the same as it had during my last visit there years before. The rising sun lent an orange glow to the twinkling waves that gradually turned to deep blue as it made its way higher in the sky. Whitecaps peaked all around us. My time at sea was peaceful and quiet, and I felt a whole new connection with the earth. I imagine sailing is the way God might travel. Most of the time, the only sounds were the subtle waves crashing into the hull and the gentle creaking of the old boat as it rocked. Then excitement would suddenly erupt when one of us had hooked something, and occasionally, a catch would be large enough that it took two or three of us to pull the creature aboard.

We brought in blue crabs and all sorts of fish. Huge fish. It's amazing the kinds of animals that lurk in deep waters. Once I caught a marlin, and pulling him in was like wrestling a monster. He glowed green under the surface, but his gray-blue dorsal and caudal fins cut through the waves like our sails through the air. He squirmed and flopped against the hull as we lifted him from the water, and I was nearly speared by his bill when pulling him onto the boat. In our struggle, one of my comrades tripped over the jib sheet, jerking the boom to the port side where I was leaning over the edge and fighting the massive fish with all of my might. The jib boom struck me in the back, knocking me over the side into the water. I emerged again, splashing and gasping for air.

"You clumsy bastard!" called the fisherman who had tripped.

"Me?" I returned in laughter. "This is your doing!"

"For every fish we catch, we have to give them a man."

"At least tell me you got him."

They all smiled as they held up my fish for display while I treaded water. It was the most exhilarating fun I could remember having in far too long. Despite our clumsiness, we had managed to conquer the monster, and it was all worth it to see the joy on the faces of the people he fed. We brought our catch back from the harbor on a wooden cart hitched behind Nomad, who was unfailingly prepared to take on any burden.

There were always boats coming and going and lingering in the harbor, and I relished watching the other fishermen as we floated past them. There were so many of us all existing in harmony—all on the same mission. One morning as we were leaving port, I was sure I saw the last president of the United States on another boat across the harbor. Of all people to see out there, I thought, imagine seeing him. It was a small rowboat, and he was alone. He looked like everyone else, sitting at the edge and leaning back against the bow, dangling one leg over the water with a fishing pole in his hands. I squinted for a better look, but we were at too great a distance to identify him with certainty. The more time passes, the more I wonder. Who knows? Perhaps I was just being hopeful.

As relaxing as it was out on the water, I had a lot of time to think about Maria. The sea reminded me of her. Sometimes, at just the right time of day with the right cloud cover, the color of the water exactly matched her eyes. She loved the water and would always choose it over the mountains, though my preference was for the latter. It had been so long that some of the little things about her were beginning to feel like more of a dream than reality. I couldn't always conjure the sensations associated with my memories, like how even in warm weather her hands were always cold, but I could hardly remember how they actually felt when I would hold them. I had to concentrate to remember her voice. Even the most valuable memories become hazy when the mind is so overwhelmed. Somehow, although I had left home largely to escape the unwarranted animosity I felt toward her, the void inside me was growing every day that I spent away from her. I had left to recover something lost, and yet I felt I was losing more. I missed the days when things had been good—when we had been so happy. How long could I stand it all without losing my grip completely? Sometimes I tried not to remember her, but that was usually even more painful.

I didn't mention those things in my latest letter to Maria, except for the part about the color of the water and her eyes. I figured she'd like that. And I wrote about sailing and fishing and the people who had taken me in, both in the mountains and on the coast. She might have even been envious, wishing she were there more than she wished I were home. Perhaps that thought was more hopeful than realistic. I couldn't have blamed her if she didn't miss me at all.

By then, my arm was almost entirely healed. The tiny holes in my leg from my accident with the alligator were nothing but scars and nearly invisible unless you were looking for them. Of all the world's dangers, it seemed that perhaps the greatest came from within myself. Of course, I still had no idea what lay ahead. I could write as many letters as I wanted, but I could not receive one, and it was I who needed the motivation to push on. The trail was always behind me, and I kept replaying her last words in my head.

"You had better come back to me. I love you."

I returned to the mountains as refreshed as I could be, given all that I was going through. After we had established their postal center and my letter had been sent off, it was time to move north. I marked my map again. Our burden would be lighter for the time being. Nomad and I would be traveling through populated areas, and there was no need to stock food for the trip. There would certainly be places to stop along the way, but I wasn't quite ready to leave that one. I hadn't felt so at home in a while. Home felt so close, but it was so far away. All of the people from my old life were becoming more and more distant, both geographically and in my memory.

"So where are you headed next, Joe?" Aaron asked as he cleaned up after a day of work. He poured a bucket of water over his head, droplets reflecting the moonlight as they ran down and dripped from his thick black beard.

"New York, I expect."

"Ah, the Big Apple. The City That Never Sleeps."

"That's what they say."

"I've got a friend up there," Jake said. "Look for a girl named Leah Jordan."

"Jake," Dave scoffed, "Do you know how many people lived in New York? Nearly nine million just within its limits. Over twenty-two million in the metro area, which is hundreds of square miles larger now. How is he supposed to find one woman?"

"Don't ask me. Joe's the great adventurer," he replied, turning to me. "Which is why you need to know this stuff," he continued, referring to our ongoing lessons on navigation by the stars. He taught me how to find Polaris, the "North Star," by the orientation of the Plough, or the "Big Dipper." I was to follow the line of the two stars, Merak and Dubhe, that make the edge of the constellation, which rotates counterclockwise around one of the brightest stars in the sky. In the northern hemisphere, north on the ground would always be directly below that star. The constellation Orion, he explained, rises in the east and sets in the west, like the sun. From Orion's belt, the star Mintaka can be used to find true east and west by where it emerges or falls on the horizon.

"Where did you learn all this, anyway?" I asked him.

"Oh, you know, I've been around," he replied dismissively. "But when you do find her, tell her to send a letter down here, eh?"

"I'll do what I can," I said.

"Whatever you can?" he asked, somewhat pleadingly. "She's very important."

8

THE CITY THAT NEVER SLEEPS

As I moved north, accents of the people I met began to change. I passed by what used to be Baltimore and then Philadelphia. I remembered reading an article once about a "greening" initiative in Philadelphia wherein fourteen thousand vacant lots were converted to green space, and in an unanticipated byproduct of urban beautification, crime rates in those areas dropped. Perhaps, I thought, a cleaner, greener atmosphere could make a person feel safer. Even a criminal.

Most of the cold urban buildings were still standing, but some had come down and had been replaced with smaller, more efficient and functional structures. I was amazed at how quickly the new development was taking shape. Masonry seemed to be the building method of choice, and buildings were erected on a grid, reminiscent of colonial America. It was beautiful. They were installing windows and doors, which meant that they had the ability to float glass and forge metal. I would have to learn more. I suppose that many of the people had fled from the cities immediately after the collapse but were gradually returning to reclaim and rebuild. Whatever rioting there had been I expected was long over.

Half the Eastern Seaboard had evolved into one massive agglomeration, and we made so many stops that it took weeks to make our way through it. I stayed with different families along the way who fed me a plethora of ethnic foods I had never before tasted. Some of them gave up old family recipes for me to bring back home. They reminded me of the "New Deli" around the corner from our old house that was owned by an Indian family with a sense of humor. It was nicer than staying outside every night, and they seemed to be used to taking in drifters. People were moving through all the time. Sometimes I was not the only strange guest in a house, but there was seldom any hesitation in inviting an outsider in. I got accustomed to having human company on a constant basis. It was far less lonely for a while.

I was pleasantly surprised when we reached what had been New York City. New Yorkers, at one time, had had a reputation for pretentiousness, but they were as gracious to me as anyone back home. I was always asking for directions; where's the nearest community farm—where's the nearest water well—where can I get some wood for a fire or whatever necessity it was that I needed—who do I talk to for this or that? That's how I met the people who took me in.

I discovered that the big city had established a registrar to ease communication and to connect the disconnected. It was a similar concept to what they had done in refugee camps after natural disasters or civil wars but with considerably more human resources and considerably less panic. It was all very organized and civilized, albeit somewhat frustrating at times.

The registrar was made up of a series of huge circus tents. Hundreds of people worked underneath to keep written records of names and to deliver messages. It doubled as the citizen catalogue and the local mail system. Their postal center had already been established for me. Lines reminiscent of the quintessential DMV office formed beneath the tents and wrapped outside, leaving many of us to bake in the sun on a hot day. I tied my horse to a tree in the shade and joined the others waiting to send or receive messages. It wasn't long before I was drenched in sweat.

"It's damn hot out here," I said to the fellow next to me.

"Almost makes you wonder if it's worth it, doesn't it?" he replied.

I looked around. Some others had had the foresight to bring umbrellas or light cloths for shade, but most had not. I figured that sweating like a dog in my shirt was no less appropriate than doing it without one, so I stripped it off and used it to fan myself.

"Well it was only a matter of time," said my neighbor, doing the same. "What's more important, class or comfort?"

"These days, the latter," I said.

After a while, others in our line and neighboring ones began to catch on, and clothing was waving in every direction. The fellow next to me pointed out that if we were to fan toward the next line over we could create more of a breeze, so we did. Across from us, they did the same, and the breeze of each fan augmented the previous one. Eventually, we had a synchronized wave passing between each line, creating a channeled draft that cooled everyone. It was a strange social event that would have piqued the curiosity of the Tralfamadorians, but it worked out quite nicely and gave us something to do while we waited. There were thousands of us waiting that day to list our names or to find a name or to send or collect messages. The time offered ample opportunity for conversation with my neighbors. I had never taken advantage of that opportunity when it had been presented to me in the old world. Lines were just for waiting.

That was how I tracked down Leah. When I finally got to the end of the line, I found myself flashing back to a day in the mall before the collapse. I had happened to get a phone call from Paul while I was standing in one such line, and I remember saying, "I love when I'm in a retail store and my wife sticks me in the checkout line and goes off to shop some more, and I get to the front of the line, the cashier is waiting for me, and my wife still isn't back."

"Did that just happen to you?" he had asked.

"That's occurring at this very moment."

I was at an equal loss at the registrar, having not considered what I would say to the stranger I was looking for before reaching the thin receptionist at the table who was trying desperately to maintain her patience in the midst of my casual Midwestern pace.

"Got a lot of people in line behind you, friend. Are you listing or searching?"

"Searching, I guess."

"Name?"

"Leah Jordan."

She wrote the name on a piece of crude brown paper and passed it to an assistant who scampered off behind her. She motioned for me to move aside and wait while the gofer dug through alphabetical lists to find the appropriate message file. After a few minutes, he returned and told me that there were six Leah Jordans listed and asked if I knew her box number. Of course I did not, so I decided to leave a message for all six. I could see the minor frustration in his face, but it was certainly not a new task.

"At least I didn't say Jane Smith," I told him. His scowl softened a bit as I began writing my note.

Jake sent me. Meet me at the well nearest the registrar at noon three days from the date of this message. I'll be the guy with the horse. My name is Joe.

Of the six Leah Jordans in the area, three had acquaintances named Jake with whom they shared a close enough bond that the hike to meet me was worth it. Two of them had come with their husbands, and one had come alone. Unfortunately, I had never thought to ask Jake's last name, so I was left identifying him only as Jake from the former DC area. That was clear enough, and once we had established which Leah was the correct Leah, the other two and their husbands left me with letters to pass on as I traveled west; one to the former Los Angeles area and one to the former Denver area. Their inconvenience was not in vain.

Leah suggested that the next time I wanted to set a meeting with a stranger I pick a brewery or a distillery. Someplace worthy of the hike in case the stranger turned up lame. Good advice, I thought. The girl sounded like fun. The well I had chosen was seven miles from her home, but she had been curious enough about her friend to make the trek. Leah and Jake had gone to school together and had remained close since, but their communication had been cut off in the collapse. I sensed that there might have been some long-lost romance between them. Perhaps career paths had led them in different directions. It's a shame when love comes secondary to such a trivial thing as money.

The thought took me back to Maria. Was it selfish of me to leave her at home while I set off to restore my dignity? Why had her love not been enough to satisfy that sense of purpose I so desperately craved?

We took the old Lincoln Tunnel under the Hudson River into the city and headed toward Leah's Long Island home. As the colossal Manhattan skyline grew around us, I realized that it was the first time I had entered one of the old urban areas since the collapse. It was an eerie parallel version of the city I remembered. The streets were busy with pedestrians, though still only about half as crowded as they had been before. There were no cars. One of the few horses in sight was attached to the reins in my hand and was walking down the middle of the asphalt streets paying no mind to the yellow and white stripes designating traffic lanes. Signal lights were still standing, but they were black. The streets were cleaner than I remembered and lined with both timeworn and contemporary architecture that seemed to mimic what our lifestyle had become.

Leah decided to take me on a detour while we got acquainted. She led me up through Central Park, which was then home to hundreds of people living in a vast neighborhood of tents. Children were swimming and people were bathing in the lake. The grass had grown tall. We stopped to pick fruit and berries from trees along the way, and then we wound through block after block of ghostly architecture from generations past. Leah's pace was slow, devoid of the urgency that used to possess the place like a religion or a cult. People smiled at each other on the street.

As night fell, we came upon Times Square, and what had once been one of the brightest and liveliest parts of any city in the world was nearly silent and vacant. There were no Asian tourists snapping pictures with zoom lens cameras. No flocking teenage girls with their hands occupied by designer purses and cell phones, each engaged in her own conversation separate from the next. The darkness of it was difficult to swallow. All of the light screens on the walls were black and lifeless. Street trees were untrimmed. Banner advertisements were faded and falling. It was one of the more empty parts of town, a place rife with old shops that no longer served any purpose. The emptiness was almost painful. So wasteful, I thought.

As the evening sky grew darker, the orange glow of firelight began to pop up on the streets and in the windows of the lower floors of buildings. Once we had gotten to know each other, Leah and I set out to have some fun that night, something she could see was lacking in my life. She said it looked like I was due for a good time. It seemed that the "City That Never Sleeps" had maintained its nightlife, and we headed to her favorite nightspot to lift my burden and numb my conscience. Leah didn't bother preparing for the evening the way the girls used to. There was nobody to impress. Back home, Maria had always followed the same routine before we would go out.

"Hair straight or curly?" she would ask.

"Half and half," I would say.

"Joe!"

"OK, curly."

"But I know you like it better straight," she would say.

"OK, straight then."

"But that takes longer."

"Well, you're beautiful either way."

"Cute, Joe. Jeans or skirt?"

"Both."

"It doesn't work that way."

"I can't win."

"I married you, that's your win. Now you have the privilege of helping me decide what to wear."

I wanted to be back there in our grand bathroom with his and her sinks and a Jacuzzi tub in the bay window, watching her paint her face with makeup that she didn't need. She was beautiful when she woke up in the morning. Just her presence by my side raised my status, but she never thought she was good enough. She was always good enough, though. Always. I wished I had told her that before I had left her.

Maria refused to leave my mind, particularly as I took a seat on a fire lit patio to drink whiskey with a woman I had just met. At the same moment, my wife was at home wondering where I was that night. Every night.

The patio matched the old brick buildings that lined both sides of the once heavily trafficked street. It was nestled behind an iron gate that stood open all of the time. Instead of speeding headlights, candles bobbed slowly past in both directions. I settled into a handmade wooden chair at a table that wobbled on the uneven masonry. Leah brought over two glasses of whiskey, served neat, and sat one on the table in front of me. She shot hers back and slammed the empty glass down on the table.

"Impressive," I said, my eyes following her as she walked around behind me.

"Thank you," she replied, resting her hands on my shoulders. "I think you need help relaxing. Drink up. It's good stuff."

She began to massage my shoulders. I didn't stop her. It felt too good.

Leah was always asking about Jake. What was he doing? Who was he with? She didn't seem thrilled with his new trade, but I assured her that somebody had to keep us fed.

"He's killing things now?" she asked. "We're going to have words about that."

"Somebody has to do it," I said in his defense.

"Well, I don't like blood. Never have, even in the navy."

"You were in the navy?"

"Yep. Jake and I met at Annapolis. He was a Jarhead, I was a Squid. He never liked guns either, but I think the appeal for him was more patriotism than war. Some guys just liked the violence until they were caught in the middle of it and realized they weren't the big men they thought they were. Jake was a true patriot. He believed in what he was defending."

"What was that?" I asked.

"A lot of things that no longer need defense."

The operator of the small distillery, a man named Eli, came to join us after a while, bringing with him a full bottle of whiskey that shifted the weight of the table. Leah took her hands off of my shoulders to pull out a chair for herself. When she introduced us, we both paused for a moment before sharing a laugh and shaking hands.

"Have you two met?" she asked.

"Just this morning," I said.

"We changed the weather over at the registrar." Eli laughed. She shook her head at his nonsense as he took his own seat.

"It's a small world," I said.

"But a big city. What are we drinking to, Joe?" Eli asked, pouring himself a glass.

I held up my glass contemplatively. Then I said the first thing that came to mind.

"Love!"

Eli raised his eyebrows and looked toward Leah. "Drink to love!" he said, raising his glass.

"Love to drink," she replied as the three of our glasses clinked. Her mouth smiled, but her eyes were sad, as if love was something she preferred not to discuss.

Eli and Leah were quite friendly. It seemed she was a regular patron and a big drinker. I never would have guessed from the looks of her, but I learned the hard way. I wanted to ask what it was she was trying to escape from. Perhaps it was the stress of the collapse. Perhaps her lost love. Or maybe it was just a relic from her days as a yuppie in NYC.

My vision blurred as the clear portion of the whiskey bottle grew. I began to relax, and my life back home followed my consciousness as it stumbled toward obscurity. The crowd on the patio around us thinned, and for hours we told stories and laughed together. Leah's hand would land on my leg to keep her stable when she lost her balance. Then she would correct her posture and pretend it was an accident.

I could see the expression on Eli's face beginning to change at the sight of her charade, but I was without my own wits and conscience. The wooden chair upon which she sat gradually moved closer and closer to mine.

"Are you all right?" I asked her.

"I'm fine," she said, taking my hand. "Are you?"

A chill shot through me. I looked up into her eyes, gazing back at me longingly.

"I love your hair," she said, leaning close and running her fingers through it, her other hand still loosely rested in mine. I glanced over toward Eli, who was looking on in disapproval. He excused himself from the table, and I looked back at Leah.

"I like yours," I replied, leaning in and brushing her hair away from her face and behind her ear. "It shines in the moonlight."

She closed her eyes and rested her cheek in my hand with a contented smile.

I woke up on a stone floor that was cold everywhere except for the blistering sunbeam that I happened to be lying in. My shirt was drenched in sweat, and my pants were covered in a mysterious orange substance and lying on the floor on the opposite side of the room. My head felt like someone had driven a chisel into my skull and was slowly prying it apart. I sat up, looking around for some evidence of where I was and how I had gotten there. Then I saw Leah making breakfast in a fireplace.

"What the hell happened last night?" I asked her.

"You drank too much."

"Clearly."

"Want some breakfast?"

"Definitely," I said, climbing to my feet.

"I don't usually take home strange men, but I couldn't leave you out there all alone with Eli. He likes to have fun with people who pass out at his place. You might have woken up in the East River, especially since you're friends with Jake. I think he's a little jealous."

"Jealous of what?" I asked.

"Oh, never mind."

"I have a sneaking suspicion that Jake is not the one who made him jealous," I said as pieces of the night fell back into place.

"You're probably right."

"Well, I've always had a weakness for Wild Turkey."

I picked up my pants and sniffed them, but my head was too congested to smell anything. I walked around collecting the trail of my socks, shoes, and belt, which were strewn about, and then carried them all over to Leah.

"What's this?" I asked, presenting her with the stain on my pants.

"That? That's vomit."

"Vomit? Whose?"

"Yours. You puked everywhere. I haven't seen anything like that since college. It was like *The Exorcist*."

"Oh, Lord," I said. "I'm so sorry."

"It's fine, at least you did it outside. My neighbor's dog already cleaned it up."

"That's disgusting."
"Yeah, well you should take a look at yourself."
"So..." I hesitated. "We didn't..."
"No."
I sighed with relief.
"You must have had a lot of sorrow to drown last night," she said. "A nice hangover will give you something else to focus on. Go get cleaned up while I finish breakfast. You're coming to work with me today."

Work was at an old brick foundry that then doubled as a float glass manufacturing facility. It made sense to pair the two, as the production of float glass required the use of molten metal. That was how their windows were made. The foundry was one of many old buildings in the city that still served its purpose. The more modern, vertical parts of the city had become the least inhabited, and some of them were eerily vacant. The oldest buildings, however, were the most similar to our new construction outside the urban centers. Architecture evolves with the needs of the user, and because our lifestyles had become so primitive, construction took a few steps into the past. Some of the contemporary architecture was being disassembled and making its way to various foundries to be recycled. They used the old metals to cast and forge new tools and components. The foundries were powered by natural gas primarily and coal or petroleum coke when necessary. Fuel sources were being extracted, processed, and distributed on a limited basis. There was even a functional wind farm, I heard, generating minimal amounts of electricity.

Leah was the person in charge of glass production at that particular facility. Once formed, sheets of float glass would be shipped to a woodworking house, where they would then be framed into windows. Elsewhere, building materials like concrete, brick, and mortar were in production. I watched their new construction industry as it took shape, requiring the unselfish cooperation of thousands of visionaries with the foresight to see the world as it could be rather than as it was. Labor without the expectation of compensation, but also without the damning authority of any oppressor, was somehow liberating. Each person worked not only for him or herself, but also for the great community as a whole. That community, in turn, provided for each member of its population.

My hangover rendered me rather unproductive, so I spent the day observing. Never before had I seen such a great variety of people working under one roof. There were three men in particular whom I watched diligently all morning, seeking to learn as much as I could about their trade to take back to the farm with me. The sweltering heat of the foundry didn't seem to affect their mood. They bantered and laughed while they worked as if they were laboring alongside best friends or brothers, though their varying skin pigments flaunted their diversity. It became increasingly evident that those three men, who clearly hailed from very different backgrounds, viewed one another not merely as friends, but as family. I was as impressed by their camaraderie as I was by their trade.

Some time midmorning, my headache and exhaustion got the better of me, and I dozed off. I awoke abruptly to the sound of a scream as one of the three men tripped while crossing an overhead walkway and went tumbling over the edge toward the molten metal bed below. A flowing sheet of glass, no longer destined to become a window, would break his fall in the final agonizing moments of his life. Adrenaline pulsed through me and I shot to my feet, but I was too late for action. Through the steam between us I caught only a glimpse of what had happened, and I was certain he had been killed. I panicked. My ears rang with the sound of his voice and then with the clanking of footsteps as another of the three darted across the steel bridge above. His call echoed around the room, though I could see nothing but a white wall.

"Hang on, we've got you!" I heard him yell through the scalding fog. The opaque world around me was spinning in slow motion.

Then the cloud of steam cleared, and I saw the man who had fallen dangling by a chain he had grabbed at the last moment on his way down. It was run taut through a series of pulleys in the ceiling, and as my eyes traced its route back to the floor, I saw the third man at the other end of the chain, pulling back with all his might to keep his friend from falling. His feet were braced against a wall, fighting the weight of the man in the air.

I raced across the room to his aid, grabbed the chain, and pulled back with him. The man on the bridge was leaning over the edge with his arm outstretched.

"Just reach," I heard him calling. "Grab onto my hand."

The man on the chain rose slowly as we heaved by the other end. He reached out and locked his fingers around the wrist of the man on the bridge, who did the same.

"Now let go of the chain," said the man on the bridge.

He closed his eyes, took a breath, and the two of us at the other end stumbled backward as he released the chain and swung his free arm onto the suspended walkway. The man on the bridge helped him climb to safety, and together they stumbled slowly down the stairs to the ground.

The four of us stood silently looking at each other for a moment, all of us panting, before dropping into a joyful and relieved laughter. Just then, Leah came running to us.

"Everyone OK?" she asked.

"Always," wheezed the man who had fallen as he raised a cross pendant hanging from his neck and kissed it. "Just making sure these fellas are on their toes."

"Well it looks like you need to be more careful with yours," she said. "That goes for all three of you, OK? We don't need any more accidents. You're lucky to be alive."

"Agreed," said the man who had rushed onto the bridge to save his friend. "We can thank Allah for his grace."

"And for waking Joe from his hangover nap at just the right moment," laughed the man who had fallen as he looked at me and extended his hand. "Thank you," he said.

I smiled and shook his hand. "Quite welcome."

Leah took me aside and told me we were done for the day. "I want to show you something," she said.

"Aspirin? Please tell me you have something for this headache." It had returned once the adrenaline had faded and my hands had stopped shaking so much.

"We don't have that. Your body is punishing you. Take it like a man. Drink some water, and come with me."

"See you soon, Joe," said the man with whom I had held the chain. "Shalom."

I did as Leah said, and we headed off. We walked block after block down the streets of the old city through throngs of people that reflected the diversity of the foundry. They all seemed to live with that same harmony that would have brought a smile to the face of Piscine Molitor Patel. Eventually we reached the water of New York Harbor, where I saw hundreds of sailboats and rowboats under the welcoming radiance of Lady Liberty basking in the afternoon sun. News had reached Leah that a fleet of boats had arrived from Europe that day and there were many people in need of places to stay. The two of us walked down to the docks and made our way into the line of New Yorkers waiting to take in homeless strangers, most of whom had undoubtedly only begun their journey. They had crossed the ocean. Then they would disperse throughout the continent to big cities and small towns from coast to coast. They would all have a journey ahead of them, not unlike my own.

One by one, boats had been docking and seafaring travelers disembarking since early morning, and they were still coming in. As we reached the front, we helped to tie up the next one and unload its passengers. That particular vessel had come from Rome. In addition to myself, Leah took in a small family who had been vacationing in Italy and had not realized the severity of the situation until it was too late. By then they had been stranded. Fortunately for them, their home was only about a day's hike from where we were, and they would just need shelter for the night. She also took in a quiet businessman named Pete.

Once we had brought them all back to Leah's flat, the family settled in for the night. Leah convinced Pete to join us at Eli's for more nocturnal mischief, which I wasn't looking forward to after the previous evening. I humored her anyway, and I'm glad I did. Over drinks, I asked Pete what the collapse had been like in Rome.

"Pretty much the way it was here, I assume," he said. "At first, it was crazy. Protests turned violent, services went out, and a lot of people cleared out of the city. I lived on a vineyard in Tuscany for a while, which was all right. If you've got to run, there are worse places to run to. Got me out of the chaos of the city. But I had to come home. My family had to bear it all without me, and every day since has been torture. I headed back toward Rome to look for a way home, but I found the boat a little way up the coast, so I didn't quite make it back to the city. Not sure what became of it. Now I've got a long walk ahead of me."

"Where's home?" Leah asked.

"Chicago."

"That's where I'm headed tomorrow," I said. "You can join me. It'll be nice to have someone to talk to."

"You're from Chicago?"

"No, St. Louis. But we moved out of the city when this all happened, to a farm in the middle of nowhere."

"Flyover territory." Leah laughed.

"Flyover territory?" Eli repeated. "Leah, you're from rural Ontario."

"It's true. I confess."

"Don't need a passport to get home now," I said. "I thought you went to Annapolis, though."

"I did. My parents were US citizens, so I was both American and Canadian."

"If you're from St. Louis, what are you doing up here?" Pete asked me.

"I volunteered to help establish long-range communication. The New World Mail Network, we call it. I've already been to the Gulf and all the way up the east coast, and now I'm headed west."

"Do you not have family back home?"

"I do."

"And you left them?" he asked, incredulous. "I've been searching for a way home for months. Every day has been a struggle to move on, doing everything in my power to get back home, and you left yours? I can't imagine the kind of will that took. Admirable."

"I had other responsibilities," I said. Only I knew the truth.

"Hey, Leah," Eli broke in, slamming his drink on the table, "let's hear the Canadian national anthem."

She stood and began to sing proudly, "O Canada! Our home and…"

"No, no, no, in French!"

"You drunken idiot," she said, shaking her head and beginning again, "O Canada! Terre de nos aïeux…"

As Leah sang, I pondered what Pete had said. What I was doing didn't feel admirable. It felt selfish. I had left home to fulfill egocentric desires under the guise of a greater purpose, and there I was, drinking with strangers a thousand miles away from my wife, one of whom I had nearly had an affair with the night before. The more I thought about it, the more I wanted to go home, and I began to realize how much I missed Maria. I had treated her so coldly, and why? Why had I let myself become that person? Was I really so weak? The guilt made me sick, and I began thinking that I might end my journey in Chicago. I might head south and leave the rest of the job to someone else. Perhaps I just needed to go home, pick a trade, and wait for the world to evolve like every other normal person. There was nothing exceptional about me. How arrogant I was to have thought that way. It was time to end the game I was playing and get my priorities straight.

The next day, Pete and I parted ways with Leah. She was leaving town, heading south to what had been DC to reconnect with Jake. They needed each other, I thought, and I was glad to know they would soon be together again. Pete and I started back to the registrar. Before we left, we had to arrange for them to send and receive mail using the new network. I mapped out all the places I had already been and where to find their provincial centers. The City That Never Sleeps had had a number of people like me come through with messages from various places, but none on a specific mission to establish a postal matrix. I left them with a letter to deliver back home to Maria in hopes that their messenger would go straight there, connecting more people and places along the way. Another messenger was sent north to connect the cities that had been Boston and Portland and places beyond. Leah would inform those to the south of the registrar up the coast. One man could begin the job, but I couldn't do it all alone. Better men and women would soon take over.

As we departed—Pete, Nomad, and I—with us came my precious cargo: the two letters I had been asked to deliver out west.

9

THE GREEN MILL

We picked up a horse for Pete while passing through Amish country in the former state of Pennsylvania. It was a slow walk for the first few days, but the company of another person was a fair trade for speed. Nomad was growing restless though, so the generous gift was a good thing for all of us. Aside from their clothing, the Amish people and their neighborhoods looked pretty much like our home at the farm. They blended with the expansive coastal commune so well that I barely noticed any change when we passed from one to the next.

Pete and I got to know each other well as we passed through Appalachia. The mountains slowed us down, but the horses carried most of the burden. My abs and lower back grew sore from leaning forward as we climbed and backward as we descended.

"What happened to miracles?" I asked, watching the sunbeams shining through the clouds ahead of us and settling on the tops of the pines. "They used to happen all the time."

"I think they still happen," Pete replied, "but in today's world, there's usually some scientific explanation. If there isn't, they say you're crazy. They say it was a hallucination. Some things they used to call miracles are so commonplace now that we don't think twice about them. People are intrigued by mystery in fiction, but in real life, they're afraid of it."

Aside from some time outside of what was once Cleveland, the trip to the Chicago area was largely devoid of human contact. Pete talked a lot about his family. He had a wife and three children, twin girls and a boy, waiting for him back at home. His work had taken him to Rome, and, like the family he had shared a boat with, he had expected things to improve, so he had tried to wait it out. Work had been important until it was gone.

"Back then," he said, "success was just a matter of kissing the proper asses." How right he was. "Look where that got us." When it all came down, he felt as though he had abandoned his family, and he wondered if they would ever forgive him. That was a feeling Pete and I shared. It was a strange coincidence that he and I were paired for those few weeks, because our lives were so similar in so many ways. The nice house in the suburbs, the loving wife, the sense of responsibility and the need for success that had come to feel so trivial by comparison. Sometimes listening to him talk was like listening to my own conscience. Hearing it from the outside gave me a bit of a different perspective on my own life.

"Family is the most important thing," he would say. "I know it sounds like a cliché, but it's true. My business is gone, and I don't even care. All I want is to be with my wife and children. I'd do anything for them. Have you ever heard of the Tabonuco tree, Joe?"

"I haven't."

"They're interesting trees," he continued. "They grow in Puerto Rico and other Caribbean islands. Their roots weave together underground so that, as a forest, their structure can withstand hurricanes, but individually, they would be doomed. Nature teaches lessons in such gracefully subtle ways."

I was excited to see what Chicago had become. Not only would I be closer to home than I had been in months, but Chicago had always been one of my favorite cities to visit. You had the big-city atmosphere with the pace and hospitality of the Midwest. Not that my hometown was a small one by any means; St. Louis had a plethora of history, architectural charm, and culture of its own—like most cities, I expect. Chicago was just bigger and sprawled along the shore of the endlessly beautiful Lake Michigan. It seemed to rain every time I would visit, and I loved the fog that would drift in off the lake, leaving skyscrapers poking through the gray ceiling block after block.

That time was no different. It was raining and foggy when we came across the outskirts of the newly expanded metropolitan area. The place was designated by a sign that I knew well. For decades, it had hung above the door to the old Al Capone hangout in Uptown. "Green Mill Cocktail Lounge," it read. Someone had removed it from the old building and propped it up out there in the middle of the highway to welcome newcomers into the city. Paul and I had enjoyed some memorable jazz performances at the Green Mill over the years. We shared an appreciation for the art that not everyone understood, and I realized how long it had been since I had heard a musical instrument of any kind. I hadn't picked up a guitar since we were back home in St. Louis. It hadn't even occurred to me to bring one with us to the farm, even if we'd had the space. Instead, I was graced only with the sound of nature's music, which played ceaselessly all around us wherever we traveled. The birds in the day. Coyotes and owls at night. Wind in the wheat and corn, water in the streams and rivers we passed over.

Just outside the old suburbs, we came across an expansive soybean field, bright green from the fresh rain, even under the gray sky. Behind it was another village of cabins not unlike the one I had left at home. Pete was anxious, I sensed, the prospect of home being so near to him then. He seemed to be filled with both joy and apprehension. We hastened our pace to reach the village, where we found a small group of farmers just cleaning up after the day's work.

"How goes it, fellas?" one asked as we rode up.

"Very well," I said.

"You guys lost?"

"Just returning home, actually," said Pete. "Well, almost, anyway."

"Where ya from?"

"Evanston. I've been gone awhile, and I figure my family moved out of town with everyone else. Is there a registrar of some kind around here to help me find them?"

"Sure thing," the farmer said. "Up in the city. We go up there most weeks. Goin' tomorrow, if you fellas want to stay the night."

I did stay, but Pete couldn't stand to waste any more time than necessary. Once they had given directions, he departed with such haste that it was as if the past weeks spent in only my company had been completely lost on him. But I couldn't blame him. He was off to be reunited with his beloved wife and children, and damned if he wouldn't spend that very night holding all four of them more tightly than he ever had before. Had I been so close to home, I don't think anything could have slowed me down either. Besides, I figured we would meet again someday anyway.

The farmer who took me in was named Matthew. He insisted on being called Matthew. I made the mistake of calling him Matt once and was briskly corrected. He and his wife had taken in so many drifters of late that they had a place in their home always made up for the next visitor. They fed me and insisted that I rest early to prepare for the morning's trek into the city.

I was awakened by the sound of a rooster for the first time ever. It was a more welcome sound than that of a buzzing alarm clock, but he could have had the decency to put some distance between himself and my window. I had become accustomed to being awakened by the sunrise.

They prayed before breakfast, Matthew and his family. I don't know why I noticed it. I had seen a lot of people praying over the last year and a half or so, more than I ever had before the world had changed. I closed my eyes, clasped my fingers, and kept silent. After we had eaten, Matthew's children set to cleaning dishes, and Matthew and I began our journey toward the city. It only took the morning to get there on horseback. The fog had lifted, and I could see the old Chicago skyline ahead of us. The Sears Tower, once the tallest building in the world, still defined the west end of the skyline with unmistakable prominence. It was called the Willis Tower then, but to my generation, it will always be the Sears Tower. Who knows what they'll call it next.

Matthew and I rode into the city on horseback, weaving through streets bordered by hanging gardens and tower gardens and urban blocks of vertical aeroponic and hydroponic farms. I had never seen Chicago so green and lush. Even in the city, with limited space at their disposal, people had learned to produce their own nutrition on a massive sustainable scale. We made our way to an old warehouse on the south side where their registrar was housed. There were a few of those throughout the city, but that was the one Matthew used. I figured it was probably the best of any to use as their provincial postal center for the New World Mail Network, as it was the most convenient to the majority of visitors from the outside. It was directly off the highway for anyone coming from the east, west, or south.

Finding the organizer of the facility was a bit of a hassle, but once I had, I was greeted with news that brought me great joy.

"We've already sent a guy south on the same mission as yours, friend," he said. "And another east. You probably passed him on your way here."

"Brilliant! You hear that, Matthew? Where have they been?"

"Don't know yet. They only left a few weeks ago."

I could hardly contain my emotions. There were indeed more just like me as I had hoped, and it would not be long before the civilized world was reconnected, if not united as one. I felt a sense of glorious pride for having been a part of such a thing. It was the paramount achievement of my life, I thought. Of course, I also felt that my own burden had been lifted. Finally, I thought without hesitation, after the long journey and the months away from my wife and family, I could return home and allow the New World Mail Network to evolve without me. My work had been done. I mapped out all of the places I had been, and the organizer offered to take any correspondence off my hands and have it delivered south, to my home, while I continued west. I had not written yet, but I assured him that I would return the next day with outgoing mail. That was not my plan, though. Instead, I planned to head straight home the following morning.

As Matthew and I rode back south to his farm, my smile could not be turned.

"What you're doing is pretty incredible," he said. "It shouldn't surprise me that it took so long for somebody to step up to the job, but I guess most people give up when they lose everything they've got. What's the point, they figure. Giving up is easier than starting over, but we've done it before, and someday we'll have to do it again. Nothing on this earth lasts forever. We're never ready for it, but the strongest few pull the rest of us out of the dirt and brush us off. Most people would be surprised to learn what they're truly capable of. In the early 1860s, the Pony Express made it possible to send mail from one coast to the other in about ten days with nothing but men on horses two-thirds of the way. Of course, their system was less complex than the one you intend to build. Our population is much larger and more widespread these days, but we learn from history, don't we."

"We do," I said, "but you give me far too much credit."

"Why's that?"

"I left home out of weakness, not strength."

"Whatever your reasons," he replied, "you're here. Poor judgment sometimes produces the greatest accomplishments, against all odds, just as the best of motives can end in catastrophe. I don't presume that all of the riders back in those days were the best of men, but they did what they had to do. The new network will probably evolve the same way theirs did, I'd figure, with swing stations and all."

"With this growing number of riders, our main obstacle will be organization," I said.

"That will come."

"They'll move far more quickly than Nomad and I can alone. Like the Pony Express, this is just a first step toward something larger, faster, and more efficient. Someday we'll have the railways again and electricity. Even cars in one form or another."

"It has to start somewhere," he said, and then he looked at me. "Someone has to make it happen. Like Ishmael said, 'For small erections may be finished by their first architects; grand ones, true ones, ever leave the copestone to posterity. God keep me from ever completing anything.'"

I felt he was trying to inspire me, but I tried to ignore it. I had made up my mind. It was time to go home.

When we rode back into the small farming village toward his home, the farmers who had been with Matthew on the previous day when Pete and I had arrived were digging trenches into a field.

"Finally!" he called as we approached. "It's about time you goons did something productive!"

"Well you two took your sweet time!" one of them yelled back. "We got bored. It's getting hot out here. Have you come to relieve us?"

"Relieve yourself," Matthew said.

"I plan to, once we're finished here."

"What are they planting?" I asked.

"They're not planting. They're laying a leach field."

"Like a septic field?"

"Yes. You ever notice how green the grass is above the leach field?"

"Never thought about it," I replied.

"Well, once we're done here and we've got running water again, our crops will thrive. In the meantime, we're using composting toilets, which are working just fine for now."

One of the farmers paused his digging suddenly and turned to me with a look of surprise.

"That one nearly escaped under the guise of a fart," he said, "but at the last moment, its identity was revealed and its plot for exodus foiled."

"Soiled?" Matthew exclaimed. "You soiled yourself?"

"Foiled, my friend. Foiled. But now I need to pinch one, if you'll excuse me."

Matthew closed his eyes and shook his head in embarrassment as the man threw down his shovel and waddled toward one of the two small sheds they used for outhouses.

"That's Lucas. I just call him Number Two," he said, "and that other idiot out there digging is Nathan. I call him Number One. Whatever happens, if he challenges you to a sword fight, decline. There's no shame in it."

The man who was still digging laughed. "Probably more shame in accepting," he said.

"They're plumbing experts," Matthew continued. "Something that happens to benefit me in my trade, so I keep them around. They needed food and a place to sleep. I needed extra hands and a leach field, for both the latrine and the crops."

I heard Lucas yell through the walls of the outhouse, "That's funny."

"What's that?" Nathan yelled back.

"I don't remember eating a football."

"Damn it!" Matthew scolded. "What did I say about that kind of talk? Have some class!" Then he turned to me to apologize for his comrade, "I'm sorry. He's very crude."

After a while, Lucas emerged from the outhouse and came to introduce himself formally. I declined to shake his hand. His hygiene was suspect. Despite their demeanor, though, Nathan and Lucas were clearly skilled in their craft. Everyone excels at something, I figure, and each person and each trade is a necessary piece of the puzzle. That's the beauty of humanity. It's just a matter of determining one's calling. That's the tough part. Sometimes it takes a disaster to find that out.

Matthew made sure that his guests washed properly before handling food, even in the fields. Cleanliness was a rule of the house, one that I was pleased to abide by. Cleanliness is next to godliness; isn't that what they say? When we sat down for dinner that night, there was a pitcher of ice water awaiting us at the table.

Ice water.

Water with ice in it.

I had never thought I would miss such a thing after the previous winter, but then, having sustained the scorching summer without a single ice-cold glass of the most basic necessity for life on earth, I could hardly restrain my thirst long enough for them to finish their prayer. When I finally took a sip, the flavor gave me goose bumps all over. It was the freshest, most delicious drink I had ever tasted.

They had a deep underground cellar where ice was stored. They would pack the walls in the winter, and it would last until the next. In the center of the cellar, surrounded by walls of ice, they could keep produce or meat, if the need arose. That wasn't common, though. Enough people relied on the area farmland that there was seldom a surplus great enough to require long-term storage. There was never a shortage, though. Matthew was what I would call a giver. He and his farm were almost entirely self-sufficient, but like Abraham, he shared his blessings with those less fortunate in those times. People like them gave the rest of us hope. Besides, there was more than enough land to feed everyone. It's a mystery why people had ever gone hungry in the old world.

Waking the next morning, I questioned the ethics behind my decision to abandon the mission and call it complete. My morals seemed confused by the planned change in course, and I decided to stick around the farm a few days, conflicted as my conscience was.

The internal debate over my destination raged silently while I worked the fields with Matthew and his family. It was a decision that grew more important and less certain with every passing moment. I didn't speak much, which was fine. My time was better spent in contemplation, and there was plenty of solitude in the crop rows.

Before sunset on the third evening, I was sitting on the porch, dicing hot peppers to use as a wildlife repellant for some of the crops. I hadn't worn gloves, and the juice from the peppers was burning my hands and face with a fury that rinsing with water only intensified. It felt like fiery needles pricking my skin everywhere. Matthew came through the door and sat next to me, squeezing the juice from a tomato over my hands.

"See how that does," he said.

"Thank you."

"See, we take care of the crops, and they take care of us."

"What was it like for you before?" I asked.

"Harder," he said. "My expenses running this place were twice what I took home, and people who didn't know better criticized us for taking government subsidies when the corporate farms were putting us out of business. You wouldn't believe what they used to feed livestock at those places and their animal factories. There were plenty of resources to provide for everyone, but where was the incentive? Sometimes we were paid more *not* to produce. The industry wasn't valued, and there was a separation between the producers and the consumers so that the only winner was big business."

"And now?"

"Now we're rich." He laughed. "We don't have any money, and we're richer than we've ever been."

I sat back and took a deep breath as the burning sensation in my hands began to subside.

"Smell that rain?" he said. "It's coming tonight."

Sleeping hadn't been easy, but that night a fine storm came through and the sounds of distant thunder and raindrops on the aluminum roof soothed my soul enough to doze off. I was thankful to be indoors. Lightning flashed shadows on the walls of the bedroom in the old farmhouse. Storms can be miserable when you're sleeping outside, but so calming when you have a solid roof over your head.

The following morning, we stepped out of the house to start work, and Matthew paused on the porch, looking out as the sun rose over the fields. It was quiet, as if the fresh rain on the ground and the crops absorbed every sound the way the ground and the crops had absorbed the rain. The air was cool and still.

"So what do you think, Joe?" Matthew asked me.

"It's beautiful," I said.

"Is this not the greenest crop you've ever seen?"

"It may be."

"I love the way they look after a storm. So refreshed. Rejuvenated."

"They're healthy," I said.

"Yup. All we use is all natural animal waste. We eat from the land, the cows eat from the land, the horses eat from the land, and when we're through with it, we give it back to the land. Who ever decided it was a good idea to pump healthy foods full of chemicals and hormones and antibiotics? As if humans could improve upon nature in a lab. Outsmart God."

I enjoyed harvesting their tomatoes. I would tug a wooden cart through the rows with me and pluck them, one by one, slowly filling it until I could barely pull it through the dirt. Then I would take it to the house, empty it, and head back into the field. There were so many of them that the work never ended. They were enormous. Bright red. Sometimes when the area wildlife got a little greedy, Matthew would spray the crops with a solution of vinegar, water, and crushed hot peppers that the animals found less appealing, but mostly it wasn't a problem. He figured the land belonged to them as much as it belonged to us, so he didn't mind sacrificing a few fruits and vegetables. Besides, a healthy wildlife population was as important to keeping us fed as the crops were.

West. South. I was deeply conflicted. On that last day before I left home, when I told Maria that I would dream of her night and day, I'd had no idea how true it would be. She was always there. But every day I was gone, she seemed less and less real. When everything you know to be true about your life is suddenly taken away or abandoned, as the case may be, even your memories start to change. Everything was unfamiliar then. Even the places we had been to before were different. I had nothing left to associate with my memories of my wife. There was no telephone and certainly no e-mail. I couldn't even receive a letter from her. There I was on a farm with a family I had never met before, completely isolated from everything I ever knew, yet closer to home than I had been in months. It would be so easy, I thought. I could be there in a week. But, I wondered, would she still take me back?

I found myself standing alone in the field with beads of perspiration running down my face, staring into the distance at the blue cloudless sky, surrounded by what I thought was the most radiant green I had ever seen. My soaked shirt was draped over the cart and my pants were drenched in sweat. My skin was tan, and my hands were calloused. Muscles chiseled, waist thin. Thick beard and long hair turning blond from the sun. I didn't look the same as I had with her. She might not even recognize me, I thought. The sun was beating down, but I was so deep in contemplation that I didn't notice it. "In the zone," they used to call it. To what zone were they referring, I wondered—some place better than here and now or just dreaming with your eyes open? I don't know how long I was standing there before I heard Matthew's voice.

"You all right out here, Joe?"

"Yes."

"Been standing out here awhile. I saw you from the house."

"Sorry."

"Don't be sorry. Thinking about that pretty girl you got back home?"

"I can't get her out of my head."

"Yeah, I know what that's like. I spent a few years overseas right after I got married," he said, pulling up his sleeve to reveal a faded "Semper Fi" tattoo on his bicep. "It wasn't easy, but we got through it all right."

"How?"

"Love and hope, my friend."

"What if I forget those things?"

"You won't forget the love. I had the same thought back then, but if it's real, it doesn't go away. Hope is the tough part. You focus on that love, and it will always come back."

"I miss her. I think I have to go home."

"You could do that," he said. "Someone else will pick up where you left off."

"But when?"

"That's the question."

"I could go home and bring her back with me. Things haven't been the way I thought they would be. People, I mean."

"That's not what I'd worry about out west. I'd worry about the earth and the wilderness. And the winter. You don't want to put your wife through that."

"I should just go home."

"Regret is the heaviest burden you'll ever carry."

As hard as it was to accept, I knew he was right. I went through my gear that evening and found the two letters I had been asked to deliver out west from the Big Apple, destined for Los Angeles and Denver. More than half of the people I had set out to reach were still severed from the rest of us. Regardless of my original motives, I realized that it wasn't about me anymore. It was no longer about satisfaction of my own self-worth. I had to finish what I had started for the good of millions. Hundreds of millions. It was my calling, something I had never experienced before. I had never done anything selfless. Nothing that had required true sacrifice, anyway. If I provided a service, there was always compensation, financial or otherwise. Not anymore.

The letter I wrote to Maria that night was different from the others. It was sweeter. I wondered whether she would see me changing through my words. The ink on the page bled with stray tears. I was ahead of schedule, I told her, and I couldn't wait to see her. And I would see her soon. I loved her.

I gave that letter to Matthew the next morning for delivery, and I set out with Nomad after breakfast.

"Good luck out there," said Matthew as I saddled up. "And God bless."

10

ALONE IN THE NORTH

The sight of another person became scarce within a few days of leaving the Green Mill. Nomad and I passed by what used to be Milwaukee and Minneapolis–St. Paul and continued northwest on the old highway. We stopped briefly outside those places and other small settlements as we came across them, but they thinned out quickly. The highway was quiet and empty. There weren't many cars left around up there. Fewer drifters passed by until eventually there were none.

The weather was growing cooler, which was a relief from what had been a scorching summer. Whether it was actually hotter than any other summer, I don't know, but it sure felt like it. All day in the sun in the humidity of the ocean can make eighty-five degrees feel like a hundred, and a hundred unbearable. It was less brutal up north as autumn approached. For a while, we had a nice breeze from behind us that cooled the sweat on my back. We traveled farther on days like that. The more pleasant the weather was, the longer we could go before our exhaustion got the better of us. When it was scorching hot or pouring rain, our endurance suffered. Sometimes I would get down and walk, and I almost had to drag Nomad to keep him going. Sometimes he pushed me. Slow days were excruciating, especially up north. All I could think about was how far we were from our next destination on the west coast, and every step was taking me farther from home.

The land was flat and green for a while, and then flat and brown. Giant hay bales lined the sides of the road and lay dispersed throughout fields. Nomad ate from them. I hunted small game and ate from trees, weeds, and farm fields. There were many farm fields in the east, but they became scarcer as we moved west. I fished when we came to water. Sometimes I starved, not because there was no food, at least at first, but because I was so anxious to move on that feeding myself just wasn't a priority. I learned to block the hunger out. My stomach had shrunken on the journey so much that I could feel the void in my bowels. I missed Maria's cooking. My own on the road didn't make me want to eat until I had to, but I needed the energy to move on. Most of the time, I didn't even bother with a fire anymore. I caught fish and ate them raw after scraping off the scales and gutting them with my knife, which was beginning to dull with daily use.

Shadows of clouds flowed like water over the fields and subtle hills. Every time one passed over, the landscape seemed to change. Bright green and glistening yellow fields lost their shine and turned to gray, but when the clouds passed, the shine would return. Sometimes their shadows brought me relief from the sun. Sometimes they brought deep sorrow.

Eagles glided overhead. Small herds of bison, cattle, elk, or moose wandered the prairie and grazed, and they usually didn't have any objection to our passing through. Heads would rise to watch, following us along the endless highway line that split the plain in two. Nomad feared nothing. He was at home in the wilderness among the beasts. When we had passed, heads would lower again as if we had never been there. Life in the wild went on.

At night, I slept out under the stars most of the time. I had quit pitching the tent weeks before unless the weather warranted it. Nomad, it seemed, could sense my homesickness, and he would move closer to where I lay as if to comfort me. I never knew a horse to express such affection and compassion, let alone one who had been wild less than a year before. I would sit up and pet his muzzle, feeling his hot, moist breath on my face, trying my best not to drag him into my sorrow.

"I'm fine, my friend," I would assure him. "We'll be headed home soon." It was like lying to a child, but of course, he couldn't understand. All he knew to do was love me, and he trusted me to take care of him. Sometimes, even the faith of an animal can be inspiring. It was comforting to have at least some connection to a creature, even if not a person. He was all I had for nearly two months in the north, and the solitude brought us closer.

I thought of a cruise we had taken once, Maria and I. I remembered standing at the bow of the ship at night, looking out at nothing but water as far as I could see, and that sickening feeling of isolation the first time being surrounded by the endless black ocean.

Like floating in space.

Nothing above.

Nothing below.

As vast and wildly open as this land was, I felt as separated from the rest of the world as Robinson Crusoe alone on his island. Despite the difference in geography, it was the state of my consciousness that mirrored that of the proverbial man marooned. During the day, I had little more to do than to ponder the world and everything that had happened. I tried to maintain a constant state of meditation, tuning out the monotonous clapping of hooves on the pavement. Anything to keep my mind occupied. A vacant mind is dangerous to its owner and everyone around him. It's counterproductive. It leads to complacency, ignorance, anger, and violence. None of those had any place in my life on the road and would only make the journey more trying. I did math in my head just for something to do. I struck up conversations with my horse.

"Nomad," I said, "if a guy on a horse leaves Chicago traveling toward Seattle at twenty miles per hour at the same time another guy on a horse leaves Seattle traveling toward Chicago at thirty miles per hour, how long before they meet?"

Wishful thinking.

"The distance? What do you mean 'rest time'? Other variables? Ceteris paribus. No, I'm sure you're the fastest horse on this road. I'm sorry. I didn't mean to insult you. No, I don't think talking to a horse makes me crazy."

Not yet, anyway.

After a while, strange dreams began to come. I dreamed about people I barely knew. People I had only seen at work. People I hadn't seen in years. People I had never met. It made me wonder how we're all connected.

I dreamed of nights with Maria when we first moved to the farm. Though we had lost everything else, we made love with a passion that transcended the friction of our bodies, her breath in my ear and the look of ecstasy on her beautiful face glowing in the firelight. It was a passion that touched my soul, inspiring the same from me, the depth of our love truly manifested in the act of the same name.

I dreamed that she had left me.

I dreamed I was in a small boat at night in the middle of the ocean—a wooden boat, with a roof and a small cabin, but no sails or oars. A giant marlin had a hold of it and was tugging it violently, thrashing in the water, nearly capsizing my vessel. I dove in to fight the fish, blinding black water all around me, but I woke before the fight was over.

That last dream was recurring, and it always happened the same way. I would wake up in cold sweats, terribly afraid in the tall grass and surrounded by nothing more than the wide open plain. The loneliness was haunting. It was so quiet. Fear is what happens to guilt and regret when you know that nobody but God is watching.

The days were better than the nights, though. Even as we moved west and the hills began to grow, the landscape was expansive and plain but so beautiful. It was bittersweet. Sometimes I wished it were uglier. To experience such profound natural beauty and have nobody with whom to share it is a feeling of equally profound loneliness. Most of the land looked as if no person had ever touched it. The only way I knew others had been there was by the road on which we walked.

There were a few small camps along the way—very small—just enough to remind me that I wasn't the last person left on earth. Often, it's hard to remember that existence is not as limited as our vision. Those times, it was exciting to see the upright spots moving toward us on the horizon, but the sight always ended in disappointment. Most of the towns up there had been abandoned, and the few people I did meet were already on their way elsewhere, looking for new places to call home. As the weather grew cooler, some were migrating south from what had been Canada. They had no more shelter or food to offer than I had. Nomad and I passed through briskly, and I hoped that those people would settle before the winter. As suddenly as we had found them, we were alone again in our eerie solitude.

Days turned to nights and nights to days, but little changed that I could see. The aurora borealis snaked across the star-spread sky, smearing the night in green, purple, and red. It was astonishingly beautiful. Most nights, I fell asleep watching it, a cosmological wonder teasing us to inquire farther outside of our own little marble in this vast universe. A sign, I thought, to remind us that we were not alone. Such a sign has driven many a man to madness, but it was one of the few things that kept me sane. What was out there beyond our world? Where did we come from, and how had we arrived at this strange point in the comparatively short history of humanity? Where would we go from here? I felt gifted, blessed, even, to experience such a marvel that only a fraction of earth's population would ever see.

The northern lights reminded me of Matthew's family and the way they prayed. I began to do the same. Strange things happen to a man when he feels he has nothing left, and the farther I got from home, the more the feeling crept in, growing like a parasite feeding on my body and soul. Throughout the days, I began praying to a God whose existence I often questioned. Though on occasion I had pondered His presence, I wasn't what I would call a man of faith. I hadn't thought to talk to God before or to ask for help when I felt alone or without hope. Self-sufficiency had become such a staple of modern culture before the collapse that it had bordered on an epidemic of narcissism, and the irony was that we had never actually been self-sufficient at all. The more we "advanced," the more dependent we had become on the things that I had come to learn were so fragile. So easily broken.

They appeared as an inescapable line of dark storm clouds, low to the ground, creeping up on us from the west until eventually the snow-capped peaks came into view. The mountains have a way of tricking you like that. I was relieved when I saw them. In that same moment, I heard the faint patter of hooves on the ground behind us and turned to find a herd of wild horses converging. There were dozens of them spreading like an organic sea of flowing manes behind us in a range of colors that shimmered in the morning sun. A low cloud of dirt and dust puffed beneath them and left a trail in the air.

"Look, your brethren!" I called to my horse over the rumble of the herd as it blended around us.

Nomad broke into a gallop, and for miles we ran among them, through the wild grass of the plain and toward the great Rocky Mountains. I was one with the herd, as if I belonged in that state of divine freedom with the cool wind gusting through my long hair like a mane of my own. For a short time, I forgot where I had come from and where I was going—even who I was. I didn't feel alone. I felt the shine of a greater being upon me, drawing me forth as a part of that great wild place. I felt as I imagine the mustangs felt. Nomad galloped with an unmistakably untamed spirit. A herd such as that had been his family before we had taken him as ours, but I had become his family. I wondered: if I were to set him free, which path would he choose?

When the herd broke away, we moved from the highway to the railroad. I hoped that that route would be flatter in the mountains. It was, but I had to keep faith in Nomad's footing. The terrain became rough as the plain moved behind us. We crossed narrow bridges, some of them so high that there was no question as to my fate if I were to fall. The tracks wound through valleys alongside beautiful alpine streams and cut long mountain tunnels so dark that, without a torch, we were blind. Aspens towered over us, the golden sunbeams breaking through them like a photo on a postcard. Their leaves glowed in the most glorious greens, yellows, and reds, accentuated by bony black-striped ashen trunks. As the sun passed over throughout the day, shadows seemed to crawl between them, peeking through to steal a glance at the strangers passing beneath.

The quiet beauty of the mountains in mid-September was indescribable, and it drew me back into that nearly incapacitating desperation and loneliness of before. My wife was more and more just a memory, evaporating from reality as the days passed. At night, I could hardly sleep, and it slowed us down. I was exhausted and starving. Even Nomad seemed sluggish, as if his energy were somehow dependent on my own.

Time dragged on—days and nights. I wanted Maria desperately. I worried about her, how she would go on without me, but I also wondered about the sense in those fears. I had thought of myself as her caregiver, but I realized that perhaps the truth was in fact counter to what I had known. I looked at myself, lost without her and losing hope. I relied on her as much as she did me. Perhaps more.

"You're the peanut butter to my jelly," I had told her. "The grapes to my wine."

"That doesn't make sense, baby."

"What?"

"I can't be the grapes to your wine. Maybe I'm the cheese to your grapes."

"You mean wine? Cheese to my wine?"

"Cheese and grapes are good too."

"Whatever, I love you."

"I love you."

Nomad wasn't much of a conversationalist. Try as I might, the greatest response I could get out of him was a peek over his shoulder at me, as if to question why I even bothered. Sometimes he would let out a snort or give me a poke in the shoulder with his muzzle or scrape a hoof in the dirt. I would walk alongside of him under the aspens, feeding him grains that I had collected along the way and talking to him. He always listened. We had become best friends in the time we had been together.

I began using my tent again in the mountains. The forest was black as death at night, and I felt too vulnerable without it, but I still couldn't sleep. Insomnia or terror, I don't know which kept me awake, but it seemed the only thing that soothed me was the monotonous rocking on the back of my horse during the day. Sometimes I would wake up on the side of the tracks with a curious muzzle in my face and a pain from the impact of the fall.

It was time to put an end to that, I decided briskly when I opened my eyes to find myself dangling with my arms tangled in the reins and my legs swinging freely a hundred feet over a rocky white-water river. Confusion quickly turned to terror when I realized where I was, suspended in the wind whipping between cliff faces on either side, the infinite sky above and death just a short fall below. Nomad stood still, looking down at me judgmentally.

"See, this is what happens," he seemed to say. "Pay attention. Get some sleep. Focus, or we'll never make it out of here alive."

"Shut up and pull me up!" I yelled.

I struggled for a better grip and reached for the saddle, but I grabbed the shotgun instead. It broke from its sleeve, exposing the two letters that I had tucked into the saddle next to it. How could I have been so careless about securing them? There I was, dangling over a gorge of certain death with one hand tangled in the reins attached to my horse, the other gripping my primary means of protection, and right in front of me, shuddering in the wind, the two envelopes that had driven me to keep moving.

They could not be lost.

It could not all be in vain.

I let the shotgun slip through my fingers into the abyss and watched as it shrunk to a speck below me. Then I closed my eyes. I counted.

One.

Two.

Three.

A gunshot echoed from the stone cliffs on either side of me, startling my horse. Nomad shifted his stance, and the envelopes came loose.

"Don't move!" I yelled.

Nomad froze. Still dangling in the air, I reached as far as I could, but my fingertips barely touched the paper sticking out of the saddle, an inch shy of salvation. Just then, I felt a gust of wind and watched the letters break free. My arm swung toward them wildly in a desperate final attempt to save the two pieces of paper I had brought clear across the continent. I closed my palm and my eyes tightly.

Deep breath.

Eyes opened.

Victory.

I stuffed the envelopes into my pocket and breathed a sigh of relief.

"Now, back," I said.

Nomad lifted his head and backed slowly away from the edge, dragging me onto the bridge. I lay there, face down on the tracks with my heart pounding and gasping for air, my body quivering with adrenaline. Nomad snorted, and I felt the spray from his nostrils on the back of my neck.

"You bastard."

I think he was laughing at me.

I fell asleep then—or passed out from exhaustion—with my face pressed against that railroad tie.

Hours later, I woke up in the darkness to the sound of the river rushing below the bridge, and Nomad was no longer next to me. I sat up and saw him at the end of the bridge, standing just beyond it, waiting. After crawling out to him, I lay down in the dirt and fell asleep again by his side.

I didn't have much trouble sleeping after that. There were still nightmares, but they didn't keep me awake. I wonder now if I may have been reaching the point of collapse. Failure. Giving up. Just lying down under the aspens, closing my eyes, and falling asleep. Forever.

About the time I figured we were crossing the Great Divide, I began to feel very ill. Food had become scarce in the mountains, and I suspect my condition was a result of the combination of starvation, exposure to the elements, and an impending emotional breakdown. The void inside me continued to grow, but it somehow seemed to extend beyond the longing for my wife and the life I had left. It was as if there was something even greater that I was missing, masked by the presence of people when they were around, but haunting my thoughts when I was alone. I wondered what was in those letters I was risking my life for. What could have been worth that? Was I crazy to have continued on when I was so close to home? If not yet, would I become crazy?

As if the torment of my conscience wasn't enough, that of the environment was equally relentless. I was certain that we were nearing the base of the mountain and the journey would soon become easier. There wasn't enough strength and stamina left in me to take much more of it. My innards were constantly subject to what I can only describe as a torturous wrenching and twisting, as if some wicked creature were devouring me from the inside out. My mind seemed to be suffering the same. When I had left the Green Mill I had been strong and healthy, but my body had reached such a grave state of malnutrition that it was feeding on itself. The little bit of fish I'd finally caught for dinner had overwhelmed my stomach, and I left the remains of my meal on the ground just outside my tent before turning in. It was a mistake. I know it now and I knew it then, but my head was not clear.

In the darkness of my dreams, I heard breath. It approached slowly and softly, growing louder and more primal as I felt my heart begin to pound in my chest. Was it speaking? What did it say? I could not understand. I was lucid, but was I conscious? Was I roaming the depths of the world of fears created by my own mind, or was I, in fact, awake? The black of night was the same behind my eyelids, and when I blinked and felt their wet, I realized they had been open.

Then came the night's breath again—the unmistakable sound of a hungry bear in my camp. In my tent, I lay silent, trying to keep as still as possible, terrified that the beast would smell me. If he were as hungry as I, he would have no reservations about taking my life to save his own, and certainly he had more will to live. I wanted to call to Nomad, but I knew that would only make matters worse for both of us. The only way to stay alive was to stay silent. If he was still alive, that is. I couldn't hear him moving, and he would not have waited around to ask the intentions of the bear.

I heard the sloppy chomping of his jaw as he ingested the meal I had inadvertently prepared for him. My carelessness was unprecedented. Had I been thinking straight, I never would have done some of the things I had. My thought process and reasoning were regressing as my body deteriorated, and it was only a matter of time before one of those mistakes got me killed. Perhaps this was it, I thought.

I imagined my wife growing old without me—the loneliness and sense of abandonment that would burden her the rest of her life.

I imagined the violent pain of those grizzly claws and teeth as they punctured my skin and began to devour me. Would it be a quick death?

Slowly, I felt around for my satchel. I slid my trembling hand inside where I kept my knife when I slept and removed it, unsheathed the blade, and held it tightly, preparing for whatever would come next.

It felt like hours that I waited in motionless silence, listening as the bear huffed around outside the tent. His nose poked the canvas in search of more food. That meager fish had been simply an appetizer, and he craved the next course. I fought to keep my fatigued body awake and my eyes open, just waiting for the moment that nose would find its way inside with me. Then what? I was too weak, too slow to react.

My eyelids fell.
I listened.
The words of John Donne were recited softly by the night's breath.

> *Death, be not proud, though some have called thee*
> *Mighty and dreadful, for thou art not so;*
> *For those whom thou think'st thou dost overthrow*
> *Die not, poor Death, nor yet canst thou kill me.*
> *From rest and sleep, which but thy pictures be,*
> *Much pleasure; then from thee much more must flow,*
> *And soonest our best men with thee do go,*
> *Rest of their bones, and soul's delivery.*
> *Thou art slave to fate, chance, kings, and desperate men,*
> *And dost with poison, war, and sickness dwell,*
> *And poppy or charms can make us sleep as well*
> *And better than thy stroke; why swell'st thou then?*
> *One short sleep past, we wake eternally*
> *And death shall be no more; Death, thou shalt die.*

I awoke again to the sunrise with the knife still in my hand. When I crawled from the tent, the site looked untouched aside from the missing leftovers, and I sighed with great relief.

But Nomad was gone. I called to him repeatedly and searched the area, but there was no sign of him. I took no sign as a good sign. It meant he was alive.

I packed up and continued down the tracks on foot through the lush, green Pacific Northwest foliage. Under an ever-changing canopy of massive sequoias and firs, I tramped through the layers of ferns and moss that coated the ground. It rained so frequently that the water droplets on the leaves and pine needles never had a chance to dry. Nomad knew where we were headed, I figured, even if I didn't exactly know. As much as I feared for the safety of my friend, I knew that my own life was in greater danger. I was growing sicker by the day, and without him, I was slower with a heavier load on my own legs.

It was a few days going, fading in and out of consciousness, before I cleared the trees at the base of the mountainside. I collapsed in the light of the sun and rolled down the slope like a limp rag in the wind, bouncing from tree trunks and sliding in the mud. By the time gravity stopped me, I was barely able to open my eyes. It was all I could do to lift myself and crawl on my hands and knees, falling to the ground again every few feet just to give my lungs a chance to breathe.

There, as I cleared the trees, was the sight that I had been waiting for so long, but I was too sick and exhausted to even feel relief. Just a short distance away was a small village of cabins, smoke rising from their chimneys in the cool autumn air.

It took everything I had left to climb to my feet one final time. I wavered from side to side, light-headed, dizzy, and nauseous, stumbling toward salvation, running on just the fumes of hope that still remained. My body was limp, my skin cold and clammy and too pale for a man who spent every day in the sun. My fingers were trembling from malnutrition.

As I came near the village, I suddenly feared that perhaps I was not the only one starving in the northwestern autumn. What if the people there were in as hopeless a state as I had found myself in—so hungry, perhaps, that they might make a meal of one of their own?

I stopped to turn away, but when I saw the faces of people around a fire turning toward me, I collapsed again. Villagers surrounded as I lay there looking up to the heavens, looking back down upon me.

"Are you OK?" one woman asked.

"I smell sausage," I whispered.

"You must be starving! Skin is hanging off your bones."

"I'm a little hungry."

"Let's get you something to eat," she said.

"I can't eat."

"Look, we have food."

"I have to keep going."

"Where are you going?"

"Seattle."

"We'll take you, just stay and eat."

"Don't eat me."

"What?"

"I have a letter to my wife. I wrote it in the mountains. Will you at least send it to her?"

"Where is she?"

"East," I mumbled, my voice struggling to produce words.

"Winter is coming. We can hold it until spring."

I pulled the letter from my pocket and handed it to her.

"You didn't have a horse, did you?" she asked.

Then everything went black.

11

"THE DOCTOR OF THE FUTURE"

The bed in which I awoke was soft and comfortable. I was tucked cozily under a warm down blanket, and I could hear wind chimes outside one of two open windows in the timber-framed room. An enchanting aroma of some sort of incense floated in the air, blending with the smell of the fire burning in the stone fireplace. There were soft voices drifting in from outside, and I could hear doors opening and closing elsewhere in the building. Bright tapestries hung about everywhere I looked, and potted greenery brought the whole ambience to life. It was raining gently, one of those rains that still let the sun through. There were thin drapes on the windows, and the sunlight made the room glow a warm orange as it bounced from the wooden walls, though the bed was situated in such a way that the sun never shone directly upon me.

I was too weak to move more than half an arm's stretch, but next to the bed stood a small table just within my reach. There sat a glowing plate full of ripe, fresh produce, and beside that, a glass of crystal clear water.

In walked a young woman in a colorful gown that matched the tapestries on the wall. She was petite with bright, happy eyes and a smile so gentle that just looking at her made me feel safe.

"Let me help you with that," she said, slicing an apple for me as I took a handful of blueberries from the plate. "Now that you're awake, I'll have some salmon and eggs brought in. Let's make you strong again."

"Where am I?" I asked, barely able to utter the words.

"A good place," she said. "I'm Mary."

"My wife was Maria."

"Yeah?"

"Is. My wife is Maria."

"Well, we're in good company. I'll be back in a bit. Drink some water."

She returned shortly as promised, taking a seat beside the bed. I did not yet have the strength to sit up, and she stayed and fed me, helping to lift my head. She spoke softly in a voice so welcome to my ears. I was joyful to finally be in the comforting presence of another person, even if I lacked the energy to express it at that moment.

"Some people carried you in here a couple of days ago," she said.

"Is this a hospital?"

"No, you don't need a hospital."

"I'm not dying?"

"Well, you need health care, that's for sure. Now eat up."

"I had a horse," I said.

"Oh, yes, we were wondering about him. He followed the ones who brought you here. Don't worry, we've got him tied up outside. Apparently, he had come to them and waited for days before you arrived."

"Thank God," I sighed as she lifted another bite of fresh fish to my mouth.

I rested there for several days before I was healthy enough to get out of bed and move around. It was a wonderful place, and Mary was attentive to my needs. The first thing I did when I was strong enough to walk was to visit Nomad, who was elated and whinnied at the mere sight of me. At first, though, that was the extent of my travels from the room. My body was painfully tight and frail, and my joints and bones ached. As the condition of my muscles had deteriorated, my skeleton had fallen under great strain. Slowly but surely, as we had traveled through the north, I had been creeping toward death with every step. Had the villagers not saved me, I was told, I would likely not have lived through the day.

In addition to nourishment, Mary provided me with physical therapy to get all of my bodily systems functional again. The nature of her work kept her close in my company, and ultimately, our resulting relationship was as much to the benefit of my mental and emotional health as the personal care was to my physical state. Though I still had nightmares on occasion, they became less frequent. Mary and I spoke often and became good friends. I told her all about my journey, of course, and about my wife and family back home. She had a family of her own there, with far more children than I would ever care to have myself, but it was clear that they were the great joy of her life.

The place was located within the urban limits of the city that used to be called Seattle. They called it a center for healing. It was separate from the hospital, which was only a short distance away. Mary's husband, Marcus, who happened to be a surgical oncologist at the hospital, would visit her from time to time at the healing center, and during my stay, I got to know him well.

Eventually, my short walks became long ones, and I began to explore the city. I found myself gravitating toward this new generation of medical people who'd had no choice but to adapt quickly once their state-of-the-art technology and equipment had become the most expensive collection of paperweights in history.

"What did you do before, Joe?" Mary asked me.

"I was a financial advisor."

"So you sat at a desk all day."

"Yes."

"And let me guess," she said. "You'd come home after nine or ten hours of sitting, have a big meal, and loaf on the couch until bedtime?"

"That sounds about right." I laughed.

"I bet you didn't get enough sleep either. Exercise much?"

"Not usually."

"See, most people were just like you," she went on. "Is it any wonder why people were sick all the time or why we had an obesity epidemic?"

"Maria's always had more of a concern for our health than I have," I said. I remembered her ridiculing me for choking down a meal-sized piece of chocolate cake after two helpings of dinner on my birthday.

"What kind of regime are you running?" I had asked her.

"I just want to keep you healthy," my wife had replied. "I need you around for a while."

It seemed, increasingly, that it was I who needed her.

"That's what I mean," said Mary. "So instead of proactively fixing our lifestyles, we reactively treated with chemicals that often did more harm than good. Television commercials for medications spent more time listing the potential side effects than the benefits, such that an advertisement for an insomnia drug sounded more like a volunteer recruitment effort for chemical weapons testing.

"And as for the hospitals," she continued, "did it really make sense to cram patients into little rooms with strangers and surround them with stark walls and cold machinery, then feed them a diet devoid of real nutrition? That was the way it worked: load patients up with drugs and send them right back to the lifestyle that put them in the hospital in the first place."

On the wall of my room in the healing center hung a framed quotation from Thomas Edison: "The doctor of the future will give no medication, but will interest his patients in the care of the human frame, diet and in the cause and prevention of disease." I wondered if, when he said that, he had any inkling of the chain of events that would lead to this revolution in the medical industry over a century later.

The hospital and the medical doctor were no longer the first line of defense against illness and disease. Instead, they took a holistic approach that didn't prescribe medicine or demand invasive procedures as treatment for every ailment. Good health began with proper physical activity and nutrition. In the healing center, I had salmon and eggs regularly. Almonds, kale, broccoli, spinach, carrots, tomatoes, apples, and berries: all of those were regular parts of my diet. They cooked with ginger, Echinacea, and turmeric, and they often served various herbal teas and other natural remedies. I wondered how some of those provisions were even available in the Pacific Northwest.

Though the healing center usually saw a patient before the hospital, there were of course some conditions that required more intensive care. The first time Marcus invited me to tour his facility, I stepped into the hospital, and the electric lights filled me with such awe and elation that I froze in the doorway to marvel at them.

"Yes, we have electricity," said Marcus, patiently waiting for me to regain control of my senses. "It's very limited right now, and only a few facilities have access. Mainly the hospital and medical laboratories, water treatment—the necessities."

"How?" I stuttered.

"Fortunately, we were already a predominantly hydro-power city. When it all crashed down, people made a real mess of things, but the infrastructure was already there. The energy source in the Skagit River never changed. It only took people to get it working again. With some maintenance to repair all the damage to the grid that occurred during the chaos, eventually we'll be back to full capacity."

"It's beautiful," I said.

He laughed. "I've got a surgery in a little while, Joe. Do you want to wander around a bit, and we'll catch up later?"

"Uh huh," I muttered, taking a seat on a bench in the lobby. I sat there for a time, staring up at the glorious white lights in the ceiling. People walked past me in all directions, but they occupied only the periphery of my sight and my consciousness. I was entranced—hypnotized as if it were the first time I had ever seen an electric light. I was sweating with excitement as I imagine Edison had been when he had finally produced that first functional masterpiece after thousands of failed attempts. It was a while before I took to my feet again, wandering the hospital as Marcus had said and absorbing the beautiful radiance around every turn.

The institution was well staffed, but the patient population was relatively sparse. Many of them had been moved to the healing center for recovery. There were nurses and orderlies working on computers again. Of course the Internet was still not operational, but the hospital's internal network was functioning as it had before. Babies were being delivered. Broken bones were being mended. Tumors were being removed. The hospital was running at nearly the same capacity as it had before, but with less strain on the staff. Not only was the electricity on, but the indoor plumbing was also functional. I must have stood at the drinking fountain for ten minutes, irrigating myself as though I had been lost in the desert.

Down a hallway lined with soothing natural art, I came across a crew of people rolling carts of supplies into the building that had been unloaded from a large horse-drawn wagon outside. On some of the boxes, "San Francisco" was stamped in ink. I followed them back out the door and onto a brick path that forked, leading in one direction to the roundabout where their wagon was parked and in the other to a beautiful, colorful garden where I took a seat on an old wooden bench to watch the birds and butterflies. There was a pond with a small waterfall flowing into it and dozens of koi swimming just below the surface. The bright foliage permitted just a peek of the surrounding city.

The new urban ambience was different. It wasn't cold and stiff. Even where humans hadn't placed them, there were elements of nature all around. When we had fled the cities, we had left the earth to do its work, and it had wasted no time. Flora had grown everywhere. When the people moved back, they built upon it with urban farms and gardens. Cities and homes were gradually fusing with the earth beneath them. The fragrance of flowers was everywhere. Sustenance flourished in abundance.

After a while, a child about four years old came into the garden and sat at the edge of the pond, dipping his feet into the water. He laughed as the koi nibbled on his toes. A few minutes later, Marcus arrived and joined me on the bench.

"You've found my favorite spot," he said.

"How was surgery?" I asked.

"Very well, thank you. I think she'll be around for some time yet."

At the sound of Marcus's voice, the child turned around to look and then cried excitedly, "Dr. Mark!"

"Hey, Timmy, how's life treating you?"

"It's wonderful!"

"I'm glad to hear it." Marcus laughed. "Did you meet my friend, Joe?"

"No. Hi, Joe."

"Hi, Timmy."

"Timmy had a tumor monster," Marcus said, "but we got that all taken care of, didn't we, Timmy."

"Sure did, Dr. Mark," he replied, laughing and turning back to the fish.

"He's a good kid," Marcus said to me.

"He has cancer?"

"Well, not anymore, as far as we can tell. After we removed what we could, we sent him over to Mary, and she got to work on his diet. Loaded him up with antioxidants. We think it's all gone now. She's like an angel."

"But you still keep him here?"

"No, he's living back at home with his family. He just likes it here."

I smiled and looked back toward the child splashing innocently in the water.

"He's not the only case we've had like that," Marcus went on. "We've got a lot more healthy people out there than we used to. Of course, we've always known ways to prevent things like heart disease and diabetes, but we're learning that even conditions we used to call incurable are not quite so hopeless. MS, RA, even cancer can often be reversed with a few dietary and lifestyle changes. Speaking of which, how are you feeling, Joe? Mary taking good care of you over there?"

"Quite," I said.

"Well you sure look a lot better than you did when I first saw you."

Once I was healthy again, I had a job to get back to. Conveniently, the hospital was located adjacent to the postal center that had been restored to serve the place, and the logistics had already been ironed out. Their postmaster watched in silence as I mapped out all of the locations of the eastern half of the New World Mail Network for them.

"So you rode all this way on that horse out there?" he asked.

"I did."

He paused for a moment as if calculating in his head. Then he said, "You know, that's like five and a half thousand miles."

"Something like that, yes."

"OK," he said, shaking his head in disbelief.

They began to dispatch carriers immediately. My next course, though, was south. Regular shipping routes had already been established between the Pacific Northwest and the Bay Area, and I wanted to hitch a ride with one of the conveyance crews on their next trip out. The presence of people would keep me sane enough on the road, and soon I would be headed home.

That was what I told myself and what I needed to believe in order to press on. But "soon" is a relative term. In comparison to the trip I had already made, what remained of my journey was shorter. On horseback, however, it was far from over.

Sometimes ignorance truly is bliss. Eventually, I would be passing through the Rockies again, but my planning was more of an immediate nature. I was always thinking of either my next stop or my ultimate destination—home— but never anything in between. There was, however, a reason the villagers who had brought me into the city would not venture east in winter, and I would come to understand that reason with intimacy.

I met the crew who had been delivering supplies to the hospital. They were loading another shipment into their wagon to be sent back down south to the Bay Area, and they offered to have me join them. There was room in the wagon for me to ride, and I thought Nomad could use the break for a while. God knew I could.

My last night in that place was bittersweet. I was anxious to get back on the road and to get home to my wife, but I liked the way the world looked from where I was. It was comfortable. There was electricity, indoor plumbing, and all the nourishment I would ever need. I wasn't quite ready to leave those things behind again, but my yearning for home would always outweigh the convenience of such comforts.

Mary brought a full dinner into my room and sat to join me while I dined as though it were my last meal. "You won't be eating like this for a while," she said.

"I know," I replied. "I'll miss it, but we'll be fine."

She smiled. "I know what you're thinking about."

"Yeah?"

"Yeah. Don't ever give up, Joe. You'll be with her soon."

"She almost doesn't seem real anymore—nothing from my old life does. But I miss her deeply. More than I miss anything else. I feel empty."

"Sometimes faith is more important than memories."

12

LEAVING A WAKE

The nightmares returned. It happened almost immediately when we got on the road headed down the Pacific coast in a convoy of wagons and horses. The saving grace was that at least I had some company for that leg of the journey, so when I awoke from those midnight haunts I wasn't entirely alone.

I dreamed that I was mowing a field of chest-high wild grass around my old house in the suburbs, but there was nothing else in sight. The city was gone. The house was dilapidated and collapsing. Maria was sitting on the grayed front porch with a glass of iced lemonade, covered in filth but wearing a myriad of gaudy jewelry—layers of gold necklaces, pearls, rows of earrings, diamonds, and glimmering stones of every color. Her face showed no expression. She just sat there, sipping her lemonade, watching me mow the infinite field.

That was the latest recurring dream, among others that became increasingly dark as we traveled. Since we had begun moving again, I missed home immensely. Beyond the cliffs beside us, the deep blue Pacific Ocean spread endlessly into the distance. I've been told that the human eye cannot detect such minute measurements from a single point so near sea level, but I felt as though I could see the subtle curve of the earth when I looked to the west. It gave me hope that perhaps home was not as far away as it felt. The tide snaked in behind white shields, approaching in rhythm with relentless perseverance like rows of soldiers into battle. Waves crashed off of the ancient sea stacks, each chiseling its signature into the rock of history and sending a chilling spray into the air that disappeared into the fog.

I felt so frail, constantly awakened at night and haunted during the day, and I was sure my weakness was obvious to my companions. What must they have thought of me? *Who is this homesick coward we allowed to ride along with us? We, too, spend our lives on the road, a job fit only for a person of great mental and physical strength. What business did he have setting off on this journey so ill prepared in every way?*

If those had been their thoughts, I would not have blamed them. After all, it was the truth. But none of that ridicule ever reached my ears. Instead, they provided all that Nomad and I required to satisfy us until we reached the Bay. Transportation. Food. Rest. Company. I tried to focus on maintaining my physical health. If I allowed that to deteriorate again the way I had in the mountains,

THE WORLD AS WE KNOW IT

I would likely not live to tell the tale. I had been fortunate that time, the villagers having been present at just the right moment. It was a blessing that I would surely not be granted again.

The road was surprisingly populated most of the way; it was usually not busy, but we passed through many towns that dotted the coast with perpetuity from north to south. Some were old. Some were new. Between them, we followed roads through forests of towering redwoods hundreds of years old, some of them with trunks so wide that they had been bored through to complete the path. Even our wagon and convoy of men on horses fit through the tunnels cut in the trees. Thin clouds hung low in the woods and glowed with the color of the sky in the afternoon. The canopy was a beautiful green ceiling with spots of blue here and there and immense red pillars firmly holding it all together.

Ezra was one of the travelers with whom I shared that time. He had a love of his own back home, Jesse, of whom he spoke as I spoke of Maria. Our love was what kept us all going, I realized. It wasn't just me. We were all hopeless without it, lost and devoid of a destination and purpose. Even the hardest of men have a weakness, whether they show it or not. Love is both our weakness and our strength. It is what separates humans from beasts.

"Are you counting the days, Joe?" Ezra asked.

"I try not to, but yes," I said. "I know the days past, but I can only guess at what's ahead."

"Don't concentrate too hard on the future. It will drive you crazy. Not knowing."

"I try."

"One day at a time. That's the only way."

It took at least four weeks to reach the Bay, which gave me time to recover my strength. I had become restless and eager to move on. The first sight of the old San Francisco skyline radiating with the sunset was so exhilarating that I nearly leaped from the wagon and ran to it on my own feet. We approached as the sun went down, and something odd struck me. There were lights in the building windows, even in upper levels of high rises. The lights were white, and they burned with consistency not characteristic of fire. They were electric. And they were everywhere. In the place from where I had just come, only the essential buildings were graced with electric power, but at the Bay, it seemed the light was ubiquitous. I had not seen such a brightly lit urban scene since before the collapse.

"My God," I said. "The whole city has power!"

"Not quite, but we're getting there," said Ezra. "We still have to be conservative with it, but the electricity came back on a few months ago in some places. This is the brightest I've seen it. They've made progress since we've been gone."

We came to a barn outside the city where the crew dismounted and began to unload the cargo they had brought back on the wagon. "This is our stop," Ezra said. "Are you staying the night or heading into the city?"

"I think I'll keep moving," I said, thanking them all for their company and the ride.

"Godspeed on the road ahead, Joe," said Ezra. "And keep the faith."

I mounted my horse, and as we trotted back onto the road, I saw a man emerge from the barn and throw his arms around Ezra, who was equally joyful at the long-awaited reunion.

The city's white aura drew Nomad and me across the quiet Golden Gate Bridge, trafficked only by pedestrians, and onto the hilly urban roads that had been San Francisco. We roamed awhile, catching glimpses of the Bay between buildings and hiking the winding brick of Lombard Street. As the hour had grown late, though, the electric atmosphere had faded, and we were nearly alone on the streets. The stars twinkled in the cloudless sky above. Beautiful Victorian architecture towered on either side of us, splashed in pastel colors that I could still see in the moonlight.

We stopped to sleep in a park, wishing not to disturb anyone at home at that time of night. Waking my new neighbors would certainly not breed a desirable reputation, and I had become accustomed to sleeping under the stars. After all, the weather was beautiful there. The temperature had hardly dropped from the day, and the cool breeze blowing through the palm trees carried in the fresh perfume of the ocean.

No sooner than I had lain down on my bed of grass, a man approached on a midnight stroll through the park, and I rose again to greet him.

"Nice night," he said.

"Indeed it is."

"I practically used to live out here. Not a bad place to sleep, I say. I'm Joshua."

"Glad to meet you," I said before introducing myself. His eyes widened at the sound of my name, though I didn't take much notice of his expression at the time.

"Seems I'm not the only one who enjoys the quiet emptiness of the streets at night," he said. "I find this is the perfect time for a walk."

"Well, I don't really have a choice."

"You new around here, Joe? You look like you've been on the road awhile," he said as if he knew it for fact.

"I have."

"Well, perhaps you've spent enough time sleeping outdoors. I've got an extra bed at my place, if you'd prefer."

Of course, I couldn't turn down such an invitation. The innocence and faith with which people invited strangers into their homes were revolutionary to the overwhelmingly suspicious and cynical worldview we'd all harbored in the past. The prevailing assumption was that everyone was to be trusted—even filthy, long-haired, bearded drifters dressed in rags.

On our walk to his home, I learned that Joshua was a schoolteacher. I had pondered how a new system of education might evolve, but until then, I had not seen any sort of organized school in any place I had passed through. Building, farming, and access to fresh water were things we required for survival. The establishment of an educational system was different. It wasn't a necessary adaptation to our newfound circumstances as everything prior had been, nor was it a desperate attempt at recovery of a lifestyle we once knew. Rather, it was a confirmation that we had moved past the world as we had once known it, accepting that it would never again be the same, and the time had come to retire the old ways to the history books.

I joined Joshua at his school the next day. I had assumed, since power and water had been largely restored, that class would be held at one of the old school buildings, so I was intrigued when Joshua led me instead to the beach on the Pacific side of the city. Students of all ages began arriving almost immediately after our arrival, textbooks in hand and enthusiasm on their faces.

"This is where you hold class?" I asked.

"For now," Joshua replied. "I find hands-on application more effective than hours of mindless lecturing. Students retain very little of that unless it's accompanied by interactive demonstration. They don't remember much if they aren't interested."

He began with a brief overview of some renewable energy sources—solar, wind, geothermal, hydroelectric, tidal and wave, biomass and anaerobic digestion—before asking his students to take out the miniature tidal stream generators they had constructed in the previous class. As they all stepped into the crashing waves, Joshua explained the mechanics behind the newly functional tidal farm that was helping to power the city. Construction had been nearly complete at the time of the collapse, but only within the previous few months had it finally begun fulfilling its purpose. Joshua motioned for me to follow, and I joined the class in the water.

Beneath the clear, sunlit surface, I watched their tiny turbines spin like a submerged wind farm. The ocean had an astounding capacity to provide for us, from food to energy, as did so much of the natural earth we had neglected. Only creativity and foresight were necessary to put brilliant ideas to action, and in that respect, we had only restricted ourselves. Money, it turned out, had failed the human race as a motivator for progress and expression of success. Our capacity for production was limited by the potential for monetary profit, so we maintained the use of archaic and environmentally devastating energy sources like fossil fuels long after better options had become available. The technology had been there, but implementation was costly to initiate, even if operating expenses were far lower in the long term than with our current methods. Wind, water, and sunlight provided enough free energy to satisfy us all. It was just a matter of harnessing them properly.

We had embarked on a new era of energy production, one in which the motivation was not money but rather the good of all people and the integrity of the planet on which we lived. It seemed we could one day thrive with all the luxuries we'd had before, but without any expense to our valuable natural resources.

Remarkably, watching the turbines shimmer as the tide rushed through them was as exhilarating to the young students as it was to me. Perhaps, had I been taught in such a way, I might have been inspired in my youth to devote my life to such a noble cause. Instead, like so many, I had not chosen a professional path until well into my college career. The decision was made then more from a lack of available time and options than true inspiration.

When the tidal stream generator demonstration had concluded, Joshua decided to deviate from the lesson he had planned.

"We have a guest with us today," he began, "who has traveled quite a long way to be here. This is Joe."

I smiled and waved as the class greeted me.

"Why don't you tell us what you're doing, Joe?"

I was surprised and unprepared. After a moment of hesitation, I addressed the class, quite unsure of where to begin my story.

"All right, does anyone know a mailperson?"

"I do," a child spoke proudly. "My dad is a letter carrier."

My eyes widened as I looked at the child.

"Really?" I replied.

"Yes. He's on his way to Salt Lake City."

"My brother is headed to Phoenix," said a second student.

"My mom is in Los Angeles. Going to Mexico next."

I was speechless.

"We've got a fully functional mail service now within a few hundred–mile radius," Joshua said with a smile. "It's expanding every day. This is the new communications industry, Joe. Ironic, isn't it?"

"Unbelievable," I muttered.
"You didn't think you were the only one, did you, Joe?"
"I knew there were others."
"But?"
"But how many are there?"
"Hundreds locally. A few dozen who leave the city."

I sat and spoke with the class awhile, sharing stories of my adventures as they shared those of their own families and friends on similar journeys. They knew much of what I had been through, having heard it all so many times before. Those of us committed to the new communication network were revered for our sacrifice, and so many of the stories I heard mirrored my own. We were proud of what we had all accomplished together and of what could soon follow because of our perseverance. The network could one day evolve from carried letters to include telephone and electronic communication again, but these first steps were vital to facilitate the possibilities of the future. In front of me was the next generation, and they were full of inspiration.

Teaching was regarded as a vital component of the growing system and had become a highly valued and prestigious career path of its own. Joshua, like his colleagues, was no longer restricted by the bureaucracy of the system but was then free to explore the full range of resources at his disposal, challenging both the creativity and raw intellect of students, rather than their ability to memorize facts and figures. Classes were larger but had taken a step back toward the ideology of the one-room schoolhouse where students of multiple age groups learned together. Not only did that allow them to integrate and expand social horizons, but it also allowed older and more experienced students to assist in teaching the younger ones, consequently reinforcing what they themselves had learned. The nature of the system inspired creativity.

"As they teach, they learn," Joshua said.

In school they studied practical subjects, many of which had never been addressed in schools of the past. There was history, math, science, and English, of course, but the application of those subjects to survival, farming, communications, mechanics, green building, and energy production was equally important. After all, application was the purpose of learning to begin with. Foreign language courses were expected of anyone who did not speak at least three fluently. Success in school was not determined by standardized tests. In fact, very little was standardized. Advancement was based on the teacher's recommendation, which rendered the teacher invaluable. College-level education was no longer the only option beyond the new equivalent of high school. The preferred course for most careers was then apprenticeship—continued learning through application.

When class had concluded, Joshua and I began the long walk back to his house. It was not so strange that we were greeted on the street by nearly everyone we passed. That, I had grown to expect in my travels. What *was* strange, however, was that all of those people knew him by name—not just within his own neighborhood, but on every road and every corner we traversed along the way. When I inquired as to his seeming celebrity status, he responded with a modest shrug.

The next day, I thought it prudent to make a contribution to that place as I had in others. Before the sun had fully risen, I embarked on the mountainous hike downtown to Pier 39, where sea lions basked in the morning sun among the fishermen loading gear onto boats. There I joined another crew just boarding their catamaran.

"We can use more hands today anyway," they said, welcoming me aboard. "One of our guys just left town."

We set off westward, tacking past the city under the Golden Gate and into the blue. It was a beautiful, cool morning with a breeze coming in from the ocean, just like the night I had arrived there. The Pacific view of the city bared a stunning fusion of human creation and that of God: feats of engineering and architecture—bridges and buildings—spread in three dimensions across a mountainous backdrop. From the shore was drawn a waving blue carpet that sparkled, fit for royalty and with an adventurous spirit. The designed elements complemented the natural, as they should. Too much faith in human creation leaves little for all that was there long before. I stood with the breathtaking view from a vessel powered entirely by the wind, traveling as people had traveled for thousands of years.

That feeling always brought me back to wonder about God. Sometimes, like the wind, his presence seemed passive, even nonexistent. Others, it emerged as if out of nowhere, moving us with overwhelming power to great new places and leaving a wake of joy and inspiration.

Aboard the vessel, the crew's lunatic revelry echoed that of the proverbial Pequod, with their timeless songs and vulgar jokes. They, too, had converged there from diverse strata and distant places. When I told the fishermen the name of the man who had taken me in, they were not surprised in the least. They as well all knew Joshua.

"Who is he?" I asked.

"The teacher," one of them said.

"Yes, but why does everyone know him?"

"When it all came down, we didn't know where to go. It was mass panic. Most people here didn't know how to hunt or farm. There was no electricity, no communication, no running water. We were terrified. I don't have to tell you what it was like. I'm sure you experienced the same things.

"Then Joshua came along. I'm not sure how it started, but people began to follow him, and as word of the teacher spread, everyone began looking to him for answers. During times of great struggle, people will look anywhere for a leader and follow the first person who steps up. It doesn't always end well. Too often that person will take advantage of the very people who entrust their lives to him, but every once in a while, there's someone like Joshua. Things grew calm again, eventually. As we adapted and learned to provide for ourselves, Joshua gradually slipped back into anonymity. Not entirely, of course. We all still know his face, but he's just one of us."

"What did he do before the collapse?" I asked.

"Joshua was homeless. He slept in parks and scavenged for food." He smiled and said, "Wisdom is sometimes hidden in unexpected places."

I couldn't help but look at Joshua differently that night when I brought the day's catch back to his home. We ate together, and he was strangely quiet throughout the meal. Uncharacteristically so, from what little I knew of him. He kept glancing at a sealed envelope sitting on a desk nearby in the room. I didn't want to probe, though. If he was planning to request that I make a delivery, it was his own business, and I would let him ask at whatever time he saw fit. Already I had accepted the responsibility in places past, and in my satchel two other letters awaited delivery. What was a third? Still, I didn't quite understand the apprehension about asking such a favor. He was, after all, providing me with a home and an education during my stay. It was only right that I repay him somehow.

Then I began to wonder why, when their network had already been so developed, he would charge me with the responsibility of a single delivery. Would it not be simpler to send his mail with one of the Bay's own carriers, regardless of its destination? Certainly, if it were a local delivery, they would be more familiar with the route and established postal centers. If it was distant, my route was indirect to almost any location, and I only had one stop left on the coast before I would head home.

I grew increasingly curious through the meal, anxious, even, picking away at the delicious halibut that I had arduously taken from the ocean earlier in the day. Occasionally, Joshua would look across the room to the envelope and then look at me as if to speak. But without a word, he would turn back to his plate and continue eating.

It became apparent that whatever he was holding back seemed to him as much a burden spoken as it was kept within. If I were to have an answer to my own frenzied curiosities, I would have to inquire.

"I see you looking at that envelope, Joshua," I said. "What's in it?"

He looked up at me silently.

"If you need me to make a delivery, you can ask. It isn't a problem. Lord knows I owe you for the hospitality."

"You owe me nothing," he said. "The sacrifices you've made are more than payment enough."

"Either way, I can take it off your hands if you need."

"It's not outgoing."

"No?"

"No. I received it some time ago."

"May I ask why you haven't opened it?"

"Because it isn't addressed to me."

"Who is it addressed to?"

He paused for a moment and took a breath.

"It's addressed to you, Joe."

13

THE CITY OF ANGELS

I was back on my horse early the next day, having slept very little that night. I spent most of it up writing. And reading the letter over and over. That is, after I had finished harshly berating Joshua. When he handed me the envelope, I saw the origination mark from Eden Valley—my home. It had been delivered some weeks prior with specific instructions to hold until I arrived. Because the postal center at the Bay knew not whom to expect or when or from where, it was decided at the time that Joshua would be the ideal custodian of the mysterious piece of mail. After all, nearly everyone still in the city knew him, or at least knew how to find him. If anyone were to hear of the stranger on a mission, it would be him. It was only by coincidence, or perhaps fate, that he had happened upon me in the park that night.

Looking back, I can understand Joshua's reservations and why he hadn't given me the letter that very night and had decided instead to wait until I was preparing to get back on the road. He, of course, had no idea what was inside. It was an unknown and mysterious thing, and he dared not venture to guess what joyous or devastating news it might bring me in a time of such personal strife so far from home. It was obviously important, he knew, based on the distance it had traveled and the orders that had accompanied it. Would it bring news of death? Some catastrophe? Those were his fears, and though he was perhaps not as forthcoming as I might have wished he had been at the time, I'm glad now that he did wait. I would not have spent that valuable time in the Bay Area had I received the letter on the night of my arrival. I would have been off again immediately.

My reaction to Joshua waiting, though, was one of anger. In truth, I wasn't sure exactly how to react when I saw my name in Maria's handwriting on the front of the envelope, and for whatever reason, anger was the emotion that presented itself. I stood in Joshua's dining room with the unopened letter in my hand, yelling terrible things at him. Perhaps that arose out of my own fears of the words that might have been enclosed. He sat quietly, enduring the abuse with no rebuttal to my volcano of tension poisoning the air as we breathed it.

I left the room to read in private, my hands shaking as I tore open the envelope, and I didn't emerge until early the next morning before the night gave way to the day.

I was gone before Joshua had risen, leaving my outgoing mail on his dining table and not taking the opportunity to say good-bye. I wanted desperately to be home, but after reading the long-awaited words of the person I loved more than my own life, I understood more than ever the importance of the two envelopes in my satchel. Regardless of what might have been inside them, it was my responsibility to ensure that they were delivered. The city that had once been Los Angeles would be my next stop.

As October rolled into November, Nomad and I traveled southward on Highway 1, the blue Pacific following alongside over the immense cliffs. Breakers exploded in white clouds below as the wind picked up from the west. The road wound like one in a painting and traced the coast, the ocean to our right and the mountains to our left. We crossed old bridges built into the cliff faces and suspended over deadly chasms, which looked as though they might collapse at any moment. I read the letter so many times that I had it memorized, and then I kept reading just to see Maria's handwriting on the page.

> *Dear Joe,*
>
> *I don't even know how to begin this letter. It's been so long since we've seen each other, and between the letters you send, each of which makes me break down into tears of joy, all I feel is fear. I know I shouldn't tell you that, but you're all I can think about. Every moment I have to endure without*

you is agonizing. I miss you so much, and I love you more than words can say. It's been hard, Joe, I won't lie. I can't even imagine what it's like out there for you. When you get home, I want to hear the real story, not the sugarcoated one I get from your letters, but for now, that will do. You were always trying to protect me.

Things are good here, though. You wouldn't believe how big this place has gotten. We've taken a few trips back home, and things have calmed down there too. I'm still calling St. Louis home, out of habit, I guess, but for all intents and purposes, the farm is home now. I guess it's time I got used to that. It doesn't feel like home without you here, though.

Everyone else seems to have settled into this new life all right. Mail comes in and goes out every day now, and I know we all have you to thank for it. They're more organized now than they were at first. A person came in today with mail all the way from California. You should have seen how happy people were at the post office. I figured since the last letter I received from you came from Chicago a few weeks ago, I could send this one back to California to wait for you. I don't know how they'll find you, but I'm hopeful.

Do you remember the day you proposed to me? I do. Like it was yesterday. It was the first anniversary of our first date. I was preparing a nice swordfish dinner for the two of us when the kitchen suddenly became very warm, and I swept into the dining room to find the table covered in candles like a shrine to a little red box in the middle. You had left it sitting there all day, insisting that I wait to open it until the exact time that our date had begun the year before and repeatedly asking me what I thought was in it. I was terrified to speculate. What if I was wrong? But I wasn't wrong. You asked me to spend the rest of my life with you, and I didn't have to think twice before saying yes. I loved you so much then, and I still do. That was the most wonderful day. Remember those days, Joe. That's how we'll get through this.

How symbolic that first year seems now. One revolution around the sun. Each such revolution seems to bring a new chapter in our lives. It was just over a year we had spent here together before you left, and, I hope, it won't be more than another since that we will have spent without each other.

I'm sorry to be so brief when there's so much to say, but I have to get this to the carrier before he leaves again tonight. I miss you so, so much, but I'm so proud of you. We all are. You must know that and never forget it. We'll be together sooner than you realize, and I can hardly wait for that day. I love you more than you'll ever know. I'll always wait for you.

*Love Forever,
Maria*

It was as if she had forgotten the awful way I had treated her before I left, and reading her words and hearing her voice in my head stoked that fire of guilt within me. The nightmares became progressively worse, and the void inside me continued to grow. Somehow, though I would have given anything to hear from Maria, that letter made things even more difficult. I was overcome with so many emotions. The more I heard about how proud she was of me and what a wonderful thing it was that I was doing, the more ashamed I felt. I didn't want to be away from her anymore. I wanted to be home, holding her. What could be worth the sorrow to such an ordinary person as I was? Who was I to have taken on this great responsibility? I was no wise man and no great hero. That was a realization I had come to months before. Rather, I was simply a person who had abandoned his family for his own pride, and my wife, in her pure, uncorrupted love, with all the time she had waited for me, was still as loyal as she had ever been. After having been away from her for so long, even the simplicity of those handwritten words on the pages made all of the memories that had been fading into oblivion real again. My love for her was overwhelming. She was as much a part of me as my heart itself and equally vital to my survival, and it made me physically ill to be without her.

At my weakest of moments with nowhere else to turn, I always felt compelled to pray, though I wasn't sure exactly who I was talking to.

It wasn't until I saw the Hearst Castle peeking majestically through the distant haze that I realized how terrible my reaction had been back at Joshua's home, and I decided to camp there that night and begin writing him a letter that I would send back at my earliest opportunity. He deserved proper thanks and an apology, but I don't suspect that he ever held it against me. That wasn't his way.

Every passing day humbled me with the beautiful things it presented—the graciousness of all the people I had met, the beauty of the landscape everywhere I went, the love that had overtaken me at the mere sight of words on paper, and then the view of that extraordinary mansion perched on a mountainside at the coast. It was life as I had never expected to live it.

About the time I saw the castle, as they call it, I also noticed an ominous dark cloud approaching from the west. By then, I had spent many stormy nights on the road, and I had learned to pitch my tent early and secure it well in the face of nature's wrath. Nomad and I hiked a short way up the mountainside in hopes that it might provide some protection from the oncoming front, and I set to work on my shelter for the night. The storm, however, came on more quickly than I had anticipated, and the wind began to pick up. I struggled to stretch the worn canvas over its frame and stake it into the ground, and by the time I had finished, I was exhausted, drenched, and freezing. The sky had begun pouring rain. I crawled inside and peered through the front flaps, watching in awe as the black clouds churned above.

The blue Pacific had faded to a dark gray under the cumulonimbus ceiling that spanned as far as I could see. It almost blended with the horizon. The white caps of the ocean had grown huge and rough, crashing into one another with force I thought could capsize the greatest of ships. Thunder boomed in the distance and clapped and sizzled as lightning spider-webbed over the water. Between strikes, I could hear the tide pummeling the rock faces not far down the mountain. Wind whistled over the canvas that sheltered me, and streams of water blew in through the holes that had formed in it over my months of travel. I sat alone, shivering in an upright fetal position with my arms wrapped around my knees as the frigid world seemed to be collapsing all around me. However uncomfortable, even menacing, it was, I couldn't help but marvel at the power of the earth at work. It was as if nature felt all of the emotions in conflict within me and had set out to share in them.

A sudden smack took down half the tent on top of me as I quivered inside, and I scrambled out of the flap to see what had happened. The gale had uprooted one of my stakes, and the tension of the line had pulled it into the side of the tent, tearing the canvas open. Fighting to stay on my feet, I grabbed the stake and tried to put it back into the soggy ground; when I pulled it back, the tear in the canvas caught the wind, yanking the stake out of my hand and the entire tent onto its side. There would be no recovering it in that weather, and as the storm grew more intense, I knew that spending any more time out there could be fatal.

Just beyond, lightning struck a tree with a deafening crack and blinding flash, bringing it straight to the earth. The ground shook beneath me when the tree landed, its branches bouncing like rubber from the momentum. Through the flaming timber, I saw Nomad galloping up the side of the mountain for shelter. I dove into the collapsed tent for my satchel and went after him. All around, trees swayed, and severed palm fronds blew across the landscape in every direction.

"Nomad, wait!" I called to my horse, but I could barely hear my own words over the sounds of the storm. Just maintaining my footing was arduous in that gale. I scrambled frantically through the grass uphill, blinded by the torrential rain and deafened by the thunder and wind gusting in my ears. The odor of burning trees that had been struck by lightning was potent in the air, and my chest vibrated with every strike. It was a total sensory bombardment that rendered me hopelessly disoriented.

Between claps of thunder, I heard a neigh of distress in the distance, and I ran in the direction of Nomad's call, trying to stay beneath the shelter of the trees on the mountainside as much as I could. I did my best to cover my satchel and protect the letters inside, but it was no use. Everything was soaked as if I had been entirely submerged in the ocean. I was too overwhelmed to be terrified, though I had all rights to be. Instead, I focused on protecting the things entrusted to my possession as if my life depended on it. In a way, it did. Without the impetus of those letters, I would have perished long before.

Suddenly, I felt a paved surface under my feet. I looked up to find the façade of the mansion towering over me with the California palms on either side of the entrance, bent within inches of snapping in the wind. Between the stone fountain on the patio and the gold-accented front gate, Nomad reared and circled. I bolted past him to the door and struck it with all the force I could muster over and over until I broke it in, and he followed me through into the grand entry hall. Behind him, I slammed the door shut again and barricaded it with any furniture I could find.

I was too exhausted to care anything for the architecture at that moment. Still trying to catch my breath, I collapsed onto the floor and lay there panting until I fell asleep, the soggy wet envelopes limp in my hand.

When I awoke it was quiet. I was nearly dry, and the colossal entry hall was splashed in bright sunlight. It took a minute to reacquaint myself with reality and remember where I was. Beside me lay Maria's letter, open on the floor and miraculously intact. Next to it were the two other envelopes, also somehow unharmed. I was dumbfounded by the fact that they had survived the storm. I'd been certain that they had been destroyed the night before as they had deteriorated in my hand, and for the moment, I had been lost and hopeless. I had watched the water dripping from the flimsy paper into a puddle on the floor. It simply wasn't possible that they were then completely unscathed.

I found myself kneeling on the floor with my arms in the air, involuntarily screaming "Thank God!" with the sound of my voice echoing in a chorus around the room. I slipped all three letters safely back into my pack and climbed to my feet, suddenly taking notice of the extravagance of the massive gallery in which I stood.

Everywhere was carved molding, ornate tile, shimmering colors, massive tapestries, and stone. It was elegant and beautiful, a work of art that deserved great appreciation. At the same time, it was an almost gaudy icon of the self-indulgence that had plagued our culture, and I thought of the place where I was headed. It made me apprehensive about what I might find in the city that had once been Los Angeles.

I remembered a party I had gone to once back in college—a noisy and crowded scene at a fraternity house that I never would have been allowed into had a friend of mine not been a member. I had stepped outside into the cold winter night, using a cigarette as an excuse to flee the sloppy charade indoors, and I'd found Paul doing the same. We had met one of the brothers of the house out there and held a pleasant enough conversation, though it had felt forced, as if he thought he was doing us a favor. He'd been telling us about some woman in LA, where he was from, who had been caught trying to smuggle cocaine in her breast implants.

"Yeah, people will put coke in anything to smuggle it," Paul had said.

At one point, I had offered our new friend a cigarette, to which he'd replied, "Are you kidding? Do you know what those things do to your lungs?" Throughout that night, I had watched him suck down half a bottle of whiskey and snort line after line of cocaine. Touché, I'd thought.

I quit smoking anyway, though. Sometimes when we're young, we think we're invincible, and some of us never grow out of that. Los Angeles, I had thought, was the embodiment of a culture built on hypocritical, self-indulgent excess—a collection of entitled and self-absorbed children with no understanding of the fact that working people everywhere else provided for their elite existence.

But had I been I so different?

Nomad and I came slowly down the mountain in the direction of the road, and next to the still-burning tree that had fallen in front of me the night before, I found that the only shelter I had brought had been taken away by the storm. Ahead lay many more clear nights under the stars and wet ones under the clouds, but it was no use concerning myself with that then.

I could hear Maria's voice reciting, "God, grant me the serenity to accept the things I cannot change, the courage to change the things I can, and the wisdom to know the difference." One by one, the things I had brought for protection were being snatched away by the very wilderness that they were intended to defend against. All I could do then was move on without them and hope that somehow, some way, I would be provided for.

When I rode into the City of Angels a few days later, the first thing I did was find a post office to send the letter back to Joshua that I had written along the way, and even more importantly, to find the recipient of the first of the two letters that I had brought from that City That Never Sleeps.

"Looks like you've got the wrong office," said the clerk at the counter when I finally reached the end of the inevitable line with which those places were always laden. "Rebekah Prophet is the name?" he clarified, flipping through pages in a massive book on the counter.

"Yes, Rebekah Prophet," I repeated, reading the name on the envelope.

"It says she's registered over at the Santa Monica office."

So that's where I went. By the time I arrived at the proper office, night had fallen and it was closed, and I fell asleep on the cold marble steps in front of the building. When they opened in the morning, I was the first one to the counter, where they offered to take the letter off of my hands. I refused, though. After all that way, thousands of miles with the letter in my possession, I had to see it delivered. That was one responsibility I would fulfill, and I wanted to see the look on the face of the person for whom I had endured it all.

Three whole days I stayed there waiting, sleeping nights on the front steps and standing days in the lobby. The postal clerks were understanding and accommodating, and they provided me with food and water while I waited, though I didn't eat much. I spoke with many in line, none of whom knew Rebekah, and I was beginning to question whether she had moved elsewhere without notifying the service. Perhaps she had died, even. The thought wasn't so farfetched. In a world without a thorough census and in which every citizen was undocumented, one person could easily go unnoticed.

It was on that third day, shortly before closing time, that I began to doze off with dwindling hope. A hand on my shoulder roused me, and I opened my eyes to find an elderly woman with radiant white hair standing in front of me.

"They said at the desk that you were looking for me."

I leaped from my seat, startling her more than mildly.

"Rebekah?"

"Yes?"

"Rebekah Prophet?"

"Yes?" she replied reluctantly.

"I have a letter for you," I said, handing her the envelope. She took it, gazing at her name and that of the city written on the front as if she was in shock. Her eyes widened, and I heard her gasp. Then I had to catch her before she hit the floor when she collapsed.

"She's alive!" Rebekah screamed. "She's OK!"

She tore the envelope open and read frantically, sobbing with joy, and then she grabbed me and squeezed until I had lost my breath.

"Thank you," she whispered into my ear. "I don't know who you are, but you're a godsend."

When Rebekah calmed down, I learned that the woman who had given me the letter outside of the Big Apple was her daughter. They had not spoken since the collapse, and Rebekah had known nothing of her daughter's safety during all of those months. Suddenly, on that otherwise ordinary day, she was graced with news that brought her as much joy as she had ever known. Her daughter and family on the opposite coast were alive and as healthy as ever.

To express her appreciation, Rebekah invited me to dinner at her home that evening. We talked about our families as we walked, and after some time we came upon a pair of great iron gates standing wide open and inviting us off the road. Across the yard stood an extravagant Spanish-style mansion glowing in the sun falling toward the water behind it.

"Some home," I said, flashing back to my night in the Hearst Castle.

"I'm just staying here a little while," she replied.

We went in the front door, and it was as if we had entered a casual and boisterous gathering of a large multicultural family. In a way, that's exactly what it was. There were people of all ages and all races coexisting under the same roof. A trio of children ran across the hall in front of us, laughing and playing as the voices of their parents called to them from a large front living room. The potent aroma of a hot meal made my empty stomach grumble.

"Smells like they've started dinner without me," Rebekah said, and she led me toward the kitchen. It was hot and noisy in the room, and there were pots and vats of food cooking everywhere like a caterer's kitchen before a wedding.

"Didn't want to wait for me, huh?" said Rebekah to the other chefs.

"Sorry, we got hungry," said one woman. "Who's your friend?"

"This is Joe. Joe, this is Anna. She owns the house."

"It's nice to meet you, Joe," said Anna. "Will you be staying for dinner?"

"If it's all right."

"Of course! The more the merrier."

Dinner was a delicious smorgasbord of seafood and fruits and vegetables that they put on the table. Their fusion cuisine came in great variety, clearly influenced by the numerous cultures represented within that household. We filled the dining room with people who hailed from all over the world like some royal dinner party, and they took me in as one of their own. It was apparent that any kind of social exclusion was the only thing unwelcome in that house, and I felt guilty over my presumptions about the city. The mansion was grand and opulent, to be certain, but it also provided a home to many families, who I learned had lost their homes to rioting during the collapse. Anna had always owned the place. She had been some kind of media executive, I figured, based on the décor of the house. When everything had happened, she had refused to leave and had rather gone to the streets to collect families made homeless and given them shelter. "I stayed because this place is my home," she said, "but it's a lot less lonely now that I have family."

When she learned of my journey, I immediately became the newest member of the family, which meant I had a place to call home as well for as long as I stayed. That would only be the few days Nomad and I needed to rest before getting back on the road, but I imagined future visits with my wife under different circumstances. The two of us could watch the sun set over the ocean each night from the terrace off the back of the house and share breakfast each morning with our new extended family, whom I grew to love during my short first stay with them.

I got to sleep early that night in a comfortable bed that they had made up for me, but first I sat reading Maria's letter awhile.

"I'll always wait for you," she said. She shouldn't have to, I thought. I could hardly wait to be with her, but soon I would be back on the road, finally heading toward home. My final delivery would be made on the way.

While the focus of life there fell unquestionably on family and the freedom to spend time with them, still I witnessed no sloth. Able-bodied adults worked, not because they were forced to, but because a person cannot fully appreciate the gifts given them without providing some of their own. During the day I joined a few of them to offer my own labor. As we walked the streets toward the new industrial part of town, I watched the people passing. I noticed how naturally beautiful they were, just like people back home. Cosmetics were a thing of the past. Our lifestyles kept us healthy and fit, and beyond that, people accepted themselves for who God had made them to be. Accepting ourselves had been the hard part in the past. Our greatest critics had come from within.

The job I was given was assisting in operating a printing press. It was a surprisingly simple mechanical apparatus. Pages were fed into a track where a cylinder with interchangeable letters pressed ink onto the paper and ejected it from the other side, all powered by a hand crank. I was printing history schoolbooks alongside a whole room full of people printing on those machines. Elsewhere, the machines themselves were manufactured by hand on an assembly line. Even parts of the process to manufacture paper were done by hand. It was the beginning of a new industrial revolution that utilized the power of the human body in addition to renewable energy.

"I like this revolution from the old world of industry and commerce," said Anna. "We threw out the rulebook—the hierarchy and bureaucracy—and it gave us all a fresh perspective. Nobody works *for* anyone. We work together. Before the collapse, there was an increasing disconnection between those at the top and those at the bottom, and the majority was not adequately provided for. They were overworked, undercompensated, and underappreciated. From the sheep to the dogs to the pigs, the human factor was lost. Everyone was just a number, not just looking down from above, but also looking up from below.

"Most of us have feelings of entitlement, whether we realize it or not," she continued. "Rich because they're rich, poor because they're poor. We don't want to hear about someone else's problems when we have enough of our own. It's hard not to be more concerned with oneself than the whole. We are, by nature, selfish creatures, and it takes a lot to overcome that, but the result is worth the struggle. After all, rich and poor—'haves' and 'have nots'—are just products of the marketplace. The trick is having enough available work for every person willing and able to do it. Where is the sense in overworking part of the population while the other part searches for a way to contribute? And, of course, each member of the workforce must understand and embrace his or her value. In the end, we uncover the cyclical fact that the welfare of the individual is dependent on the harmony of the whole, and vice versa."

Their system eliminated most of the positions of middlemen, putting those workers to better use, and we knew exactly where our products came from because the producers themselves were the sources of acquisition. Wheat came directly from the farmer who sowed and harvested it, clothes from the clothier who knitted them, tools from the blacksmith who forged them, and so on. Without any generally accepted currency, many places I visited operated on a barter system so simple and honest that it didn't require oversight from some governing entity. We employed the old farmers' market ideology for nearly every type of product, and it worked splendidly. As it turned out, people liked to know where the items in their homes came from. It brought the community together and bred a greater respect for every trade.

That harmony was reflected everywhere and particularly in the home of my family there. They openly discussed their diversity, struggles, and triumphs, and I witnessed the realization of Dr. King's dream as their children ran throughout the house playing together after dinner.

"We learn from one another, as do our children," said one father in his calming West African accent. "Do you have children, Joe?"

"Not yet."

"Someday?" he smiled.

"Someday."

"Good. They give us purpose," he said, looking at his wife next to him and rubbing her pregnant belly. She smiled back at him as he continued, "My children made me understand my own capacity to love. And through them I understand the way God looks upon us, with unconditional love greater than we can imagine. He has given us a gift here. A gift of rebirth. We must not waste it."

The morning of the next day, as I was preparing to head out and most of the other members of the family had already left for the day's work, I heard a muffled scream through the door to my room. I paused to listen for a moment, hoping that perhaps the voice I'd heard had simply been that of one of the many children at play. Then it came again, that time undoubtedly the sound of a woman in distress. I threw on my shabby pants and darted from the room barefoot and shirtless, passing the open doors of vacant bedrooms down the long hall toward the loft overlooking the entry hall. I wound down the staircase, the screams growing louder as they echoed from the walls.

Entering the great room, I saw a cluster of children huddled together in silence, watching from a distance as Anna knelt over the pregnant mother whom I had last seen with a serene smile on her face the prior evening.

"Push!" Anna demanded.

"Where is my husband?" the woman screamed.

Anna turned and saw me.

"Joe! Go find him!"

Without a word, I dashed out into the yard and mounted my horse. We galloped down the driveway and out the gate and then hit the streets, headed toward the printer where I had worked with the father the previous day. Pedestrians jumped from our path as I yelled ahead to warn of our fast approach.

"Look out!" I bellowed. "The baby's coming!"

We arrived at the building miles away, bystanders diving to avoid the barefoot and shirtless lunatic leaping from his horse and dashing through the doors. I cleared my way through the building to the room of printing presses.

"Abidan!" I called through the mass of workers. "Your wife is in labor!"

Everyone froze and turned to look at me, and then back toward the man just as crazy as I who was hurtling clumsily through them to reach me.

"Now?" he yelled.

"Now! We have to go!"

I heard cheers from behind as the two of us sped out through the doors still swinging from my hasty entry and Abidan hopped onto Nomad's back.

"Come on!" he said as I stopped short.

"You go!"

Without hesitation, he was off, and I was left to walk back on my bare feet.

I must have looked like the proudest bum on earth waddling through the streets with my head high and most of the skin on my body bared to the sun. By the time I returned, the house was quiet again. I came in to find the cheerful mother and father on the sofa swooning over their newborn daughter, who was asleep and wrapped comfortably in their arms. They looked up to smile at me and then back down to the product of their love. In another room, I could hear the other children playing. Anna was in the kitchen preparing lunch for everyone.

"How about that?" she said when I came in and pulled up a chair at the breakfast table.

"How about it," I sighed.

"Makes me want children of my own."

"Does it?"

She laughed. "Not the labor, but what comes after. Speaking of which, aren't you getting ready to head back on the road?"

"I am."

"Well, have something to eat before you go. I'll make extra to take with you."

The City of Angels was already operating a complete communication network throughout the southwest, which meant I could skip the trip to the city that had been Phoenix, where I had originally planned to make a stop. The network was growing at a rate faster than I could ride, and new carriers were beating me to my destinations. I was sure that they had already reached every city I had planned to pass through on my way back.

It was then I realized that the mission to establish the New World Mail Network had been accomplished. It had happened so gradually as I traveled that it had lacked the climactic, triumphant moment I'd hoped for, but I guess that sort of thing only happens in movies. I was glad, though. That meant a shorter trip northeast from there toward the Rockies, and I would be passing through the city that had been Las Vegas instead.

I sent a letter home, the last that I would send on the journey, letting them know that I was finally on my way back. Any more correspondence mailed from then on would likely not arrive more than a few days ahead of me, and I saw no use in that. I thanked Anna, Rebekah, and the rest of my family there for their hospitality. As I packed to leave them, home was finally a real place, not some fantasy I dreamed about but would never see. I had less than two months left, I figured. Perhaps half that if Nomad and I could maintain the pace. I told Maria that I loved her and that we would be together soon.

In all my excitement, I had neglected to consider the dangers of the winter and the wilderness over the distance of nearly two thousand miles between there and home.

14

IN BLOOM

Traveling the barren desert between those two cities was like two weeks in purgatory. We covered less ground each day. Nights were cold, and though the days weren't unbearably hot, the sun was blinding. Decent shade was almost nowhere to be found, so when we did come across it, Nomad and I always took the opportunity for rest, whether it was under the occasional Joshua tree or the north side of a rock formation. It was bittersweet that my shelter had been taken up to the heavens, as we would not see rain for a while, but my water skins ran dry quickly.

Cactus fruit and the gel of aloe leaves served as nearly our only sources of both food and water, and Nomad relied on me to prepare them so that they would be safe to eat. The latex from the aloe leaf, I quickly learned, was to be avoided. The body is designed to let us know when we've eaten something harmful, so I made adjustments as necessary. Likewise, the prickly pears had to be peeled before ingestion, and after enough raw Opuntia, I began cooking it to lower the acidity.

Still, sustenance of any kind was not abundant enough to keep either of us healthy. As thirsty as I was, I could only imagine Nomad's suffering. The long, narrow road behind us looked identical to the road ahead, and I began to question our progress. It sometimes seemed as though we weren't moving at all but just walking in place, day after day. Between the highway signs, which were few and far between, I often watched the sun to be sure that we were still headed in the right direction. Not far north of the road we traveled was the place they called Death Valley. I prayed for our deliverance, wondering if there was anyone out there to hear me.

Even through the agonizing hunger and thirst and the loneliness that accompanied them, the beauty of the desert was undeniable. There was something divine about its untouched landscape and the cloudless blue sky above that shone with millions of sparkling diamonds upon the fall of night and blood red in between. It was strange how the farther I moved from civilization, the closer the heavens seemed. I marveled at the fact that any kind of vegetation and animal life still managed to thrive out there despite the dry, harsh conditions. Life, I realized, adapts to whatever environment with which it is presented in order to go on. In the eloquent words of Ian Malcolm, "life finds a way."

Then the half-buried skeleton of another traveler gone astray reminded me that the same is true of death.

A sign reading "Welcome to Fabulous Las Vegas, Nevada" had been knocked down and was lying sideways on the grassy median separating inbound and outbound traffic on Las Vegas Boulevard. I imagined smiling faces in cars on one side of the road and frowning on the other. That town, I figured, had been one of the first to come down when disposable income had gone the way of the dinosaur—with a sudden and fateful blast. I find it ironic that the terms "America's Playground" and "Sin City" once referred to the same place.

I decided that as long as I was there, I might as well stay on the strip. Why not try to enjoy my visit? Not that I was a gambler, really. Not in the Vegas sense, anyway. Besides, I figured that wouldn't be much of a thing anymore. Even with the redevelopment of so many industries, I still had not seen a dollar change hands since the collapse. I was more interested in the city itself—the people, the lights, the colors, and the architecture.

The sun was just setting as I approached the Bellagio fountain spewing an aquatic symphony that called the attention of every passerby. The orange glow in the west silhouetted the palatial hotel. Colorful lights again splashed across streets and buildings, then powered predominantly by the Hoover Dam and various photovoltaic facilities up and running again, but the ambiance was somehow different than it had been before. In the air was a celebration, not of debauchery and hedonism or of an escape from reality, but of love. A newly constructed plaza off of the hotel restaurants overlooking the fountain had been completed just before the collapse. Upon it was a wedding ceremony in progress, where cheers erupted with the "I dos" from the bride and groom.

I entered the lobby after leaving Nomad with a valet outside, which I found strange, but as horses had replaced cars, so had stables replaced parking garages. They would provide him with feed and water immediately, as he had grown weak during our time in the desert. I was nervous still, leaving him alone, but the valet assured me that there was nothing to be concerned about. They had not had a single incident of thievery, probably because everything in that town came free.

Reluctantly, I left him, in dire need of my own mending. I walked in with an awkwardly foreign appearance under the Chihuly glass ceiling, glowing like a garden of colorful jellyfish above my head, screaming of an intruder. Immediately I felt out of place. I was filthy and dressed in rags not fit for such an elegant establishment. I hadn't bathed since the coast. At the front desk was a pitcher of water, the entirety of which I gulped down as they were setting me up with a room overlooking the strip and providing me with a list of complimentary restaurants. It was surreal. I felt briefly like a child without a care or responsibility whose needs and wants were all satisfied with no requirement that that satisfaction be earned.

"How long will you be staying with us?" asked the clerk at the desk.

"Only a night," I replied. "I'm just passing through."

"I hear that more often than I used to. Travelers passing through are the only reason our little oasis still exists out here in the middle of nowhere. Probably a lot of folks wouldn't be alive if they hadn't found us on their way to greener pastures. Where are you headed?"

"Southern Missouri."

"Really? This time of year? You may want to rethink a winter jaunt through the Rockies. Let me know if you decide to stay longer. We can set you up with some temporary work."

Nothing was stopping me then, though, and I didn't pause to consider his warning. My first order of business was hygiene and hydration, and then I would fill my aching stomach. After taking advantage of the complimentary food and drink, most of which had been brought in from California, I decided to join the public wedding reception on the plaza outside. It seemed to be an open invitation affair, and I could use a distraction. There were plenty of those to go around.

By then it was well into the evening, and many of the guests were sufficiently liquored up. I didn't intend to find myself in the same state, but one usually doesn't. The more I drank, however, the more my mind drew back to the memory of my own wedding day—Maria's beautiful face, slipping the ring onto her finger, the sound of her sweet voice when she had said, "I do." It brought me nearly to tears, and I drank more in hopes of driving out the memories. They were just too painful.

"So who are you with?" asked a friendly fellow who had taken a seat at the bar next to me. "Bride's side or groom's side?"

"Neither, actually. Don't tell anyone."

"Not here for the wedding?"

"I just needed some company," I said.

"And drinks, I see. What do they call you?"

"Joe."

"Ah, Joseph, a name as suitable for a humble man as it is for a king. Which are you?"

"The former. At least I'm trying to be."

"Well I'm Zeke," he said. "I don't know them either."

I laughed.

"In fact, I'm not sure anyone here does," he continued. "People are drawn to love, though, especially these days. We've always had lots of weddings in this town, but half of them were just charades."

"If you consider the divorce rate," I replied, "I'd say half the marriages anywhere in this country are charades."

"Agreed. Whatever happened to 'till death do us part'? Why is it that a spouse is the one expendable family member who can be legally disposed of for any cause, or even none? Seems to me that the ease of divorce defeats the entire purpose and meaning of marriage and, by default, family. And without family, what do we have? Look at that beautiful bride and groom."

I took a drink and turned toward the newlywed couple dancing in the center of a crowd on the patio.

"It's like they've forgotten what happened here," he went on.

"What was that?" I inquired.

"You'd never know it now, but this place became a war zone after the collapse. Literally. We're isolated in the desert, you know? Not much farmland out there. Not much fresh water. When deliveries quit coming in and the public water turned to sludge, people turned on each other, and that was before the heat of the summer. Gangs took over, fighting to the death for the last bits of whatever it was they needed at the time. Food. Water. Women. That fancy fountain there? People drank it dry. Then the gangs used the plaza for public executions, and there was a mass exodus of honest people to the desert. The ones who left knew their chances were slim out there, but they had to be better than staying. Bodies were piled in the basin where the fountain once was and where it is now."

"What happened in between?" I asked.

"Eventually, we realized that nobody was going to win if it meant someone else had to lose."

"We?"

"I was as much a part of it as anyone," he said, taking a drink. "Hard to believe that plaza where all those people are dancing was not long ago painted red with blood."

I watched the newlywed couple. The love was plain on their faces and in their smiles. They were entirely absorbed in a world of their own. It was as if they had forgotten not only the hundreds of people watching them, but also the entire collapse and all of the struggles we had all faced over the course of the last two years. We couldn't run from them or leave them behind, but perhaps we could learn from them. Perhaps we could even fix the things that had gone wrong. Despite the trials we had faced, love had managed to prevail in that place. Perhaps, if given the chance, love would always prevail. That radiant couple was entirely unfazed by the changes in the world as if those changes didn't matter. All that mattered was their love for one another. With that, they could overcome any obstacle. I knew that kind of love all too well.

"They look like they know," Zeke said. "You shouldn't get married unless you know."

"Do you know?" I asked him.

"I did. And you?"

"Yes," I said, looking at the ring on my finger.

"Where's your wife?"

"About fifteen hundred miles east of here."

"Miss her, don't you?"

"Every day."

"Been gone awhile?"

"The better part of a year," I replied.

"You look it."

"The flowers were just blooming when I left."

"We've still got plenty of flowers in bloom."

"Back home they're wilting."

"The flowers are always wilting somewhere," he said, "but they're always blooming somewhere else."

I had failed to take into account my recent dehydration and the months that had passed since the last time I'd had a drink; it must have been with Leah. The liquor was hitting me hard.

"Zeke," I said, slamming my drink down on the bar, "are you up for an adventure?"

"Ah, a man who has been through bitter experiences and traveled far enjoys even his sufferings after a time."

"What?"

"Never mind. What sort of adventure, Odysseus?"

"Something to sober me up."

"I've got just the thing," he said. "Come with me."

We stumbled out of our chairs, past the party and the fountain, and onto the strip. All around us, themed hotels towered, block after block of extravagant complexes representing places all over the world that were experiencing the same things we were. How different they certainly were from before. Everything had changed, and perhaps not in the abysmal way that it had seemed in the beginning. People, I thought, had somehow grown wiser.

We'd been mischievous when we were young, as youth naturally are. Many times we had been irresponsible, even. We had driven fast, taken risks, and broken rules, always in search of thrills and in love with the rush of our defiance of authority. There had been a time when I'd kept the company of rebels—people who took pleasure in destruction. We hadn't considered our karma. Losing honor to greed. Losing health, both physical and emotional, to promiscuity. Losing friends to drugs and lies. The world always taught lessons in response to our mistakes. It was up to us to accept them.

People will always be people, though, as I would learn that night. We each have our own ways of coping with internal struggles, sometimes by means of self-destruction. The worst way to face those struggles is alone.

Zeke had a favorite spot where he liked to sit and watch the world as he knew it. That spot was on the rooftop of a restaurant that gave him a clear view down the strip in both directions. I was a little uneasy when we exited the door at the top of the stairway into the breezy desert air, but Zeke was no stranger to that place. He had spent many nights there. Watching. Waiting. Wondering where he might go next. It was evident that Zeke had been lost for some time, all alone in the crowded, electrified oasis. He took a seat on the ledge and dangled his feet over the side.

"Come on, sit down," he said.

"I'm good back here. I've had my share of confrontations with gravity."

"You'll balance better on your ass than on your feet. I saw all those glasses in front of you. Come on, don't waste this view."

Reluctantly, I crawled to the edge of the rooftop and scooted my feet over the side. The view was indeed glorious. The atmosphere glowed with neon lights and extravagant hotels, and behind them, the mountains were silhouetted by the moon. Below us, the streets were alive with pedestrians, but no cars—a hybrid culture of modern and primitive technology that was fascinating to observe from the outside. From above.

"I told you," said Zeke. "A whole new perspective."

"I haven't done anything like this since I was young and invincible."

"I know what you mean. It's interesting how, when we're children, we have adults in our lives who we look up to with the belief that they have all the answers to life's infinite questions, and yet we rebel with insistence on our independence. Then we grow up and realize they didn't actually have the answers at all, and neither do we. It's a terrifying revelation. Sometimes we see how childish adults can be, and we're glad we were too innocent to see that as children. We would have had nowhere to turn for role models. Really, we're all still children. The real growth happens in the next life."

A gust of wind blew across us, catching my beard and long hair, and I gripped the ledge as my stomach dropped.

"Don't be so nervous. You're not going anywhere," he said, standing up. "But I am."

"Oh yeah? Where's that?"

"That remains to be seen. Do you ever wonder about gravity, Joe?" he asked, spreading his arms like wings and scooting his toes over the edge. "Why are we so drawn to earth?"

"Gravity draws us to one another as well," I replied. "Why don't you take a step back, Zeke?"

"It draws us to the thing with the greatest mass. What is there greater than the earth?"

"God, maybe? I don't know."

"Ah, yes. Can gravity explain then why we're drawn to God?"

He closed his eyes and spun in a circle. The wind whistled in my ears.

"If you're not careful, you'll learn very soon," I said. "Sit down, Zeke."

"God!" he called, his voice echoing off of the buildings around us, "Why do you bless us so, only to take those blessings away from us? What good could possibly come from this misery?"

He was shaking as he spoke to the sky, laughing and crying at the same time. He stumbled, nearly falling over.

"Zeke, sit!" I insisted. "You're too close to the edge, and I don't want to see you die tonight."

"O ye of little faith, don't you believe I can fly?"

He began flapping his arms, looking at me and then over the ledge. I didn't know what was happening. Granted, I had only known him a short time, but how could such a seemingly normal man have taken such a turn? What could possibly have driven him to that madness? I stood up and backed away, trying to coax him in the direction of the stairs.

"Let's go back down," I said. "You've lost it."

"Precisely my intention," he replied, turning away and looking into the night. "Would it be so bad? We all have to die someday."

"Don't do it, Zeke. Please."

"I didn't want to die alone."

"You don't have to."

"I'm not. Tonight's my night. Good-bye, Joe."

He stepped to the edge, closed his eyes, and took in a breath, and I saw him disappear in silence.

It happened too quickly for me to react, and I was left standing there in shock. I was speechless—frozen. The lights blurred. I heard screams from the street below.

I had never seen a person die before, and surely not by his own choice. It was, without a doubt, the most horrible thing I had ever witnessed. I vomited and collapsed onto the rooftop in a cold sweat. So many thoughts rushed through my head, mostly of Maria. Where was she then, as I was watching a man jump to his death? She was so far away. I thought of the marlin in my dreams.

I don't remember going down the stairs, but when I reached the street, I saw a crowd of people gathered. A path cleared, and out came two horses hitched to a cart upon which Zeke's limp body lay. They passed quickly, and between the heads in the crowd I could hardly see him, but I watched them disappear down the road. I sat on a nearby bench and put my face in my hands.

Some time later, I felt someone take a seat by my side.

"Can you believe that?" said a voice.

I was silent.

"He's lucky to be alive."

"What?" I asked, looking up at the man next to me.

"What are the odds that he would land directly on the canopy?"

I turned toward where Zeke had fallen and saw a hole in the canvas awning just over the front door of the restaurant and the blood spattered on the pavement below it.

"Where did they take him?" I asked.

"The hospital, I imagine," said the man, pointing in its direction.

Leaving him there on the bench, I ran as fast as I could. I scrambled into the lobby out of breath and asked where they had taken the man who had just fallen off a building. He was in surgery to repair several compound fractures and some internal bleeding, so I waited. I slept there in the lobby all night, forgetting the elegant hotel room that had been prepared for me free of charge.

In the morning, they said Zeke had been moved to a room for observation, and I was allowed to see him.

"Quite a night," I said when I came in. All four of his limbs were in casts, and there was a brace on his neck. His face was purple and swollen.

"Yeah," he replied, turning his eyes away from me.

"How are you feeling?"

"Hungover. And broken."

"You look it," I said with a laugh.

"This is where she died," Zeke said, looking around. "It happened shortly after the collapse, when we lost power. Somehow, when you lose someone you love like that, suddenly everything else you've lost doesn't matter."

I nodded.

"It's so hard to go on after that kind of loss. Sometimes I think life isn't worth living. I have to wonder why she was taken from me."

"Perhaps so that she would never have to feel the pain you're feeling."

"But so young?"

"I like to think that some people are just too graceful for God to leave in a world that often seems so far away from him. Sometimes he takes them back."

"I like that. She was that special to me."

"Someday you'll know."

"Yes, someday."

I left town with my horse that day, having never slept in that beautiful hotel room. The city was just as it had been when we had come into it. Nomad and I trotted past the restaurant from which Zeke had jumped, and they were outside patching the canopy. His blood had already been cleaned from the sidewalk.

15

COLORFUL BLESSINGS

Is it worse to be lost at the beginning or near the end of a long journey? In the desert, I decided to leave the highway and take what I thought was a short cut. Since I was not in a car, there was no reason we had to stay on the road, I thought. I had mapped out a new route for us through the desert and judged by the date on my watch that we could make it through the mountains to the city that had once been called Denver before the winter really got bad. How we ended up on the south side of the Colorado River, I still have no idea.

My determination to finish what I had begun was so intense that it blinded me to my periphery. By the time I realized that the Grand Canyon was supposed to be on my right side, not on my left, we would have wasted more time trying to correct the mistake than we would moving on as we were and making adjustments accordingly. I didn't remember crossing at the Hoover Dam, and I certainly had no recollection of a romp across the canyon. Yet there I was, within eyeshot of the path I knew I should have been on and unable to reach it. So close, yet so far away. I was dismayed at the discovery, to put it lightly. That mistake would be more costly than I realized at the time, putting us days behind where we would have been had we simply stuck to the old highways as planned. Sometimes only a few days, minutes, seconds, even, can mean the difference between life and death.

The air grew increasingly cool, but the colors of the day were hot. The sun bounced from the canyon walls, highlighting horizontal stripes in all shades of red, yellow, and orange. The nights, though, were so cold they struck fear even into the earth and transformed everything to deep blue and purple. I shivered in the frigid wind of the desert, wondering each night if the icy reaper would take me in my sleep. It felt as though my life were slipping away every time I closed my eyes. In the dead quiet darkness, I could fade into oblivion, my fate never to be known to a soul on earth.

Yet each day I awoke with the rising sun, rolled my bed, and packed it away on the back of my horse to continue on. The canyon was one of those sights that could never be adequately explained with words or justified by a photograph. Even seeing it with my own eyes, it was impossible to comprehend something so extraordinarily immense. It was breathtaking. Millions of years at work and it was still eroding and evolving, still not complete, and it never would be. The canyon is like humanity in that way.

My nightmares became worse as the nights passed. I dreamed that I had returned to the farm only to find it abandoned. There was no one waiting for me, yet the stream still flowed behind the cabin, and the birds still spoke from the trees.

Shadows crept across the landscape and canyon walls as the sun passed high in the sky. The brown vegetation quivered in the desert wind that drowned out the sound of the river rushing below. The terrain got rough. I could feel rocks slipping under Nomad's hooves as we hiked steep paths, but it never seemed to make him as nervous as it made me. It was a tense ride for a while. I tried to stay far enough from the canyon to keep us on flat ground, but its shape was serpentine with legs that sprawled miles from the main and left us with constant obstacles to work around.

As we climbed through one of those subsidiary gullies, we came across a mystical waterfall nestled within the landscape, as if it was kept a secret by some divine native culture. It spilled between the red canyon walls into a brilliant turquoise pool surrounded by lush green cottonwood trees and ferns that crawled across the vertical rock faces. A rainbow glowed in the mist above the pool and drew my eye to where it cascaded into a series of others and continued to flow down further into the canyon.

Beside the large pool, I saw a young couple in their midteens seated with their feet in the water. From where I stood on a cliff above I could hear their voices and their laughter faintly. I was momentarily puzzled. It was strange, I thought, to come across people in such an obscure and hidden place as that one, buried within the canyon and many miles from any civilization that I knew of. As curious as the situation seemed, I had grown so accustomed to hospitable people and it had been so long since I had experienced any hostility from my fellow man that I had no apprehensions about meeting those two. Nomad and I headed down toward them, and as we drew near, they heard us coming.

"Make haste, newcomer!" said the boy. "The hour is approaching! I've not yet found the chance to eat today, but I'm peering over the edge of consciousness. Join me."

"Oh, hush," said the girl. "We ate this morning."

"Peyote does not count as a meal."

I got down off my horse and walked to them, introducing myself.

"Where is this?" I asked, my eyes scanning the red walls towering around us, framing my view of the blue sky.

"Havasupai Reservation," said the girl. "Where are you from?"

"East of here. Just passing through."

"Did you take a wrong turn, or were you looking for the scenic route?"

"Wrong turn."

"Well join us anyway," said the boy.

"I need to keep moving," I said. "It's still light out, and I'm behind schedule."

"Wouldn't it be a shame to stumble upon something so beautiful merely by accident and leave without taking the time to enjoy it?"

It didn't take much to convince me. Besides, it was my best chance for a night of sleep indoors with warmth, assuming they had homes to go back to. I went into the water to cleanse myself of the filth I had accumulated along the way before meeting any more people. Then I stayed with them to dry in the sun beside the waterfall.

While the pair was clearly present physically, they seemed captivated by the world they shared, which was not quite the world as I knew it. My perception of the world had changed in a profound way, as had that of my new companions and undoubtedly every other soul on earth. Physically, it was the same place we shared, but conclusions I had drawn throughout my life had brought me to only one variation of everything it could be. I had come from a place far away. I had led a very different life, lived in a very different culture and a different time with a different education. I had traveled far, gathering wisdom, I could only hope. I had known love deeper than I could have ever anticipated and only truly understood its importance when it seemed so far away. Certainly their years, though fewer than mine, had taught them lessons very different from my own and different even from each other's.

I sat and watched awhile, marveling at the wonders of nature, something I had seldom done in my past life. Over the recent months, however, I'd had little else to do while on the road. It's amazing the things a person learns about the world around him when he takes the time to appreciate it. There is so much life and color and beauty, even in places where, at first glance, they may be overlooked.

Nomad stood nearby, so still that his coat camouflaged him with the canyon walls. A falcon soared overhead, searching the earth for prey. Above the pool, with the waterfall behind it, the rainbow hung perpetually in the air. It was truly a heavenly place. Experiences of such beauty before had always been fleeting. There had always been some place to be, some responsibility preoccupying me. I hadn't had the time to ponder such seemingly trivial things when there was progress to be made elsewhere.

I fell asleep in peace there by the waterfall. My teenage companions woke me later and invited me back to the village to join their tribe for a great feast. We followed a trail alongside a turquoise creek, which led eventually to the most remote town I had ever seen, surrounded by an earthen fortress. It was the sort of place that would never be found unless you knew exactly where to look. There was something magical about it all, as if I might turn my back and, in one moment, find that everything had vanished into thin air.

The village was populated by native people whose ancestors had called it home for hundreds of years before Europeans had ever set foot on this continent. They spoke English to me, but to each other they spoke a language as mysterious and beautiful as the world around us. In front of a church with a barrel roof and a stone façade were dozens of people at work, preparing and spreading a grand banquet on a yard of tables. They put me to work immediately. Whenever that happened, I never took it as an insult. That sort of greeting seemed to me more of a true invitation into a family and culture than simply serving me as a courtesy or charity. I never wanted to hear anyone say, "Sit back, relax, and have a meal on us." Taking anything for free did not come naturally. I didn't deserve to be served. Rather, more and more, I saw myself as a servant.

Looking around at the abundance of food before me, I remembered our weekly trips to the grocery store back home. Maria had always wanted my company, but Saturdays at the market had summoned my empathy for agoraphobes. Why had everyone chosen to do their shopping at the exact same moment that she had?

"What do you need to get?" I had asked in objection to our last-minute shopping trip before our last Thanksgiving dinner at home.

"I have a whole list. I'm not going to read it all off to you."

"So you expect me to follow you blindly to my doom?"

It used to be so easy to go to the store and buy food. There I was, ironically preparing to share my next Thanksgiving dinner on a Native American reservation with the very people whose ancestors had been robbed of their land so many years ago by foreigners like me. Still, their warm hospitality had not suffered. The feast before us was abundant, somehow even more so than it had ever seemed in the past, and it came in varieties to satisfy everyone present.

Despite the plentiful provisions before us, the people lived in simplicity. They had inherited the ways of their ancestors, hunting and farming the land, which provided all the sustenance they needed. Décor was natural and beautiful, but never excessive or grand. I remembered a time when Noah's family was moving and their old home had developed such an accumulation of useless junk that he had finally rented a roll-off trash container in order to clear it all out while everyone else was at work.

"I just need to get rid of all of it," he had said. "I feel like starting with a clean slate would be better than to keep throwing things away one by one to get to the good furniture." Those were problems we would one day look back on, cock our heads, and wonder how the human race had ever reached such a point.

The banquet rivaled that of the Cratchits' Christmas present. There were at least two hundred people, making it easily the largest family gathering I had ever been a part of; many were old, many were young, but all shared the place together. Before we ate they gave thanks, and I couldn't help but join them in the sentiment. Their respect for what they had been given was like the proverbial old man's for his fish. I wondered with whom I had more in common. Was I a fisherman, fighting with my life to catch that great creature, or had I all along been intended to be snatched from my natural environment, everything I had to offer taken to sustain the lives of fellow mortals?

We're all created to share this earth into which each of us will eventually return.

I felt the joy of home with those people, though everything about them and that place looked very different from the place I knew as home. I sat with Zach and Hannah, the boy and the girl I had met earlier, and with their families, all of whom were amazed by the tales of my travels. Sometimes I thought I was talking too much, but they kept asking more questions, eager to know every detail of what I had gone through. What captivated them most was what had happened at home during and immediately following the collapse. It had been very different there. They had seen it all on the news, of course. Tourists had stopped coming, and eventually they too had lost all of the amenities sourced in the world outside, but they had never been forced to leave. There had been nothing to run away from there. They had adapted to the change, and life had gone on.

"In the spirit of this day," Hannah asked, "what do you have to be thankful for, Joe?"

I smiled as I thought for a moment, and all eyes at the table turned to me. I thought of Maria first, the greatest blessing of my life, and of the rest of my family back home. I thought of all the wonderful people I had met along the journey and the generosity they had shown me. I thought of my horse, who had become a life-saving companion when there had been no one else to turn to. I thought of what I had learned about survival and self-sufficiency and about my improved physical capability that had resulted from a grueling existence, keeping me alive even when sustenance was scarce in the wilderness. I thought of the love I felt everywhere I went that seemed to burst from every color of the earth. I thought of the future that awaited me at home and of the purpose I had gained through the loss of some comforts and material possessions.

Then I said, "Everything."

Hannah smiled. "Me too," she said, and then she looked at Zach and took his hand.

"Me too," he said.

"Me too," said Zach's father. And then his mother echoed, and then across the table, Hanna's mother, father, sisters, and brothers. The chorus grew with every mouth on down. Parents, grandparents, and children. Their gratitude was as profound as it was true. What a blessing it is to simply recognize one's blessings. So seldom had I done that before. The things I'd had and the times I had suffered were all just the way it was; I didn't ask why. But life itself was a gift, along with everything that made for it, even those tribulations that had once seemed hopeless.

After the meal, I was given a bed by a warm fire and turned in early to take full advantage of it. That would be the best opportunity for sleep that I'd had in weeks and would have for weeks more. But exhausted though I was, I could not fall asleep that night. A mysterious anxiety overwhelmed me, and even with the bountiful meal that had filled my stomach, I was somehow starving. It seemed there was a hunger within me for something more, something greater than I had ever known. Perhaps, I thought, I was on a path to a place I had never intended to go.

Sometimes a person has to be lost in order to be found. Only by losing my way had I found the place where I learned to give thanks for my many blessings. Still though, that spirit, that God, the recipient of my thanks, remained a mystery to me. Although I didn't know that great power, I thought that I was beginning to understand its ways. Curiosity and longing were consuming me, almost literally, as that hunger in my stomach refused to subside. No matter how much food I digested, my suspicion was that it wouldn't until I had an answer as to what exactly I was still missing.

Despite my fatigue, my restless mind could not be put at ease. Quietly, so as not to wake my hosts, I crept outside to see the stars in that beautiful desert sky. I had followed them there on nights I couldn't sleep, using Jake's lessons to let them guide me. They always made me feel so small, yet so important to have any role at all in this great thing. I walked a path through the canyon foliage next to the turquoise stream and back to the waterfall where I had been earlier in the day, and I sat beside that pool again to absorb more of the mystical air of which I could not get enough. The sun would rise and fall and rise again, and the water would always flow. In the darkness, the falls looked like a white wall with a fog where it met the earth, and the crystal floor between that wall and me sparkled with reflections of the glowing moon and dancing stars.

Some time had passed when I began to hear sounds that transcended the spray of the falls before me, and the stream running beside. They were curious sounds, those of wild animals I had not seen in the day. I heard the distant howling of coyotes echoing from the canyon walls. Then came the hooting of an owl. I looked toward the cottonwood from where the sound had come, and I saw his dark figure on a branch high above, silhouetted by the moonlight. He left the branch and spread his wings, gliding in perfect silence across the night sky and coming to rest in a nearer tree, and what hung about him there took my breath away. There were dozens more like him, perched in silence, and they all seemed to be looking down upon me. What could they want, I wondered. What was their interest in me? I had never before seen such a great parliament of owls.

As I watched them, I heard a sandy sounding rattle, and I looked behind me to find a diamondback rattlesnake not more than a few feet away. I sprung to my feet and began backing slowly toward the water, hoping he would not follow. He stayed there, watching me like the owls overhead, the howling coyotes never ceasing. They were becoming louder, and I knew they were drawing near. Then came the sounds of pattering paws. They appeared at the rim of the canyon—a whole band of coyotes—and stopped there, looking down upon me as well. It was as if I were some wild spectacle out there, drawing critters from far and wide for a glimpse.

The snake's rattle ceased, but from the shadows behind him more approached in a winding slither, tracing the contours of the earth and the rocks. As I began to step back into the water, they stopped as if to request that I stay. It occurred to me then that perhaps they meant me no harm. But what had drawn them to me?

Between the snakes crawled dozens of desert scorpions that emerged from beneath the rocks like circus clowns from a Volkswagen. They would distract the snakes, I thought, and I could make my escape as they made their meal. What happened, though, was exceedingly odd. The snakes took no notice of the abundant game among them. Instead, predators and prey alike harmonized on the stage before me, and I realized that they were not my audience, but rather I was theirs. There was a percussion of rattles and paws and tiny feet—songs of hoots and howls—a grand performance of nature in profusion before me. It was mysterious and strange, and I suddenly felt a spiritual connection with each of those creatures. I was no longer fearful. I stepped from the water again and took a seat on the red ground to watch the glory of the earth unfold.

Next thing I knew, I was waking up beside the embers that remained from the night's fire back in the room I had been given to sleep in. The sun was up. I had not felt so alive and refreshed since I could remember, nor so excited to resume my journey. Perhaps that feeling itself should have left me with reservations, suspicions, even, but at the time, I saw it as yet another blessing. I read Maria's letter again, as I had hundreds of times by then, and it only excited me more. I couldn't wait to see her again. My desire was so great that I ignored the warnings of the people who insisted that heading into the mountains alone that time of year was a foolish undertaking. Rather, I was inspired by something within that I thought divine. Nothing would stop me. Nothing *could* stop me. I shared a final meal with my hosts, thanked them for their hospitality, and set off with Nomad toward the rising sun.

16

FAITH

Snow began to fall about the time the mountains came into view, a few days northeast of my last sighting of another person. Days and nights passed as we began to rise, but it didn't let up. A bit of precipitation, though, could not discourage me. I was determined. Nomad, however, seemed for the first time more anxious than I.

"Come on, my friend," I would say. "We're going home. Just over the mountains and across the plains." Even the sound of my voice didn't seem to ease him. His anxiety grew with our elevation.

By then, we had found the road again, though it wasn't long before I only knew it by the path cut through the pine trees. The pavement was covered in a steadily accumulating layer of snow. The sky turned gray, and the frigid wind began to pick up, which slowed us down. I was growing hungry, a feeling surely shared by my horse, but food had become scarce as the winter had overtaken the mountains. Once again, my ambition had gotten the better of me.

It got bad quickly. What began as a light dusting was soon one of the worst blizzards I had ever experienced, and there was no place to turn for shelter. We had no choice but to move on. Nomad was noticeably burdened by my weight in that weather, so I dismounted to walk beside him. Our footprints disappeared in the snow and wind almost immediately behind us, and the road ahead continued upward.

I couldn't help but blame myself for the position we were in. After all, it was my own arrogant mistake that had put us there when had I insisted upon leaving the path paved for us to roam the unfamiliar desert without truly knowing the way. Had we stayed on course, we would have reached old Denver on the other side of the Rockies by then, perhaps even the plains.

The thick clouds and blowing snow blocked the sun in a way that made it difficult to discern night from day. The world was always black and white with shades of gray. But even at night, the white ground helped us to see where we were going. We were exhausted, but if we were to stop for too long, the cold might have killed us, so we kept moving.

"Don't worry, my friend," I repeated again and again. "It's just over the mountains."

Finally, after days of hiking up and down through constant atmospheric torment and sleeping briefly in hollows I had dug in snowdrifts, I saw a dark spot through the falling snow in a wall of the mountain. We made our way to it and found that it was a cave, not exceedingly deep but tall enough for us both to fit without much effort. Inside was little relief from the cold, but at least we had escaped the wind and snow. I could feel my cheeks again. Strangely, within the cave I found a hoard of dry wood that I assumed had been stored there by a previous passer through the area. I started a fire and lay down to rest for the night.

I was half-asleep when I heard Nomad's hooves shuffle nervously. Outside the clouds separated, momentarily framing a pitch-black and heavenly white painting of the glowing moon cut in half by the silhouette of the mountains we had already passed over. As if imitating the growling of my own stomach, I heard what I thought was Nomad's hunger speaking.

"We'll find food soon," I whispered. "I'm sure of it."

Just as the separation in the clouds began to close again, I saw the glint of two eyes outside the mouth of the cave. My empty stomach became ill as fear washed over me. They were the eyes of a demon, I thought. The eyes of death looking upon us. I reached slowly for my knife and gripped it tightly, its blade by then dull and chipped from so many months of slicing meat, carving bone, whittling wood, prying stone, and clearing foliage. My hands trembled from cold or terror; I'm not sure which. Whatever it was stayed watching awhile, as I watched back.

In such a state of exhaustion, just keeping my eyes open was laborious. Though my soul sustained the will to live, my eyes had nearly given up. Sometimes the mind gives up before the body. Sometimes the body leads the mind to its demise. It's strange how the two so often seem to work independently of one another. The eyes outside, though, were intent and alert, and there was no question in my mind that I would be forced to face the beast, whatever it was. It could be moments, it could be days, but it was only a matter of time.

I clutched the knife, preparing for the strike, but the more I considered the present circumstance, the more I questioned the wisdom of waiting. On the defensive, I was at a disadvantage, I thought. Surely suffering the winter's famine as much as I, those eyes saw me as prey. They needed me weak and vulnerable, and they were as desperate as I was to stay alive. If I'm facing a fight, I must face it head on, I thought, and I crept slowly into an offensive stance, guarding my territory and protecting my horse in his weakened state. A sort of primal instinct came over me, and the fear I had felt transformed to the methodical plan of a predator hunting prey.

We sprang at the same moment, the eyes and I, falling to the snow in vicious combat just outside the mouth of the cave. The black and white world was sprayed with red as teeth and claws fought steel, and from the woods, more glowing eyes emerged. Sounds of snarling, howling, neighing, and screaming echoed from the cave walls, silencing as soon as they hit the snow outside. What saved my life, I believe, was that the first wolf had his eyes on my horse for his meal.

I don't know how many there were, but the rest of the pack continued to attack after the first lay dead in the snow. Two went after Nomad as he reared and neighed, and I sprung to his defense, slashing wildly at any beast that drew near. As the pressure of teeth sunk into the frozen numbness of my arm, I dropped my knife. Two more wolves came after my legs and torso, and more surrounded as I fell to the ground, trying to fight them off. They ripped my clothes and gnawed at my flesh, my world of vision blurred by powder-coated fur. With my left fist, I struck the snout of the wolf on my right arm, and he released long enough for me to grab my knife from the snow. Then he came after the arm that had betrayed him. They tore at me from all directions.

I had but one bladed hand to fight wave after wave of hungry predators, and try as I might to fight for survival, my fate, I thought, had been sealed. The rush of adrenaline began to fade, and my body went limp like the exhausted gazelle at the rear of the herd. For a moment, as I accepted my fate, the sounds of war were silenced. In the snow falling from above, I saw Maria's face looking down upon me with that beautiful smile.

"Not yet," I heard her say. "Not yet."

Suddenly, I heard the pounding of hooves and distressed yelping as Nomad trampled two of the wolves attached to me, and I felt my blood pump through the pits left by their teeth as they disappeared into the woods. Others backed away, standing watch and waiting for a moment to strike again. My horse circled in my defense, fending them off until only one remained. With a final stab of my knife, the last wolf on my arm had had enough, and he followed the rest of the pack as they left me lying again in the cold quiet of the snowy night.

Nomad somehow emerged unscathed. I, on the other hand, was covered in gashes and puncture wounds by the time the sounds of howling and yelping faded into the distance. My clothes were black with blood, as much mine as my foes'.

At least we had our meal; the first wolf had been left for us. Nomad was not much of a meat eater, but we had no other options then. The beast would fill our stomachs and keep us going for at least a few more days. I lay in wait through the night, just in case the pack decided to return. The next morning I cut up the meat, and we ate again by the fire and then left it burning there as we set off again. I found myself looking up, giving thanks for the sustenance and asking for guidance through the rough terrain ahead. Through the pain of my wounds, I limped on, feeling the blood leaking from them and running down my body beneath my clothes. It was caked onto my skin, freezing red before it could dry black. A gash on my neck. Punctures in my torso. The signature of a full mouth of teeth on both arms and my right thigh. I hoped that the cold would slow the flow, but it could not go on for long, I thought. I would die from the loss of blood before the winter killed me. Behind me, a short trail of pink snow and footprints showed where we had been.

Two days later, we were famished again, and somehow the deadly cold blizzard raged on. Starvation was an adversary I had come to know well. I had become quite good at simply putting it out of my mind, but that only works for so long. We kept moving, me limping along even more slowly beside my horse, and I began to wonder if the snow would ever cease. I had taken the coat of the wolf, which Nomad and I wore in turns, but even that barely retained the warmth of life.

The place reminded me of an article I had once read about a Russian family that had fled to a remote woodland part of Siberia some time before World War II. After losing his wife, this man and his two daughters and son lived out there without any other human contact, surviving by scavenging for food. They hunted without weapons, tracking their prey until the prey gave up and lay down, and they nearly starved over the length of many lonely winters. Forty years they sustained together in the tiny cabin they had built before a team of geologists from an oil company happened to pass over in a helicopter while scouting the land. During all that time, the family knew nothing of world events and international affairs. Within a few months of being introduced to modern "civilization," the father, the son, and one of the daughters had died, and rather than integrate into society, the surviving daughter chose to return to the Siberian wilderness. That was the last anyone saw of her.

I feared then that the frozen wilderness might hold my fate as well. My toes were numb inside my shoes, and I suspected that they were frostbitten. Perhaps I might lose them. I kept the wolf's fur tight around me, and I wondered if there was another soul up there with us somewhere, suffering the same as we were. Perhaps I was not the only man so foolish. Even my horse knew better, but he had trusted that I knew the way.

"I'm sorry, my friend," I said to him, "but it's too late to turn back now." He knew it, and we pushed on.

How deep was the snow beneath my feet?

How low were the clouds above my head?

How far was Heaven from the top of the mountain? Had I reached the summit of Olympus? Was I among the gods?

It was Nomad who collapsed first, his massive body crashing into the snow beside me, leaving a white puff as though the precipitation fell upward for the moment. In my next step, I did the same. We lay there face to face, hearing only sounds of heavy breath and wind, freezing and starving to death, and as I stared into his black eyes, my thoughts drew me to that sunny weekend at the farm just before it had all begun. Before the markets had melted down and the world as we knew it had been lost forever. Those last few days when I had thought life was perfect, and I'd found everything I would ever need. I saw Maria lying out there by the stream behind the cabin, the yellow sunlight beaming from her fair skin. The beautiful, contented smile on her face. I saw her head turn when she noticed I was watching her, and she sat, propped on her elbow, and lifted her sunglasses to look back at me.

We gazed at each other across a short distance awhile, saying everything that needed to be said without words at all. Then, as if to provoke some climax, her lips spoke in silence, "I love you."

This was it. The end of it all. My death would not be entirely in vain. I had accomplished what I had set out for. The system was working, and perhaps the recipient of the final piece of mail I still carried had already received the same word from the writer back east. I regretted the risks I had taken. I had been too impatient to wait for winter to pass before taking on the Rockies, and that impatience had brought me to my ultimate demise. I was broken. Such a short time ago, I had been certain that I would see my wife and family again so soon, but how wrong I had been. I'd been doomed from the start. The day I had left so many months ago would be the last I ever saw of my wife.

You had better come back to me.

Though I may have succeeded in my service to the New World Mail Network, I had failed my wife in the most profound way. How long, I wondered, before she replaced me? Would she ever? More likely she would wait years, alone as her hair turned gray; alone as her skin wrinkled; alone as her bones became brittle and the frame of her body shrunk. She would wait, every day watching and wishing for my return. Then, eventually, she would die even more alone than I was at that moment, still with the question of my fate unanswered, and it was all my fault.

I love you more than you'll ever know. I'll always wait for you.

Her voice spoke the words she had written, echoing in my head as I lay dying in the snow. I looked at my horse, the moisture freezing in his nostrils. Tears turned to ice on my cheeks.

"I love her so much," I said to him. I coughed blood, and I could see the snow darkening around my head as it ran from my mouth. "I'm sorry I took you here, but you couldn't understand. You trusted me, and I failed you too."

I turned my eyes to the sky and spoke, choking on the fluid in my throat.

"They say you work in mysterious ways," I said, "but I've never felt so betrayed. If you're out there, how could you have let this happen? What good is everything I've learned now? How could you have me come so far only to die alone in the woods so distant from my home? Why have you abandoned me?"

Perhaps I was waiting for an answer, but I didn't say anything else. We lay there in silence for a time that felt endless. My breathing slowed. Nomad closed his eyes. The world around us was quiet as the gray clouds passed overhead, and my body was slowly absorbed by the snow.

†

"Look, he's opening his eyes."

"All right, children, why don't you go outside and play? Build us a snowman. Make some angels. Someone add a log to the fire on the way out."

"I'll do it. And I'll get him something to eat."

"Yes, I'm sure he's starving."

"The venison? Some bread and cheese? And sweet potatoes?"

"Yes, and some water. Not too cold."

"OK, don't let him move too much. He'll tear the stitches. Does he need another pillow?"

"I'll ask him."

"OK, I'll be back with the food. Let's go, children."

I heard small feet tapping on the floor and soft innocent voices as they left the room. It hurt to open my eyes. The snow had stopped, and a bright white light beamed in through the windows of the cabin. A woman was sitting next to the bed with a joyful smile on her face, watching over me.

"Is this Heaven?" I asked.

"Unfortunately not. Do you need another pillow?"

"No, thank you," I struggled to say.

"Comfortable?"

"Yes."

"Good. Just rest. We'll take care of you."

I lifted my arm to look at the date on my watch, but it was no longer on my wrist, and I realized I had lost it during my fight with the wolves.

"Stay still," she said. "You don't want to open your wounds again. It was tough enough to stop the bleeding the first time."

"What day is it?"

"Christmas Eve. Our hunters found you buried in the forest on their way to their 'lodge.'" She laughed. "It's really just a cave where they sleep when they're out on long trips. You were on their path. They only saw you because of the red snow everywhere. What were you doing out there all alone?"

"Trying to get home."

"Well, you'll want to stay here until the weather warms up. I'm Elizabeth."

"I'm Joe."

One of the other voices I had heard came back into the room with a plate of food and a pitcher of water. She was a bit older than the other.

"You're awake," she said. "I was beginning to wonder if we might have to take you back and bury you again. I'm Ruth."

"Don't say things like that to strangers, Mom," said Elizabeth. "People will think you're crazy."

"Nonsense," Ruth replied. "My humor is rare and precious."

Elizabeth shook her head and turned back to me as I finished off the water that her mother had brought and shoveled food into my mouth. "Slow down," she said. "I know you're starving, but your stomach can't handle that much at once."

I took a breath then and looked at her before asking the question, the answer to which I was afraid to hear.

"Was my horse OK?"

But her reply was not what I expected. She looked at me inquisitively, and she asked, "What horse?"

"The one that was lying next to me."

"You were alone when they found you."
"I was alone?"
"Yes."
"There was no impression? No tracks?"
"No, nothing like that."

I leaned back again and closed my eyes, and I fell back asleep.

I awoke a second time hours later to the sweet sound of song. I was alone then, the sun was setting, and the voices of carolers just outside graced the room with soft angelic echoes. "God Rest Ye Merry Gentlemen"—"Little Drummer Boy"—"Silent Night." The first thing I thought of was the letter from the east, and I looked around the room for my satchel. In a corner by the fireplace it lay upon a chair, its leather glowing orange on one side and purple on the other.

Without a doubt, I knew I was in good company there. They had saved my life, a life so desperately in need of saving. At that time two years earlier, I had been nine hundred miles away, hunkered with my family by a fire and burning everything we owned just to stay warm. I had been without hope and devoid of purpose. Confused and terrified. Weak. Helpless. So many words could describe the feelings that overcame me then, none of them good. And two years later, though many of them still applied to my current state, hopeless, somehow, was not one. No, it was hope that had kept me alive, even in those moments when all had seemed lost.

My mind fumbled with the possibilities that could explain the mysterious disappearance of my horse. My fears of losing him had been realized, and fault fell upon me alone. As if it were a punishment for those choices that had led to that dreadful loss, I was fated to finish my journey on foot and alone. No friends. No family. Still, though all logic directed me to presume him dead, it was inexplicable that his body had not been found next to mine—that there had not even been a sign. Somehow, I felt I had not seen the last of my friend, the nomad.

Elizabeth came into the room again and asked how I was feeling.

"I'm OK," I said. "A little better."

"Good."

"Any sign of my horse?"

"No, I'm sorry."

I sighed. "I'd like to go outside."

"Why? It's so cold."

"I'd like to hear the carolers better."

"All right," she smiled.

She wrapped my body tightly in a leather cummerbund to keep my stitches in place. Then I took her hand and stumbled out of the bed before putting on some warm clothes that had been brought in for me.

We stepped out the door into the snow, and when I looked up from the stoop, the sight of the snow-blanketed mountain village was breathtaking. Hundreds of log cabins spread throughout a meadow, a black, white, and green forest of aspens and firs surrounding it. Windows glowed orange with firelight, and red ribbons hung on every door. Handmade ornaments adorned the trees. People walked the snow-covered paths holding candles, wearing smiles, and singing, all bundled warmly in scarves and hats. They would step aside for horse-drawn sleighs that left tracks and hoof prints winding between cabins. Children built snowmen and ran laughing, rolling in the frozen white powder. It was a winter wonderland as I'd always imagined but had never seen.

The sky was deep indigo and so clear that I thought I could see every star out there. What was left of the sunlight sprayed purple stripes across the snow as it fell behind the trees to the west. We followed a pillar of smoke in the distance and walked to a place that seemed to be the center of the village where a large bonfire burned, surrounded by villagers swaying arm in arm and singing Christmas carols. It all brought a smile to my face. For a brief time, I forgot the loss of my horse, the trials of my journey, and even the desperate longing for my home and family. Dare I say, I was happy?

It was there, standing among those joyful people, that I began to realize the importance of faith.

Why is it that, whether suffering the burden of something terrible or reveling in wonderful news, even a person without faith is compelled to ask, "Why has this happened?" Is it because, in our hearts, we know there is a reason? In everything I had been through, perhaps God had not abandoned me after all. I watched their fire burn like a passionate heart—resilient, persistent, consuming the fuel of life and bringing warmth to all who open themselves up to it. I wished for my own heart to emulate that fire. I looked back at the person I had once been, and I felt ashamed. That passion for life had been lacking in my own, and I somehow felt more whole having lost all of the items I had collected and used to define a life past. Perhaps the true meaning of life, I thought, contrary to everything I had once known, resides all around and within us. We just have to search for it.

"Seek and you will find," said Elizabeth as we stood watching the fire.

"I've been seeking a long time."

"And what have you found?"

"Something. I'm not sure yet."

She smiled and said, "Then keep looking."

So I did. From that moment, I absorbed everything I could about that joyous place as I spent the evening with them in celebration, and it dawned on me that they were no different from the people anywhere else I had been. What was it, then, that had suddenly brought that wave of joy into my own life? Was it the simple fact that I was still alive, or was it the knowledge that even in the worst of times, I was never as alone as I had thought?

The celebration continued into Christmas the next day. We ate and danced and sang hymns and carols, and we prayed. I wondered silently why, though I had never really opposed the presence God, I had reserved my time and thoughts for things deemed more imminently important.

Perhaps it was because I'd had doubts, and I had not wanted to waste the one life I had revolving on an axis of something, someone, that might not even exist. But more and more, as I saw the good in humanity, those doubts were fading. People had come together with love so profound that it would have been called a miracle in the old world.

By the evening, I was exhausted from all I had absorbed that day, and we made our way back to Elizabeth's home. Over yet another Christmas feast, I explained what I had been doing in the mountains—that I was headed to Denver to deliver a letter.

"What's the name?" she asked. "A lot of us here came from Denver."

I took the envelope from my satchel and handed it to her, and I watched her eyes widen when she read the name. She slowly lifted her head and looked at me.

"I know him," she said.

I cocked my head and eyed her with suspicion.

"You met him today," she went on.

"That's not possible," I said.

"Why?"

"It just isn't."

"Are you walking OK?" she asked.

"Yes."

"Let's take it to him."

"Now?"

"Yes."

She handed the envelope back to me, and I slipped it safely back into my satchel. The two of us donned our winter garb and headed back out into the snow. The festivities outside seemed never ending, and even as the sun set yet again, the merriment continued to glow like the fire that was still burning in the center of the village, its light still bouncing from the happy eyes and rosy cheeks of the smiling faces around it. I followed Elizabeth that way, and we drew into the crowd of neighbors huddled closely together to keep each other warm. They ate from steaming cups of delicious stew, still sharing stories and laughter.

Elizabeth began asking around for a man named "Adam." I had met so many people over the last day that I could hardly remember each of their names, though I had done my best, and I searched my memory for one named Adam. Nothing came to mind. I thought that peculiar; I had always made a point to remember the names of people I met. It was good practice, not just in business but also in life, and by then I had accumulated so many names and faces that my list could rival that of a small country's census.

When Elizabeth finally found Adam, I heard her call to him from the distance. She pulled me through the crowd to a bearded old man who reminded me of Abraham back home. I recognized his face as soon as I saw him, and I knew why I had not remembered his name. It was because he had been introduced to me simply as "our pastor."

"Adam, do you remember Joe?" she asked him.

"Of course I do," he replied with a smile.

"Well, he's got a story you wouldn't believe."

His smile grew, and he motioned for us to follow him. Adam led us to another cabin, where he lived, and the three of us sat down next to a warm fire. The cabin was sparsely furnished but still cozy. Old worn books were strewn throughout, along with a stack of his own journals that rested in a corner on the floor. The air smelled of freshly baked bread.

"All right, Joe," said Adam, "let's hear this story."

"Before I begin," I replied, "I have something to give you."

"You do?"

"I do," I said as I again pulled the envelope from my satchel, delivering it finally to its recipient, who had unknowingly awaited its delivery for some months—so long that they had felt like a lifetime to me. The moment it left my fingertips, my job had been fulfilled. It was the last act in my career with the New World Mail Network, and one in which I still take pride. What I had been a part of for that brief time of my life was a wonderful and beautiful thing that would ultimately grow to benefit and serve every soul on earth. That was my contribution to the evolution of humanity, one that, though perhaps more suited for a bedtime story, was no more or less important than those made by the billions of others who walked the planet with me. We had suffered together, and together we would overcome.

As Adam took the envelope from me, his hands began to tremble. He stared at the handwriting on the front awhile before opening it and unfolding the pages. He read silently, his eyes beginning to water, page after page quivering between his fingers as he turned through them. Tears rolled slowly down his cheeks. It was as if he were holding his breath. Elizabeth and I sat still, watching him in equal silence, waiting for him to finish. When he reached the end of the last page, he finally released a sigh and took a breath, and then he looked up at me.

"You've given me the greatest Christmas gift I've ever received," he said.

I never knew what was written in that letter or Adam's relationship to its writer, but he insisted that I spend the rest of my time in the mountain village with him. I took up residence at his cabin for nearly two months. During that time, not a day went by that the sun didn't grace us with unobstructed light and warmth, but the beautiful white snow never melted.

I opened my mind to learn from Adam, and through his lessons, I began to cultivate a newfound faith based on that love that, though I had witnessed it everywhere, I was only beginning to understand. It was eternally simple, yet at the same time eternally complex, breaking the barriers of physics and anatomy to touch the divine. It was a gift from God, he said, that reached beyond what could be observed and proven into a spiritual realm that could not. Love and compassion are among the most basic human emotions, far more prevalent within most of us than competition and violence, yet those were the things that had seemed to dominate life in the old world. Some might have attributed that to a decreasing faith in God and an increasing faith in the individual, but humans are naturally flawed beings in the flesh. None of us is self-sufficient, and pretending otherwise does nothing but separate us from one another, from our past, and from what our future has the potential to be. As we had continued down that path, it had become more and more difficult to see where we'd begun. Ancient civilizations had had a grasp on this truth that seemed to have been lost when we started craving "progress," but love is the one and only thing that can truly fulfill any person. It is a need that every one of us shares, and as much as we may try to fill the void with synthetic things, deep down, we know there is no substitute.

We're all drawn to God, Adam said, though sometimes we may not want to admit it. Regardless of where we come from, the color of our skin, or the kind of music we listen to, we all find beauty in nature. It's universal. And we each harbor our own ideas about the best way to hold a relationship with the divine, if we hold one at all. Those of one may not suit the next, but perhaps that's the way it's meant to be. After all, if everyone shared the same customs and beliefs and the same interpretations, what would be our purpose here? If we already knew all the answers, what could we learn from one another? Where would we find the opportunity to grow? There is one thing, though, on which most of us agree despite the differences in our origins, and that is that God is love.

My own way was found there in the mountains, where I began to learn about God as they knew him, and I opened the "good book," as they called it, that Adam gave me on Christmas Day. Beginning the first day, as

I read passages with that vast congregation, the raging hunger within me only grew. I felt an exhilarating rebirth of my soul, and gradually I became more at ease, more at peace, and more willing to accept life as it came to me. There was so much more to it than I had ever opened my mind to. I let go of the past and my want for worldly possessions, and rather, I craved a spiritual life I had never before known.

Two years earlier, Christmas had brought me a new home at the farm. This one brought me a new home spiritually. Between the two had been a journey that would forever shape the ways of my life. From that moment, I was to embark on a new journey: a life devoted to love and enlightenment. It was as if my wounds had been healed, both those physical and emotional. Although I could still see the stitched and bandaged holes in my flesh, I began moving again without pain.

Adam's teachings of faith brought me comfort in trying times, though not every day came as easily as the first. My mood swung constantly between overjoyed and deeply anxious. On the one hand, I wanted nothing more than to be home with Maria, but it was still far too dangerous to leave in the winter and face another storm. Yet despite my lack of options, there was a kind of peace about the place that I had never before experienced. The book from which Adam derived all of his wisdom contained an answer for every woe.

When he could see I was nervous and missing home, he would say, "Can you add an hour to your life by worrying?

Don't worry about tomorrow—it'll worry about itself. Each day has enough trouble of its own. Have faith."

That was the refrain with which he ended every thought and concluded every departure. "Have faith," he would say. "Don't lean on your own understanding. There are great things happening that we don't yet know."

I did my best to have faith, as he said, and the more I heard those words, the more real they became. I studied daily with Adam, learning his interpretations of ancient tales. He taught of a healthy lifestyle, including foods and recipes, derived from the same stories and parables that enriched us spiritually. They were full of lessons applicable to every facet of life on earth.

"God knows we'll face trouble, Joe," Adam said. "You and I and everyone else with whom we share this world. But remember, He'll never leave us. He's always present, even when we refuse to accept Him. So cast all your anxiety away. Send it up above, and find peace in where you are now. You're never alone. Have faith."

The days I spent there were quiet, and even in the dead of winter, all of our needs were fulfilled. We had food. We had warmth. We had shelter. Most of all, we had each other. The relief almost didn't seem real after what I had been through when I had thought I was alone. Though the majority of my time was spent with Adam, there was not a passing between sunrise and sunset that I didn't see Elizabeth at least once. She was always watching over me. We ate together and shared stories of the past and of our families, with whom we would all soon be reunited. Had I not been so desperate to see my own, I would have certainly enjoyed a longer stay in the mountains. Life and time, though, interfered, as they so often do.

Eventually the weather grew warmer, and the day came for me to head back to the road. I knew it the morning when I awoke, suddenly restless yet again, as if I'd been inspired by a vision in my sleep that had slipped away when I had opened my eyes. It was time to go home. Adam also knew it when he arose to find me wide-awake by the fire at dawn.

"I'll make breakfast before you set off," he said, and Elizabeth joined us for my last meal in the village.

I had come to accept that my horse would not be accompanying me home, but I hoped that he was still somewhere out there, wandering—still a nomad on an endless search for something greater. The people of the village offered another horse to complete the journey, but I could not accept that generosity. I knew they needed her as much as I did, and there could be no replacing my own. I would walk, laden no longer with the cargo I had carried all that way. No knife. No bow, and no arrow. No fishing pole. My map and the journal I had been keeping to log the days and track my stops were gone, taken by the winter. Instead, I carried the one item that had been found with my drained body in the snow: my satchel. Inside were the letter from Maria and the old, worn Bible.

"Take care of yourself," Elizabeth said as I prepared to depart.

"I will."

"And come back to visit. In the spring next time."

I laughed and turned to Adam.

"Thank you," I said. "You've also given me the greatest Christmas gift I've ever received."

"Have faith," he replied, smiling.

I was the Prodigal Son, headed home with a new understanding of the foolishness of my old ways and an enlightened sense of life and its purpose. That purpose was, put simply, to love.

17

LOVE

"And now these three remain: faith, hope and *love*. But the greatest of these is *love*."

"*Love* is patient, *love* is kind. It does not envy, it does not boast, it is not proud. It is not rude, it is not self-seeking, it is not easily angered, it keeps no record of wrongs. *Love* does not delight in evil but rejoices with the truth. It always protects, always trusts, always hopes, always perseveres. *Love* never fails."

"Therefore *love* is the fulfillment of the law."

"Dear friends, let us *love* one another, for *love* comes from God. Everyone who *loves* has been born of God and knows God."

"You have heard that it was said, 'You shall *love* your neighbor and hate your enemy.' But I say to you, *love* your enemies and pray for those who persecute you, so that you may be sons of your Father who is in Heaven. For He makes His sun rise on the evil and on the good, and sends rain on the just and on the unjust."

"Hatred stirs up dissension, but *love* covers over all wrongs."

"Dear children, let us not *love* with words or tongue but with actions and in truth."

"*Love* is as strong as death."

"*Love* the Lord your God with all your heart and with all your soul and with all your mind."

"Give thanks to the Lord, for the Lord is good. His steadfast *love* endures forever."

"Whoever does not *love* does not know God, because God is *love*."

I read as I walked with my face down toward the road, and the more I read, the more I realized that the book I had been given was not at all the book I had once thought it was. In all honesty, I had been afraid to open it—afraid of what it might say. My assumptions had been made of ignorance, based on the religious radicals who were only so prominent because they screamed the loudest. The meek are seldom heard, but their truth is so much simpler. You cannot tell people they need God and expect them to listen and understand. What you *can* do is show them His love. This, I learned, was not a book of judgment or of vengeance. Its words would never justify bigotry or hatred. Rather, it was an evolving epic series based on one central concept—love—the word appearing hundreds of times within and as a consistent theme throughout the many testaments, parables, psalms, and letters composed by dozens of authors over a course of several centuries.

The walk was much slower on two feet than four, but those pages kept me occupied as I shuffled on. They kept me sane as the ground leveled out and the seemingly endless plain lay ahead. They kept me hopeful as the weather warmed and the days lengthened. The long road behind me had delivered great knowledge and, I hoped, great wisdom as well. Wisdom and knowledge are two very different things. It is common for a person to possess one without the other, but often we assume that a person abundant with one is abundant with both. It can be a dangerous assumption, leading us in our naïvety to believe untruths spoken by people we trust. Of those two virtues, we must ask which is more important.

I watched the crops begin to pop up from the ground on either side of the road. Grass began to green, and trees filled out with leaves. Food became more abundant as vegetation came to life. Animals came out of hibernation, and the world sprang anew, as it always had. The flowers are always blooming somewhere. Under both clear blue skies and the dark clouds of springtime storms I walked, day after day, homeward bound. The sun of the next day would dry me from the previous day's rain, and though it would inevitably rain again, the sun would always return. I passed flat fields with farmhouses, silos, and windmills. Hay bales spread across gently rolling hills. Herds of cattle. Wild horses. I would hear the patter of hooves from behind and watch as they passed by with magnificent beauty and speed, and I would smile and keep on walking, just another creature of the earth. All of that was juxtaposed by billboards still strewn along the sides of the road, then falling apart and falling down. The green signs divulging my distance from this city or that city were beginning to fade and rust. I wondered how long it would be before there was no longer any evidence remaining of the old world. Someone once told me that if humans suddenly vanished from the face of the earth, it would be ten thousand years before everything we had left behind was gone. What if, I wondered, we initiated the revolution on our own and then stuck around to watch it unfold?

There was one particular horse I noticed, from a distance at first. She looked familiar somehow when I saw her watching me, walking warily alone through the tall grass of an adjacent field, glancing over toward me occasionally as if to ensure that her path mirrored mine. She followed from early morning until I made my bed in the grass to sleep while she observed from across the road. Her company was comforting, reserved though it may have been. She remained at a distance the first day, but on the second I saw no sign of her. As I moved east, I scanned the surrounding landscape from sunrise to sunset, hoping that she might return, but she seemed to have made her own way, so I continued on mine a bit lonelier.

The next day, to my great delight, she appeared again in the distance; and again the next, drawing a bit nearer each morning. In a week or so, she reluctantly made her way onto the road, on the opposite side first, and then she crossed the median over to mine. When I would stop, she would stop. When I would eat, so would she. When I would wake, she would be waiting there, her shadow shielding my eyes from the sun. The longer she stayed with me, the fonder I grew of her presence, though I still could not make sense of it. She was not threatening, but rather she seemed curious about me, perhaps even more so than I was about her. Mostly I wondered why she felt so familiar. I had never seen the mare before, but her seemingly omniscient eyes reminded me of Nomad's. It was as if she were watching over me.

As we walked together, I began speaking to her. "Good morning," I greeted her as each day began, and she would reply with a nicker. I would tell her tales of my travels. It kept me occupied and reminded me of where I had been, the things I had done, and the people I had met and grown to love. She was eager to listen. Sometimes we walked in silence, and that was OK too.

"What brought you here?" I asked rhetorically one evening as the sun was setting behind us.

As if on cue, I began to hear voices in the distance, carried by the thin evening air—singing voices. I looked toward a far-off wheat field standing tall, having not been harvested the previous season, where thousands of tiny yellow lights glowed and flickered in the gentle breeze. As the night fell, we drew closer, the lights growing brighter and the voices stronger. I left the road and the horse followed, headed into the golden field shining in the moonlight.

The harmonizing vocals of "Hallelujah" seemed to seep between the stalks as I pushed them aside to make a path. The grain grew taller than my head, blocking out any view but that of the stars above. Through it I was drawn by the sound of a simple song in a simple place, both eternally beautiful even without the compliment of one another. I was quiet with my steps—as quiet as I could be—the horse following as delicately as possible.

We came to a clearing where the wheat ended, overlooking a vast meadow of gentle hills. There, spread across the meadow, was an astounding sight: an immense circle of people—thousands of them, maybe tens of thousands—all holding candles and swaying together as they sang. Those on the rim opposite me were so far away that they were invisible, except for the tiny flames flickering in front of each of them. From the center resonated a magnificent sound, where all of the voices projected to a single point around which they all orbited. Only by listening from that single point could one truly comprehend it all, but finding myself near enough to feel it and hear it from any perspective, I could at least begin.

I emerged and began to walk the circle's perimeter, the mare still close behind. No heads turned to inquire as to our presence. It was as if not a soul noticed us, too entranced by their own song to be distracted by anything outside of the perfection and beauty of their world. The light of their candles cast their shadows behind them, betraying no flaw, no gender, no race or religion, and no evil or pain. Each was of equal value, fitting into its own perfect place as part of a sum greater than its individual parts. Without any one, the circle would have been broken.

I wandered through their shadows for what seemed like miles in the dim light of the candles and the moon. The wheat on the other side of me began to sway as the night breeze suddenly picked up, and just then, a separation appeared between two of those shadows next to me. I stopped and gazed through the opening they had created, directly between them to that single point in the center of the meadow. They did not move back, nor did they turn to look at me. All just stood singing as they had been.

I looked to the horse, who gazed back at me for just a moment. Then she lowered her head, turned away, galloped back into the glistening wheat, and disappeared.

Awestruck and intrigued by the surreal sequence, I was compelled to join their circle and fill the space that had opened as if to invite me in, and I found myself almost involuntarily swaying and singing with the mysterious choir. I didn't ask questions, nor did my neighbors. We simply sang together through the night with all the love in our hearts.

In the soft grass of that meadow was where I awoke the following morning, and in the fields, people continued to sing and dance. There was no village that I saw—just trees and crops. Down the hill, musicians played woodwinds, the sounds of which were in the air everywhere. Music was perpetual and ubiquitous. What little was said came through song, and everything they did was a joyous and spiritual celebration.

Life there seemed to be divinely inspired and powered. Love was everywhere. The settlement was so massive that I questioned whether it had boundaries at all. Perhaps it spread into eternity. There were no plots of land or places to claim as one's own, but rather home was everywhere. I watched as an old artisan constructed a pan flute by hand, which was given to me to share in their joy and so that I would always have a piece of the place, and, together, we made music through the day. When night fell again, I slept in the open beneath the stars.

The next morning they were gone—all the thousands of people and all evidence of any settlement. As abruptly as they had appeared to me from the road, they had vanished without a trace, and my only assurance that they had been real was the pan flute in my hand. Placing it within my satchel, I again headed east.

18

HOPE

The first marathon runner didn't live long enough for a victory lap. They say that as soon as his message was delivered and his mission complete, he dropped dead.

People still ask me how I made the last leg of the journey—over five hundred miles—in five days on my own two feet. Honestly, I say, I don't remember. I had been tracking the dates between the time I had left the mountains and my time in the mysterious community of the plains. From that point, all I know is the date I left there and the date I returned home. Everything in between is blank. But, I say, anything is possible with faith and love. They're an inseparable pair. Real faith does not come without love, and real love does not come without faith. As long as we hold onto those, there will always be hope for tomorrow.

I remember hearing voices as I drew near Eden Valley, and then the sight of the old gravel road off the highway. The bright green foliage of early spring radiated in the afternoon sun. As I wound through the woods, I saw children playing. In clearings, there were cabins that had not been there before and people I didn't recognize at work in the fields. There were more people as I drew near the site of the old farm, passing me on the road and nodding with smiles to greet me. None of them knew me. They knew not that I had lived there and left before they had even arrived. They knew not where I had been or what I had done over the last year while they had built their new homes and new lives. I wondered if they had heard of me.

Down the road, I walked through an increasingly dense population, and what I came upon was a whole town that had grown from what had begun as a single cabin. There were buildings everywhere of timber, stone, and brick. In the center of town stood one with a sign in front that read "Eden Valley Postal Depot." People filed through the doors to deliver and pick up mail, a carrier on horseback leaving just as another arrived. From where had he come, I wondered, and to where would she go? Perhaps Canada or Mexico. Beyond, even.

Quietly I roamed past the communal canopy and past the place where we used to make fires that had become the town circle. I followed the old creek, still rushing strong behind the buildings, the thick woods where I had lost my first deer still flourishing on the other side. Perhaps that was where Gabe and Mike hunted at that very moment. I passed the stables where the town's horses were kept, undoubtedly where I could find Noah. Nearby, a new market had been erected where farmers distributed their harvest. They came and went with horse-drawn carts, as I imagined my old friends Daniel and John did daily. Birds sang from rooftops and scavenged for leftovers dropped on the road along the way.

Then I came to Paul and Sarah's cabin, clearly aged and weathered by comparison to every other structure around it, but still standing solid. So many things had changed since I had been gone, but even more had not. The building looked the same as it had on the day I had left. Overhead, clouds moved in and drew a shade from behind the old cabin and across the road, and I turned to see as they passed over Maria's and my front door, there before me.

My body began to tremble at the sight of my home as it became suddenly real how close I was to seeing the one I had been longing for throughout my journey. The one who had kept me moving when I thought I could take no more. Maria and all that she meant to me had become a fading reality, one that I had been more desperate to grasp with each day that had passed, but had inevitably slipped further and further away. At times, my memories of her had felt no more real than the terrible dreams I had experienced along the way. Yet there I was, in the moment I had been yearning for since that first day a year ago, finally realized.

I stepped slowly toward the front door, then hanging on metal hinges, glass windows on either side. Fighting the sudden weight of my arm, I lifted it to knock, my knuckles still quivering as the sound echoed in my ears. What an unglamorous way to make my return. I was filthy, dressed again in tattered rags. My hair was a mess, my beard unkempt, my body thin and frail, nearly empty handed, save for the satchel with my two most precious documents and the wooden pan flute inside. There was no grand welcoming party, and I would not have expected or even wanted one. My single and petrifying need was to see my wife, as wonderful and as beautiful as she had been the last time I saw her.

At the door, I stood waiting for an answer for what seemed like an eternity. Then, behind me, I felt her. I turned away from the door and toward the road. There, frozen in disbelief, Maria stood in the middle of it holding a basket of freshly cleaned laundry. A gust of wind caught her hair, glistening in the sunlight as the clouds broke above. In all her simplicity and innocence, she was the most beautiful sight I had ever seen, and I fell in love all over again.

She stood there gazing back at me for a moment, speaking not a word. Then she dropped the basket, and toward each other we ran, faster than I had ever run before; faster than I had scrambled for my life from the alligator; faster than my legs had sprinted after Thomas when he had stolen my horse; faster than Nomad had galloped with the herd in the north; faster than my heart had beat when the storm had overtaken us on the Pacific coast; faster than my hands had struck the first wolf in the mountains. We embraced with a passion of lovers long lost but finally reunited, a passion for which there is no greater metaphor. Our arms had never before held one another so tightly as they did in that most glorious, most redeeming moment of my life.

As we stood there in the road holding each other, rain began to fall. It was a gentle rain, like the one I had awoken to when I was saved in the northwest, the sun still beaming through the falling droplets as if the sky itself were crying with joy. Around our feet, her laundry blew in the wind, and we didn't let go as the rain drenched us.

"I love you," she muttered in my ear in the sweetest of voices.

"I love you," I whispered back.

She cried, and I felt her warm tears mix with the cold rain on my shoulder.

"I waited for you," she said.

"I knew you would."

"You really can't leave me again."

"I won't. Ever."

Love had never felt so real as it did in that moment. We shared then, and still do, a love as strong as I imagine two people in this world can, and having been without it for so long, I truly knew that I could not live if it were permanently taken away. Without love, there was no life. Without love, there was no hope for our future. I knew then that we would be together forever—not just Maria and me, but the human race as a whole. We had suffered together, and through love, we would overcome all of our tribulations and all of the terrible things people had done in the past to one another and to the world we called home.

I opened my eyes, and through the blur of my own tears, I saw Paul and Sarah standing in front of their old cabin, watching us with blissful smiles. Gradually, the rest of our family and friends began to arrive, and we celebrated our reunion until the sun went down, Maria never releasing her grasp on my hand. I had never slept as peacefully as I did that night with her at long last again in my arms, right where she belonged.

I settled back into life in Eden Valley, still not entirely set on an occupation, but I was OK with that. I'd had enough of postal work, and it was time to move on to something new—preferably something at home that time. Finding where we belong is all part of the journey, and we should not be distraught over an unknown end but celebrate all that we can learn along the way. I had made plenty of mistakes, and I still do. I had taken paths never before traveled, but with the rough terrain came lessons that I never would have learned had I always followed the roads paved by others.

Though I still sometimes inquired, it didn't matter how the collapse happened. Nobody placed blame. We were all guilty, and recognizing that was the first step toward rebirth. Then we had to forgive ourselves, learn from our mistakes, and continue to learn as we inevitably made more. We had been graced with an opportunity to start over with a contemporary knowledge of what works and what does not, and though humanity had been given this opportunity many times before, this time we had finally recognized the gift it was. As we rebuilt, we began to reprioritize. The care of people came first. Our construction and manufacturing methods focused on sustainability—a symbiotic relationship with the earth. We began to produce energy from renewable sources, and it wasn't long after that Eden Valley had electricity, telephone services were functional, and we reconnected as a whole with the outside world. We could have moved back to our old house by then, but it no longer felt like home.

A new economy emerged across the world, dominated by providers of food, construction and fabrication, nutrition and medicine, energy production and distribution, education, and communications. There was no white collar or blue collar and no feud or animosity between classes. Equal respect was paid to every person in every field because all were recognized as equally vital to our prosperity.

More of us learned to play musical instruments, create beautiful art, and speak foreign languages because our schedules afforded us the time to learn and achieve the things we had always aspired to but never could before. The obligations and responsibilities of that old life had been too demanding. But life had been simplified. We exercised our minds learning, reading, writing, telling stories, and enriching ourselves through interaction with people and spiritual exploration, and we celebrated frequently with festivals and feasts. There was so much to celebrate.

Once our basic necessities were satisfied, it was an easy life to adapt to. The functionality of the system was dependent on the participation of every person, but leisure was as much a part of it as work. There was time for parents to raise their own children and to provide them with the attention necessary for socially functional youth. Likewise, the elderly were provided for in recognition that their contributions had already been made. There was time for us to expand our minds and to think in abstract terms, unconstrained by deadlines and competition. There was time to enjoy and experience all that life on earth had to offer and all the natural beauty of our world—to focus on the things that were truly important.

Maria and I often spent our evenings doing just that, sitting on a nearby bluff and watching the sunset over a sprawling green valley. We would bring a bottle of wine made from our own vineyards and gaze as the colors of the sky changed and faded into the night. On occasion, Paul and Sarah would accompany us.

"The *Farmers' Almanac* predicts a good year," said Paul one evening.

"It can't be any tougher than the last," replied Maria.

"He means for the crops," I said.

"I know what he means."

She took my hand and held it tightly.

"It's so beautiful out here," she said. "I didn't used to think I could live in a place like this."

"Me neither," Sarah laughed. "Now look at us. Is this what it means to lose everything?"

"Not everything," Paul replied, still gazing into the orange glow to the west. I took another sip of wine as the light dimmed, and we were all quiet for a while. Far below, a family of deer grazed in an open field, and above them, a skein of geese sailed northward, calling to one another as they passed us by.

"If we're going to stay out here, we'll need more wine," said Sarah, breaking the silence. "Maria, come with me."

My wife reluctantly released my hand, and the two of them left Paul and me on the bluff.

"It's still the same, mostly," he said after some time.

"What's that?" I asked.

"The world, I mean. The sun still rises and sets. Rain still falls. The trees still grow and abscise with the changing seasons. I like deciduous trees for that. They grow until the winter gets too cold, and then they shed their leaves. They stick around for rough times, dormant but alive and present. Come spring, they begin to grow again, from right where they left off."

"It's a rough life," I replied. "Isn't it?"

"I think it can be. But they can bear it. And aren't you glad they do?"

He opened his hand toward the vast forest in the distance that provided us with fresh air, food, and shelter, asking nothing in return.

THE WORLD AS WE KNOW IT

"I am glad they do. It's like Heaven up here."

"Some call it that. Some call it nirvana—paradise even. Others just call it 'the way the world should be.'"

"How do you think it happened?" I asked.

"It was a long time coming, I think. We knew what was wrong, but sometimes people need a push to make a change. The two most defining characteristics of human nature are in constant conflict: our quest for love and our obsession with power. The question is, which will be allowed to prevail?"

"I like to think we've answered that question."

"It's answered every day in everything we do. There's no single moment when one conquers the other, but an endless battle that rages on day after day. We learn something from every trial, and we can only hope those lessons lead us in the right direction."

"Sometimes I'm ashamed of the things I do," I said. "The more I consider my life, the more I realize how often I make choices that aren't representative of who I am. It's excruciatingly difficult for most of us to live according to our own beliefs—to practice what we preach, so to speak. So we become hypocrites."

"You're not alone there, my friend. The important thing is that you recognize your faults and use them to better yourself. Every generation is accused of unflattering things by the one before it. I remember when they called us lazy and apathetic." Paul laughed. "Civilizations evolve and collapse, for better or for worse. Cultures and styles do the same. We tend to forget as much as we learn, but human nature doesn't change."

"We never knew what we had."

"That's the way it goes," he replied. "Until you have to earn something—*really* earn it—you don't truly understand its value, even if it was right in front of you the whole time."

"I heard all sorts of theories while I was away. Mostly, they said the collapse was caused by a lack of faith. Presumably, they meant faith in the economy, the government, faith even in each other. But perhaps it was a lack of faith in something even greater. Sometimes the moments when all seems lost are precisely when the greatest faith is found. It's these moments that define who we are and where we go once we've dug our way through to the other side."

"Perhaps you're right."

"How ironic that we always associated such a collapse with the end of the world. It turned out to be the beginning."

Paul smiled, still watching the sun fall behind the hills as the indigo-colored sky crept over our heads.

"It's time to forget what we've left behind and reach forward to what lies ahead."

A native of St. Louis, Missouri, Curtis Krusie graduated from the University of Missouri with a BS in human environment sciences, with an emphasis in personal financial planning and a minor in architectural studies and environmental design. An avid photographer, music fanatic, and great admirer of architecture, he is also an advocate for green energy and design, as well as natural, holistic health. He and his wife, Bryn, enjoy traveling the world and running full and half marathons together.

A firm believer in the healing and redeeming power of faith, love, and hope, Krusie was inspired to write his debut novel, *The World as We Know It*.

Made in the USA
San Bernardino, CA
15 April 2015